Hyperforce

By Ralph L. Angelo Jr

Contents

Dedicated to my dad who introduced me to the world of superheroes' and comic books. I hope you're looking at all of this from heaven and smiling.

Chapter 1

Starfall

The small silver spacecraft fell out of space, its hull glowing with reflected heat. At the helm, a young man, in his middle teens sat fighting the controls. His long jet black hair fell over his shoulders, and his face contorted madly.

"Prince Bol-ton, can you hold our course?" the grizzled black man standing behind his pilots' seat asked nervously. His fingers bit into the top of the high backed chair, his bald head sweated and his white van dyke trembled with each vibration of the ship.

"Better buckle up Mar-Cus. This is going to be a rough landing."

The older man nodded silently, locking himself into the seat next to Bol-ton's.

"Check the stabilizers' Mar-Cus. I think the last ship that attacked us clipped us good."

"You are correct, my Prince. The forward stabilizers' are non-functional."

Bol-Ton stood from his flight chair, "Take the controls, I'm going to try to bring us in another way."

"Prince Bol-Ton, what are you doing?"

"Only what you trained me to do Mar-Cus." he turned toward the older man with a half grin, "Pray that you taught me well."

The older man turned toward the front of the out of control craft and began wrestling with the controls.

1

Bol-Ton walked to the center of the small ship, seemingly unfazed by its jostling, and raised both his arms out to his sides. He wore a bright silver bodysuit and a flowing silver cape. He closed his eyes and spoke aloud, "Anti-grav field." A nimbus of light appeared about him, energy enveloped him from within and then spread outwards from his body to finally pass through the small vessels hull.

"The ship is stabilizing." Mar-Cus announced.

"Yes, but we're still coming in too hot. I-I can't control the speed." the silver clad boy stammered, "Our forward momentum's too great."

"You can do this Prince Bol-Ton. Add a null-motion component to your anti-grav field."

The boy nodded, his eyes still closed, "Null-motion." he repeated. The energy slipping off of his body changed colors slightly, and the ship seemed to slow down.

"You're doing it, my Prince. You are doing it."

"So hard…" the boy muttered, as the silver cape he wore shook and vibrated with every movement of the ship itself.

"We are slowing down, but not enough. You must change your energy to an anti-inertia field."

"T-trying." The straining youth replied, sweat dripped from his forehead now, "Anti-inertia, a-and force field." he grunted.

Mar-Cus turned to him at the last, but had to return his gaze immediately to the front of the ship. With a sickening tearing sound the small silver craft ploughed into a green field. Tearing up the field itself before settling into a hill of dirt dug up by its own forward momentum.

The ship hissed and sizzled, its hull steaming in the
bright light of the day. For many moments nothing
stirred and all that was heard was a constant popping
sound. Then slowly a hatch opened on the side of the
ship, sliding aside into the hull itself. Out stepped the
young man in the silver body suit and cape. He half
carried the older man, his mentor and teacher Mar-Cus
from the damaged craft. Both men struggled to a soft
hillock several feet away and then sat down upon it,
looking pained and tired.

"We must leave this place and quickly, my prince."

"I-I know Mar-Cus. But we both j-just need a
moment…"

The older man turned toward the sky and pointed,
"We do not have a moment, my prince, look!"

Out of the sky dropped two large, blood red, smooth
wedge shaped ships. They landed only a few hundred
feet from the two men and immediately hatches opened
all about them, disgorging groups of eight foot tall metal
behemoths. Smooth shaped and similarly red skinned as
their ships, their domed heads and shoulders seemed to
meld together fluidly, and as one the twenty metal
monsters began to advance on the two men.

"Mar-Cus, what do I do?"

"Precisely what you have trained for, my Prince.
Your time is now. This is the hour of your greatest
challenge. The fate of our world lies in your hands."

"I understand my teacher."

Bol-Ton stood and narrowed his eyes. He stared at
the advancing wall of metal and steel.

"Warbots." he grunted.

"Aye my Prince, and you are all that stands between them and the destruction of hope for our world."

"They will not find me wanting."

The silver clad boy threw his hands forward, shouting "Gravity swell!"

The ground beneath the Warbots feet suddenly rolled like a carpet being shaken, heaving the Warbots into the air to land heavily with a rumble like thunder across the field.

But they all immediately rose to their mechanical feet and continued to advance. They lifted their arms, pointed them at Bol-Ton. Glowing yellow energies leapt from those dreadful arms spraying toward the Prince.

His training immediately kicked in, his arms swung up before him and he shouted "Force field."

A glowing wall jumped to life between Bol-Ton and his enemies. Their powerful beams splashed against his shield.

But with each powerful, concussive blast, the youth was forced back step by step.

'I am getting too close to the Stargrazer. I must take to the offensive.'

Bol-Ton leaped upward and began to fly above the Warbots, his silver cape streaming behind him majestically.

"Laser blasts, heavy grav beams, concussive blasts." he mouthed in quick succession. The robots below him rocked with each blast of energy leaving his hands. Some exploded spectacularly. But still there were too many.

"Behind you my Prince!" Mar-Cus shouted from his hiding spot near their small ship, the 'Stargrazer'.

The Warbots unleashed hellish energies at Bol-Ton's back.

"Force shield" Bol-Ton blurted out, but it was too late. His shield only blunted the force blasts. He was knocked unceremoniously from the sky and landed hard upon the ground.

'*C-can't think straight. Can't concentrate my powers…*' he struggled to his knees and tried to right himself.

The silent crimson monsters approached raising their powerful metallic fists above their heads, ready to crush the boy when a streaking blue and white form hurtled through the sky and plowed into the group of half ton robots, scattering them like wheat before the scythe.

"Get away from him!" the newcomer roared. He reached up above his head, his mane of long brown hair blowing behind him; both his fists held high, he brought them down, hammering the ground with an explosive fury that scattered the Warbots yet again. For a mile around people stopped what they were doing fearing an earthquake had just struck their area.

"Who are you? Bol-Ton asked as the massive blue and white garbed figure helped him to his feet.

The big man smiled, for big is what he was. He stood six feet eight inches tall and was massively muscled, "My name is Captain Power." He replied.

Metal groaned behind the two men. As one they spun and unleashed energies from both their hands. From Captain Power it was a blast of furious maroon energy that punched through the nearest Warbot with astounding force. Prince Bol-Ton shouted, "Laser blast" and bright bolts of concentrated light streamed from his fingertips slashing through the Warbot nearest him.

"What are you called?" Captain Power asked his newfound companion.

"I am called Prince Bol-Ton, but I prefer Starbolt."

The remaining Warbots began to encircle the two heroes.

"Very well then, Starbolt it is." Captain Power answered.

A Warbot lunged for Captain Power, but instead of punching it or blasting it, he grabbed its arms and a bright glow grew about his hands. Almost immediately the Warbot seemed to disintegrate until only a pile of metallic ash lay on the ground where the Warbot had stood.

"You disintegrated it? Are there no end to your powers?"

Cap chuckled, "Yes, Starbolt there are. But you don't seem to be so wanting in the power department either."

The youth shouted "Force bolt." hammering another Warbot backwards.

"These things are tough, I'll give them that. Strong too." Cap commented.

"So would you two mind another couple of sets of helping hands then?" an unfamiliar voice called from above.

Both men turned as two new heroic figures descended from above, one was dressed in gold and white with a cape. He was slim but athletically muscled. The other was smaller, younger looking, perhaps the same age as Starbolt. He wore a blue and red armored suit with red metallic underarm wings. Both men wore masks that left their mouths exposed, though the gold and white suited man also had his blonde hair showing through the top of his mask. The younger man's red mask covered the top of his head.

"Who are you two?" Cap asked.

"I'm Solaron," the gold and white hero replied, "and this is Dragonfly."

The younger man nodded, aimed his arm, and with a smile fired a blast of withering energy that dropped the Warbot he was facing in its tracks. Then he touched the back of his gauntlet and fired again, this time explosive fletchettes streamed from the back of his hand, exploding again and again against the Warbot. With a huge explosive belch the hulking Warbot fell over, and lie there unmoving.

Cap engaged another of the towering metal titans hand to hand, while Starbolt soared overhead blasting more and more of the Warbots with various energy bolts.

"What do you do?" Cap called to Solaron.

"Me? Oh I'm just a living star, that's all."

He aimed his hands together at an onrushing Warbot and fired a powerful blast of solar energy, melting through the things hide immediately.

"Oh is that all?" Cap asked with a grin. He cocked his right fist back and slammed it forward, through the armor of the Warbot he was fighting. Then he drove his other hand in and tore the silent mechanized brute apart in a furious explosion of metal and showering sparks!

Captain Power turned his head and watched as Dragonfly grabbed a Warbot by its arm and began spinning it around and around in mid-air, "Not bad kid," he shouted, "Now throw it over here."

"You got it big guy-." Dragonfly replied, releasing the hurtling Warbot directly at Captain Power, who drew back his mighty right fist and slung it forward shattering the Warbot into a million pieces.

"Wow, I see why they call you 'Power'." Dragonfly offered with a grin.

"There's only a few of these left, what do you say we mop them up and discuss what's really going on here?" Cap replied.

"Agreed." Solaron added.

"May I ask a question?" Starbolt inquired.

"Of course." Solaron replied.

"Are all your people empowered thusly?"

Dragonfly guffawed, "Not quite Bolty."

Solaron shot him a withering look, then answered the silver suited youth, "No, Starbolt was it?"

Starbolt nodded affirmatively.

"No it's a very rare, very recent phenomenon upon our world."

"Anti-grav blast," Starbolt spoke, sending several more Warbots floating up into the sky, where Solaron, Captain Power and Dragonfly obliterated them from a distance. "May I ask another?"

"Go ahead." Solaron replied again.

"What is this place called?"

"Well, judging by your playmates here, I'd have to think you're not from around these parts. So I'm going to start by telling you this is the planet Earth, and that you and your ship landed in northern New Jersey, which most people call the nice part of the state."

"Ahh, New Jersey. Very good."

The heroes once more landed together. The Warbots were all destroyed and lay shattered all about the plain they had fought upon.

"So is that it? We won? Fight over?" Dragonfly asked.

"Not quite," replied Starbolt, "Zaring comes."

"Who or what is a 'Zaring'?" Dragonfly asked.

"A warlord upon my world. He has captured my parents, and chased me here. He seeks to kill me for I am heir to the throne. Once he does he can rule my world by right of challenge."

Another ship descended now and landed by the others the Warbots came in.

Out strode a powerful looking man with thick dark hair and a full beard. He wore a dark red suit of armor reminiscent of the Warbots' look, though he wore a cape of matching color. In his hand he held a glowing, spitting, crackling double headed axe.

In a booming voice he said, "Return Bol-Ton to me and none of you has to suffer any longer. I will leave your backward little world in peace. Refuse... and I'll make slaves of you all!"

Captain Power and Solaron both stepped forward simultaneously and then looked at each other. Cap tilted his head and nodded toward Sol. The golden garbed hero nodded in agreement and stepped out toward the brutish Zaring. "We do not take kindly to threats Zaring-"

"My name is General Zaring, golden man. I do not care what you do or do not 'take kindly' to. You will hand the youth over to me or I will take him."

"That hasn't worked out so well for you so far, has it, Zaring?" Captain Power prodded, purposely leaving the title 'General' off.

The powerful looking man smiled evilly, then pointed his axe at Cap, "I like you. I believe I will kill you first."

"Really? Give it a whirl, Red."

Cap walked toward his enemy, Solaron grunted, "Wait. We don't know what kind of powers he has."

"Beware his 'Neural axe'." Starbolt shouted.

Cap turned back, surprise written across his face, "His what?"

Zaring didn't hesitate. He lashed out with the sizzling, crackling axe while Cap had his head turned. He slashed Cap across the chest with it. Instantly Cap howled with pain and was sent hurtling through the air to land unceremoniously in a heap.

Solaron quickly turned to Starbolt, "What does that thing do?"

"From what I understand, it scrambles the neurons in the brain." The youth replied.

Cap lie there quivering, his eyes rolled up in his head.

"Anyone else?" Zaring roared.

"Let me take a shot at him." Dragonfly began to take a step forward, but Solaron's hand shot out and grabbed him by the wrist.

"No. We do this as a team. Ostensibly the strongest man here was defeated in half a second by this guy. Now we do this the smart way."

Zaring stood patiently awaiting his next challenge, the axe sounding like a loudly arcing live wire.

Solaron stepped forward, "Go home General Zaring. This boy is under our protection. You will not take him from here."

"You are funny Golden man I wi-"

"I'm not interested in what you will or will not do.", Sol interrupted this time, "Get off my world, or we'll throw you off of it."

"Really? Then let us play Golden man."

Zaring charged Solaron. But the white and gold clad hero shot skyward, out of reach of the blade. Instantly Sol leveled both hands and unleashed solar blasts at his enemy, slamming into Zaring's armored chest, and sending the brutish alien sprawling.

But Zaring was not done yet, he was on his feet almost instantly and aiming the top of his axe at Solaron. Instantly a blast of energy shot out the top of the axe at his enemy.

But Solaron was faster, instantly he changed tactics, creating a gleaming shield of solar energy. The neural disrupter sprayed against his shield harmlessly.

"Come and fight me upon the ground!" Zaring shouted.

"Sorry Zaring, I fight on my terms, not yours." Sol replied. He tapped the back of each gauntlet twice and fired energy from his hands again, but this time it was a heavy dense looking energy, crackling in its own right. It also had a decidedly different effect on the general. These solar blasts were force beams; they struck like battering rams and hammered the armored brute badly. He was smashed backward uncontrollably this time.

11

Nearby Captain Power slowly regained his footing, "What hit me?" he asked the red and blue clad Dragonfly.

"That axe," the young hero replied, "It's a neural something or other according to Starbolt."

"Where is Starbolt?"

Dragonfly suddenly looked around, having just realized the silver suited youth was gone. "I-I don't know. He was right here with me watching Sol take this guy on."

Cap spun around, immediately locating the missing Starbolt, "There he is. He's with an old man."

Starbolt was helping Mar-Cus away from their ship.

Zaring fought his way to his feet, saw where Cap and Dragonfly were staring and shouted, "You will not escape me so easily, Prince Bol-Ton." He hurled the neural axe across the field toward the boy, seeking to tear him asunder with its searing touch.

Three things happened very quickly; in the blink of an eye Captain Power and Dragonfly raised their arms and fired their respective energy blast, Caps being a powerful force blast, Dragonfly's his disruptor beam. The third thing was Starbolt raising his right hand and shouting, "Force Field", as he held the old man up.

The two energy blasts knocked the axe from its trajectory, but it still haphazardly careened into the hastily created shield, though it would have missed its intended target.

Now everyone turned toward Zaring who stood there shocked at the speed of which they all reacted.

"I've had enough of you." Captain Power growled.

Flying through the air like a missile, Cap fired off a powerful right at Zaring, instantly shattering the armored chest plate the villain wore. A left cross splintered more metal from his rapidly disintegrating armored suit.

"Cap, duck!" Dragonfly shouted.

Instantly the big man responded, dropping low as improbably the neural axe flew of its own accord back to Zaring's hand.

"I will slice you to pieces, you fool." Zaring slashed at Cap again and again, and each time Cap stepped back, not wanting to be shocked again by the terrible power of the neural axe.

"Look up!" Dragonfly yelled.

Cap stole a glance away from his slowly circling foe and saw two more troop transport vessels coming down.

"Dragonfly, Starbolt, with me." Solaron called.

"What about Mar-Cus?" Starbolt replied.

"Back in your ship, that's the safest place for him right now, as long as it's not going to explode."

"No, it is safe." the older man himself replied.

"Go back inside sir, we've got this." Sol reiterated.

Mar-Cus nodded and disappeared back within the small ship.

"Do you have room for two more?" a new, female voice asked.

Sol looked up and was almost startled by the two people descending toward them. They were so different from one another that the contrast was shocking. The girl who spoke was beautiful with silver hair and a red and silver costume with a short silver cape. But her brutish companion was something else altogether. He was stocky and wide, standing under six feet tall, and was

13

covered in black fur. Upon his back leathern wings akin
to a giant bat beat the air slowly. He was shaped almost
like an ape, but his face looked almost like a cats, but
flattened. His ears were definitely cat-like. He landed
next to the girl and immediately the wings on his back
shriveled and disappeared, as if they had never been.

"The more the merrier. I don't know where you two
came from but I'm glad you're here. I'm Solaron, this is
Dragonfly." The younger hero smirked and winked at
the girl. She rolled her eyes.

"This is Starbolt," Sol continued, "And over there
fighting the lunatic with the glowing axe is Captain
Power. Those eight foot tall robots exiting those two
ships along with the troops running towards us with
them are the bad guys. You are?"

"I'm Silver Shadow, this is Creature."

Sol nodded at both of them, "Glad to meet you. We
can talk pleasantries later. Right now we have an
invasion to stop. Find an enemy and stop him quickly. If
anyone gets in over their head, call for help. Let's go
people."

The Warbots began firing energy blasts from their
arms at the heroes, but immediately Solaron erected a
solar shield.

Starbolt shouted, "Force beam!" as he flew skyward.
He hammered the robots repeatedly from above. Silver
Shadow and Creature both attacked the troops that were
emerging from the transport ships and not the Warbots.

Creature grunted and lashed out powerfully, his
heavily muscled arm slammed a trooper in the side of his
head. Blood sprayed everywhere and the man screamed,
clutching his ear.

Silver Shadow ran toward the approaching warriors and then placed her fingers around both sides of her head. From her brow a glowing beam of white energy appeared that stunned each trooper where he stood, dropping him to the ground, instantly unconscious.

'She's using a telepathic stun bolt.' Sol thought.

'Yes I am.' Her feminine voice replied within his mind. He smiled at this.

Now Solaron streaked skyward and touched each gauntlet once, resetting them to the middle of three firing positions and unleashed a barrage of solar power from each fist. Searing blasts tore through the ranks of the Warbots, decimating them instantly. The once pastoral field was a war zone now. Heroes streaked through the air fighting mechanical monstrosities while others attacked a seemingly never ending wave of alien warriors.

"How are you doing?" Dragonfly called to Solaron.

"I'm fine; keep your head in the game, don't worry about me." Sol replied.

The sound of the battle was thunderously loud. By now the police had arrived first and then they called the National Guard, who had called the army itself. The entire area was mayhem and getting worse fast.

In the midst of the man to man fighting was the being called Creature. His shape and form seemed to grow and shrink and change shape with each attack. His hands grew savage claws that shredded flesh and armor, but retreated into the tips of his fingers. One of the alien warriors fired a blaster and hit him in the side, but before he was hit it seemed as if his fur disappeared and that a hard, natural armor rapidly grew to replace it.

15

Silver Shadow walked amongst the alien warriors, downing them with her stun bolt. But one warrior dodged her attack, having seen it one time too many. With a grunt he attacked her, slashing at her with his glowing pike weapon.

"Surrender woman and I will not kill you."

"Surrender yourself, jerk."

She kicked at him then, a perfectly executed side thrust kick that caught him in the gut. The alien doubled over in surprise. With a quick chop to the neck she downed him permanently. Solaron watched out of the corner of his eye and nodded his approval.

Inside his cowl he heard Dragonfly's voice through the transmitter they both wore, "This is starting to go on a long time."

"Getting tired?" Sol replied.

"Yes, and I'm not the only one. We're all slowing down, even you."

"It's a long battle. We need to end this quickly."

A new voice broke in on their conversation; it was Starbolt, "I can end this."

"How?" Sol asked.

"My namesake power, the Starbolt, but you all must clear away when I tell you, or you'll be killed. But I need some time."

"Well, I dunno about the getting killed part." Dragonfly replied, "But I *can* buy you some time.

Dragonfly hovered in mid-air, his boot jets pumping; he reached his left hand over to the right side of his metallic underarm wing and grasped it, pulling it free. It locked into position, looking like a red metal crescent. He hurled it; it sliced through the air, like a carefully

16

aimed cue ball it careened through the metallic monsters below slashing through them at the legs, cutting one leg off of each one. They fell over, unable to stand again. Dragonfly's attack turned them into useless lumps of steel. The wing turned around and flew back to him, reattaching itself to his back.

Starbolt settled upon the ground in the midst of the battle, Solaron and Dragonfly kept the Warbots away from him. He stood and concentrated. His arms were held tight in front of his chest and his fists were clenched. His eyes were closed and he shook with concentration.

Nearby, Captain Power continued to trade blows with General Zaring. His powerful fists clanged off of the shattered armor again and again.

"You seem to be weakening, Captain," Zaring chided, "Give up, surrender, and I will make your passing quick."

Cap smiled, ducked a swing of Zaring's axe and unleashed a powerful right to his foes unprotected jaw. Zaring tumbled a hundred feet though the air to land in a heap.

"Did that seem weak to you Zaring? Let me know so I won't hold back any longer."

Cap grabbed a defeated Warbot in his hands and pulled it above his head. His hands glowed momentarily and the armored behemoth disintegrated at his touch. Then he flew toward Zaring.

Solaron saw everything that was happening around him. Even Captain Power's disintegration of the deactivated Warbot. *'He just absorbed its mass. He recharged himself.'* Sol thought with a grin.

The battle continued to rage. Solaron hovered in the air and continued to harangue the ground forces with his blasts of raging solar heat while the rest fought upon the ground.

Silver Shadow seemed to be poetry in motion when not using her mind numbing telepathic blast. She moved through the alien troopers with lightning fast martial arts combinations that were a marvel to see. Solaron continued to be amazed by her.

Her monster-ish companion was something all-together different though. He attacked like a ferocious wild beast slashing and hammering at his foes, while unleashing fantastic and horrible howls and growls between each attack. At one point he stood alone with unconscious or wounded enemies all about him, but half the field away were more Warbots disembarking the transport ship. With a mad howl he began to run toward them, dropping to all fours. His limbs changed shape to that of a cat of some kind. He ran across the field at close to eighty miles per hours from Solaron's estimation.

'This is incredible,' thought Solaron, *'the different and varied powers on display here. That man, that 'Creature' is some sort of shape shifter who takes on supercharged aspects of animals, and it appears he does it subconsciously for the most part.'*

Solaron turned his attention back to the young man all of this began with, *'Starbolt is still standing there trembling, looking like he's about to give himself a stroke.'*

But then the boy in question opened his eyes up, and they glowed! A bright white light lit his eyes from within before he spoke, "Now!" Starbolt shouted.

Solaron, Dragonfly, Silver Shadow and Creature all took to the sky. Captain Power stood his ground still exchanging powerful blows with Zaring.

Then Starbolt exploded, for want of a better word. A wave of power burst from his body in all directions, devastating everything they came in contact with. The Warbots were torn asunder instantly by the blast. The enemy troops who did not get out of the way of the blast were disintegrated where they stood, their cries frozen in their throats.

In the midst of it all Captain Power held Zaring aloft by the front of his armor with his left hand and unleashed a powerful right to Zaring's face that snapped his head back and sent him flying through the air and into the side of one of his own transport ships. Cap turned and shielded his eyes with his forearm as the explosive wave rolled toward him, "What's this all about then?" he asked no one in particular.

Captain Power stood his ground as the Starbolt passed around him, he took a step back but held his own, though his blue and white cape with the twin lightning bolts emblazoned on its back was now in tatters.

Solaron landed next to him as did Dragonfly, "Are you all right?" Solaron asked, seemingly impressed.

"I am. See to him though." Cap pointed to Starbolt, who was down on all fours in the now barren and devastated field. Silver Shadow and Creature were there first, landing next to the downed hero, Creatures' bat-like wings once again shrunk and disappeared upon his landing.

Solaron stole a glance at Captain Power again, who now rested with his hands upon his knees. Then Cap stood up, flew into the air with great jets of energy blasting out of his legs and landed in front of Zaring. There was a derelict Warbot lying there smoking from Starbolt's ultimate attack. Captain Power back fisted it out of the way as if it were cardboard.

Zaring slowly tried to stand, using the ship he was leaning against for support.

"End of the road, Zaring." Cap began.

"You are an incredible being Captain Power. Never have I beheld such strength and durability. You are truly astounding. I salute you." Zaring threw his right hand out in front of him with his hand opened. Cap stared for an instant and then turned around a heartbeat too late. The neural axe flew directly toward Zaring's hand, with Cap in the way.

The axe struck Cap, he arched backward as the blade's crackling energies played about his body, wracking him with unimaginable pain. Then he dropped to the ground on his hands and knees, fighting unconsciousness.

"You see mighty one? I win anyway. For all your might, all your 'Power' you are still helpless against my neural axe. I may not be able to kill you, but I have defeated you. Now I take my leave of you, earthman. But be aware I *will* be back, and I will have that boys' hide."

Across the field the rest of the costumed heroes were now running and flying toward Cap and Zaring.

Zaring saluted them all sarcastically and stepped into the transport ship he was leaning against. It instantly powered up and shot skyward.

Cap fought his way to his feet, swaying drunkenly.

"Are you okay?" Solaron asked.

"I've been better." Cap replied angrily.

He turned and grabbed the Warbot he had batted aside and disintegrated it, absorbing its mass and re-powering himself. It was an action he repeated on another devastated Warbot close by. He turned to Solaron, "I'm going after him."

Captain Power shot into the air faster than any man made missile had ever traveled. But right behind him were Solaron and Dragonfly.

Solaron looked over his shoulder and said, "Dragonfly, make sure you engage your re-breather."

"Already done Unc." Dragonfly quickly replied.

"Codenames only." Solaron barked tersely.

The three heroes rose quickly through the atmosphere, but Dragonfly was starting to be left behind by both other men.

"Go on without me, I'll catch up, I'm just not as fast as you guys."

"Just look for explosions, I'm sure we'll all be seeing a lot of them." Solaron answered.

Captain Power continued rocketing after the transport ship. He burst through the remnants of atmosphere and beheld a huge, black ovoid vessel in orbit. The transport ship entered a waiting hatchway. Captain Power did not hesitate. He flew forward at incredible speed and slammed into the two thousand foot long vessel with both fists. Instantly he shattered their shields with that one blow.

Aboard the ship General Zaring ran to his command center, "Status?" he yelled to dark suited support staff all about him.

"Shields are down; that being, he flew into the 'Claw of Vengeance' shields and shattered them with one blow. What kind of a being-"

"It matters not!" barked Zaring, "get us out of here before that maniac destroys our light speed ability!"

"Full light speed now." the second in command reiterated.

Outside the hull Solaron had caught up with Cap, *'I can't talk to him, can't reach him without a communicator. I'll fly above him; let him know I'm here.'*

Solaron passed above Captain Power; the two men locked eyes and nodded to one another. Dragonfly finally caught up as well.

"Randy! Electron power bursts now."

"Who's the guy who's always insisting on code names?" the red and blue clad youth replied, "An' you know I like to call 'em 'Dragonblasts'."

"Whatever you call them, just use them, now." Solaron replied.

All three men cut loose upon the almost half-mile long ship. Energy leapt from each of their hands. Searing solar heat, crushing force blasts and the atomic structure destroying 'Dragonblasts' of Dragonfly.

"Sir, our hull is about to give way!" Zarings' second roared.

"Get us away from here *now*!" General Zaring reiterated.

The ship leapt forward, seemingly stretching into infinity, then snapping back together, disappearing from sight of the three men.

"Head back to New Jersey," Solaron began, "Cap will follow." Solaron waved to their long haired companion, who nodded stoically and followed them down.

Some moments later they landed in the same field which was now encircled by military, police and media.

Starbolt sat upon the open hatchway of his own ship. Nearby nothing remained of the alien transport ships but mangled steel.

"What happened to 'em?" Dragonfly asked when he touched down.

Silver Shadow turned to look at the smoldering ruins strewn about the field and shrugged, "They all self-destructed I guess after you guys left."

Starbolt looked up from where he sat; the older man Mar-Cus had an arm on the young man's shoulder, obviously concerned.

"Did you catch them?" Starbolt asked.

"They escaped, but not without a lot of damage." Captain Power replied.

"I don't think they'll be back too soon." Solaron added.

Creature stood behind Silver Shadow growling softly while he scanned the crowds in the distance who were starting to make their way closer.

Solaron noticed what he was looking at and nodded, "We should get out of here. There'll be too many questions. Questions we don't have answers for right now."

Cap looked at the approaching police and reporters and slowly nodded, "You're right. Let's get out of here. But where can we go? We're going to need to talk."

"I know," Sol answered, "I have a place and it's not too far from here." Sol turned to Starbolt, "Is your ship able to fly?"

The boy nodded, "Self repair systems have made it flight worthy again." Starbolt replied.

"If not, I'll carry it." Cap grumbled.

Surprised, Solaron turned to him, "Could you do that if you had to?"

"Easily." the big man answered.

"Let's get out of here." Silver Shadow added, "We'll travel with you two." she pointed at Starbolt and Mar-Cus.

The four of them entered the Stargrazer. An instant later it lifted up vertically. Solaron and Dragonfly led with Captain Power behind them and behind him the Stargrazer. They all streaked into the sky and disappeared.

The gathered crowd watched in awe as the heroes flew away into the distance. A reporter turned to a pre-teen boy who was standing behind the hastily erected barricades and asked him, "What did you see?"

The boy was practically bouncing up and down with nervous energy, "Oh they were so cool! An' strong! Did you see how fast they all were? They were like, 'Hyper'!"

A smiling, jovial man with a shaved head sitting on a BMW GS motorcycle was questioned next, "What did you see sir? First, what's your name?"

He replied, "My name is Brian. I only was able to see the end of their fight, the police kept us away, but I've got to tell you, they were a 'Force' to be reckoned with. These guys were tough."

Hyperforce

The reporter smiled, thanked the man and moved away, turning toward the camera, "There you have it. You heard it first here viewers. We've all just seen the birth of a new age of heroes living amongst us. Super-Heroes if you will. There have been sightings and uncorroborated reports up until now. But now we know. There are super-powered beings amongst us, and as per our first hand viewers on the scene, we're going to call them 'Hyperforce.'"

Ralph L. Angelo Jr.

Chapter 2

Getting to know you…

Solaron and Dragonfly flew through the late afternoon sky, heading east and leading the way for the others.

Within minutes they all descended toward an observatory in secluded northern New Jersey.

A hanger deck beneath the observatory that was made to accommodate helicopters was opened remotely by Solaron allowing the Stargrazer to find its way and land.

Captain Power, holding the bottom corners of his cape spread wide, settled down softly behind Solaron and Dragonfly.

"Nice place you've got here. What is all this?"

Solaron smiled, "Welcome to the New Jersey Solar observatory. We study the sun here."

Creature exited the small ship followed by Silver Shadow and then Starbolt with Mar-Cus limping and leaning on him heavily.

Solaron smiled at the two aliens, "Follow me, and Marcus is it? I'll take a look at that leg for you. I have a feeling your physiology is surprisingly very human-like"

"Ah, you are a Doctor?" Mar-Cus asked.

Solaron shrugged, "I am. I have a few different degrees. One is as a medical doctor. But I seldom use it.

I prefer investigating what's out there." he waved toward the sky.

"You must be in your glory right now." Captain Power smirked.

"You have no idea my large friend." Sol replied.

The group entered a steel door Solaron unlocked with a special code on a key pad and then a retina scan.

"There's a conference room to the right, all of you have a seat. Dragonfly, get them beverages from the kitchen. We have coffee, soda, iced tea. I think there may be some frozen meals you can micro if you're hungry in there, or we can order up a pizza. I'm going to take a look at Marcus' leg before we begin. Oh, and Dragonfly turn the TV on in the conference room and look for any news coverage on us. I have a feeling there's already a newscast with our faces on it being broadcast."

Everyone else filed into the conference room and sat in the high back, plush desk chairs that encircled the table which was in the rooms' center.

"So what are we here for?" Silver Shadow asked bluntly.

"I would assume for real introductions." Cap replied.

"Grrrrr,
what...do...we...need...introductions...for?" Creature growled.

"I kinda think Sol may be askin' you guys if you wanna make this some kinda permanent thing." Dragonfly answered. He had just re-entered the room carrying a platter with coffee and beverages upon it.

Cap leaned back in his chair and the left side corner of his mouth rose up in a half smile, "I have to tell you, I wouldn't be opposed to it. We took on those aliens and pretty much embarrassed them. Heck, the three of us drove off that space ship pretty nicely."

Starbolt looked around at the people sitting near him and exhaled, "I might as well tell you my story first then. But I prefer to wait until Solaron returns with Mar-Cus before doing so."

"I have no problem with that." Cap offered.

"Where are you two from?" Dragonfly asked Silver Shadow.

"Oh…from around. You know, here and there."

"Could you be a little more evasive?" Dragonfly replied, grinning.

Solaron and Mar-Cus entered the conference room with Mar-Cus walking on a crutch with his knee wrapped.

"It's just a bad sprain. A few days and he should be okay." Solaron began. He looked about the room. Captain Power sat relaxed and confident in his chair, Silver Shadow looked cautious. Creature growled and grunted, and seemed almost antagonistic. Dragonfly continued to smirk while trying to make eye contact with Silver Shadow, and Starbolt looked almost like a cornered animal, the way his eyes nervously darted about the room.

Sol sat down at the head of the table took a deep breath and began to speak, "I'm called Solaron as you all know, but my real name is Ronald Anderson. I'm a solar energy research scientist. The reason I'm telling you this is because you are in my home now. Yes, I own this facility. I made a lot of money on some patents in regards to a few devices I created for research. I'm taking a big risk telling you all who I really am, but it's easy enough to find out who owns this place once you leave."

"How'd you get your powers?" Captain Power asked.

"About a year ago there was an accident in here. A spy organization attempted to steal the battle suit Dragonfly is wearing. In the ensuing melee I absorbed a lot of solar radiation, which consists of many different wavelengths and bands of radioactivity. In essence I became a living star."

"What about him?" Cap pointed his thumb at Dragonfly, "Is that all suit or what?"

"No. Some of his abilities are his. The same disaster merged his DNA with that of a dragonfly, at least some of it. He has super strength, speed, reaction time, as well as something I call spectroscopic vision. He can see things across the spectrum normal vision cannot. The suit does all the rest."

Dragonfly sat there and smiled broadly. "Yep, I have all sorts of powers. But my biggest one is my attraction from the ladies." again he smiled at Silver Shadow. Creature growled in a low rumble in reply.

"All right both of you settle down. Romeo, get yourself under control." Cap ordered.

Dragonfly looked down at the table top but continued to smirk. Creature eyed him a moment longer then looked away.

Cap looked around the table and continued, "All right, we know about you two, I'm called Captain Power, I think the reasons were obvious out there. I'm incredibly strong, almost unbreakable, at least as far as I

30

know, and I fire force beams out of my hands. I fly by channeling that same energy out of my feet."

"But you have to recharge by absorbing matter to add to your mass." Solaron added.

"You caught that huh? I kind of figured you did."

"Yes I tend to notice everything around me. I always have for some reason."

"Okay that's good to know. Yes, I do have to recharge depending on how tough a battle I'm in. I tend to know where a lot of junk yards and dumpsters are for that reason. Sometimes I'll absorb the mass from a derelict buildings wall if I have to."

"Understood, that's how your powers work." Sol nodded thoughtfully.

"What about you two?" Cap asked, looking at Silver Shadow and Creature.

"I-I'd rather not say." Silver Shadow replied quietly.

"That's okay, Silver. There's no pressure here." Sol raised his hands up before his chest, palms out, reassuringly.

Solaron turned toward Starbolt and Mar-Cus, "But I really would like to hear your stories, if you don't mind."

Starbolt smiled weakly, "Very well." he sighed before beginning, "I am Prince Bol-Ton of the planet Exalander. That madman we fought is a warlord upon my world. He kidnapped my parents and seeks to kill me in battle. Then he can lay claim to the throne."

"Why not just battle your father, who I assume is the king?" Cap asked.

"My father is the king, yes. But I am next in line. If he were to battle and defeat me because of the laws of my world he would win the throne."

Sol asked, "What about the fact that he kidnapped your parents?"

"You must understand, my world is feudal, even though highly advanced. In many instances everything is decided by right of arm. His kidnapping them, as long as he does not harm them under his care, means nothing. It is just a right of challenge."

"So why didn't you fight him? I think you'd whup him." Dragonfly asked.

"He is not to be trusted." Mar-Cus interjected, "He told my young student that he would have his parents killed anyway if Bol-Ton defeated him in fair combat."

"So he wanted Bol-Ton to throw the fight." Cap surmised.

"Yes Captain, that is correct. All he cares about is power and to rule. He wishes to make Exalander his own, and then reshape it in his image."

"But wouldn't he risk the wrath of any other authorities upon your world by killing them? You said he was in no danger as long as they didn't come to harm."

"I have to believe he would kill my parents, or rather have them killed by his lackeys the moment I defeated him. Perhaps he does not care if he lives or dies? Perhaps he has transport in place to whisk him from our world the instant the deed is complete, I do not know. But I do know I cannot risk their lives."

"Why didn't your father take him on?" Sol asked, "I have to assume he has the same abilities you do, and is probably a lot more practiced at using them than you are, no offence meant."

"None taken Solaron," the prince replied, "My father passed his abilities on to me at the time of my ascension. That is how it is with my powers. They are passed between father and son. Mar-Cus had been training me since before father bequeathed my powers to me. I am well trained, but in truth, this was the very first fight I had been in up until this day."

Solaron was surprised by this revelation, "Really? You handled yourself very nicely out there." he looked at Mar-Cus, "You trained him well." The older man nodded his thanks and smiled.

"So what now?" Silver Shadow asked.

"Well," Sol began, "seeing as how the media has already anointed us 'Hyperforce' I suggest we accept the name and become a team, unless you have any objections?"

"The media did what?" Dragonfly asked.

Sol reached for a remote on the table and powered on a large screen TV that was across from the table, on it were reporters that had been at the site of the battle. Everyone listened intently and heard the audience at the battle come up with the 'Hyperforce' name. Solaron muted the volume.

"What do you all think? I personally can't think of a better name than that. Also to be honest, I think what we did out there was nothing short of incredible."

"Yeah, I was pretty cool." Dragonfly nodded and smiled.

"This guy can't be your son, who is he to you?" Cap asked.

"Dragonfly is...-"

"He's my uncle." Dragonfly blurted out. Solaron immediately looked at him in annoyance.

"Relax Uncle Ron, these guys are cool."

"Thanks for your vote of confidence kid, but in the future don't be so forthcoming." Cap advised, "We may be 'cool' to you, but you never know who isn't. Let's face facts; none of us know each other. If you noticed I haven't shared my real name. There's a reason for that. I also understand why your uncle did, because he chose to take us all under his wing into his home. That still may have not been the smartest thing to do under any circumstance, but I have a feeling it was his olive branch in trying to build trust amongst us. I'm not going to give you my real name right now. But I will eventually when we see how far this goes and if we end up enjoying working together. Is that fair?" Cap turned and looked at Solaron.

Solaron met his gaze, "You don't have to tell me your real name, it's not important to me. You're Captain Power, that's all I need to know you as."

Cap nodded, "For now that's fine. But if this lasts and goes as far as I think it has the potential to, you'll learn my name. I'll happily give full disclosure, as you have."

"So now what? Do we throw a party or something?" Dragonfly inquired.

"No, no party." Solaron replied, "But I took the liberty of ordering a few pizzas. I know I'm famished after that fight. I think, if there are no objections, I'd like to continue to get to know you all better."

Starbolt raised a hand, "I have a question."

"Okay, ask away." Solaron replied.

"What is this 'pizza'?"

Dragonfly broke out in an ear to ear grin, "Buddy are *you* in for a treat."

***

An hour later they were still seated about the table finishing up the three pizza's Solaron had ordered. He was in his street clothes now as he had to go to the door to accept the pizza delivery.

"So is your ship repairable? It seemed to fly here without any issues." Solaron asked.

"It has extensive self-repair and diagnostic devices on board. It will tell us where it will need servicing if the self-repair systems cannot complete the repairs." Mar-Cus replied.

Solaron nodded between chews, "Interesting. I'm going to offer you two quarters here to stay in, since you have nowhere else to go. In fact any of you who want to stay here are welcome too. I have plenty of rooms below ground. When I had this place built I treated it like a below ground hotel in case other scientists needed a place to stay while using the observatory."

"That's not going to be a problem now?" Cap asked.

"No. No one has stayed here in a few years. Right now it's myself and a support staff using the observatory now, that's about it. With the Hubble and the IOS up there, well let's just say there are other options to using a ground based observatory these days. Still we have an extensive scientific grant from the government as well as a few outside companies that buy into our data feed. That plus the aforementioned patents I registered have not made me want for money in a while. This place more than pays for itself now."

"Can…we…stay…here…too?" Creature rumbled.

"You're more than welcome Creature. Both of you are." Sol looked at Silver Shadow when he spoke.

"Thank you," she replied, "We do have a place near the city, but with Creature's…condition it makes it very hard on both of us, but more him than I."

"You and your brother are both-" Solaron stopped himself as everyone looked at him in surprise, no one more so than Silver Shadow.

"I'm sorry, as I already mentioned I do tend to notice things, and I noticed he's very protective of you, as a brother would be. Not as a boyfriend or husband. I just surmised you two were siblings."

"Y-you're right," she stammered in surprise.

"It's okay Silver, you are amongst friends here. Bonds forged in the field of battle and all of that."

"Do you live here too?" Captain Power asked Dragonfly.

"Me? Naah. I live nearby though."

Cap nodded thoughtfully.

"What about you?" Dragonfly asked the bigger man.

"I live in the city. I go to school there, actually."

"You're a student?" Silver asked.

"Yeah, third year college."

"How do you not get noticed? I mean you're huge." Silver replied.

Cap smiled, took another bite of his fifth slice and replied, "Not all the time."

Solaron turned toward Prince Bol-Ton once again, "So I have to ask, what brought you two to Earth? I

36

mean I have to assume there are a lot of inhabited worlds out there with much higher levels of scientific and futuristic accomplishments. Worlds that are centuries ahead of us. I mean we've barely stepped off of our planet at this point. Yet you two came from God only knows where. Why here?"

"Because your world is entering an age of heroes." Mar-Cus replied, "As evidenced here in this room, great things are about to happen on your planet. We needed allies in our coming battle; we sought them here because we watched your world for decades, knowing this part of the cycle of existence was becoming closer and closer for your world. Now it is here. The age of the hero."

"So wait, is this a cyclical thing? All worlds reach this point?" Sol leaned forward and asked.

Mar-Cus nodded, "Most do. When conditions are right upon a world heroes emerge as needed. You all did not just gain your abilities today. Chances are, living as close as you do to one another you would have met at another time, another battle. I apologize if our appearance here was the impetus for this meeting of heroes, but we would have been captured and my young protégé would have been forced into a fight he could only lose on several levels. We in truth had nowhere else to turn, but your world. A world that did not know us as fugitives from a madman. We, rather I had hoped that someone of strength and abilities would appear to aid us when most needed."

"You guys were against like fifty to one odds." Dragonfly replied, "We couldn't just leave you to get your heads beaten in."

Mar-Cus turned toward Dragonfly and smiled, "You are so different from my young charge. Though you both appear to be close or near to the same age. You are enjoying your augmented abilities, and they are not a burden to you. I am pleased for you Dragonfly. Starbolt, Prince Bol-Ton is different in that he has the weight of an empire on his slim shoulders. I wish he were allowed to grow into his abilities as you have been."

"Mar-Cus, it is all right." Bol-Ton interrupted, "I accept my place. Someday I will rule my world. The madman Zaring will be gone and peace will reign again, for however short a time before the next conflict."

"You say that as if conflict is what is cyclical in life." Captain Power commented.

"It is Captain," Mar-Cus replied, "Conflict never leaves us during our entire existence. Whether we are fighting a physical foe or are at odds within our own minds, there is always conflict. Even in our final moments upon this mortal coil we are in conflict. It is the one absolute, the one constant in this life, this existence."

Everyone was silent for a moment until Dragonfly finally commented, "Wow, that's heavy."

Cap looked at Mar-Cus and Prince Bol-Ton, "You two are a little fatalistic aren't you? I mean sure we get in conflicts every day of our lives. Hell, getting the common cold is a conflict. But I don't worry every minute between conflicts. I live for the moments in between; the times I'm having fun. When I'm with the people who are important to me or doing the things I love to do. That's what matters, not waiting to draw my sword again and again and nothing memorable in between. I hate to tell you, this life we have? Being a superhero? It's dangerous. People have died doing this. We're not guaranteed anything in this game, especially not tomorrows. Only our skill and training is what sustains us for the good times, when we get them. Yes, we can be hurt and perhaps killed on an off day. But being the absolute best at what we do prevents that. That doesn't mean it all has to be grim and nothing but training, training, training either."

Bol-Ton raised his right arm up and waved his hand, "May I say something?"

"Of course, this is not a classroom. You don't have to ask permission to speak." Solaron answered.

"Well, I just want to say that this 'piz-za' is the most delicious food I have ever eaten."

Everyone burst out laughing, except for Bol-Ton. Even Mar-Cus was laughing until his eyes were tearing.

After a moment Solaron stood and said, "C'mon I want to show you all one other thing. Follow me."

Solaron led them all to a room which had several clear, empty tubes in them. There were two tubes that had clothes in them. One set of clothing was actually Solaron's costume. The other was a simple set of street clothes.

"What's all this?" Silver Shadow asked.

"Show them Unc." Dragonfly said.

"Sure. Watch closely now." Solaron touched his belt buckle and instantly his street clothes disappeared and he was fully clothed in his costume. In a flash of light the inside of the tube now held his street clothes he had been wearing.

"That's…amazing." Captain Power admitted.

"Anyway, if any of you want to make use of these, feel free. I'll set you up with the requisite item that will be keyed to your specific finger print ."

Cap smiled, "While I would love to make use of that, I can't. Because of my specific power set I need my costume under my clothes when I change. Otherwise things get torn up and I end up standing there buck naked."

"I can make it work you know."

"Can you? If you can make it all work for my specific case I'll gladly drop by with my spare costume and we can give it a go. I'll still want to have at least one at home, just in case this breaks down."

"Which one do you wear the most? Are they all the same?"

"No, I have my first costume which is black and gold with nautical or swashbuckler style boots. Then I have a red one I like, and then there's this one."

"This one's your favorite?"

"Yes, it is."

Sol nodded, "Go home, fix your cape or replace it, whatever you're going to do with it and bring this one back, since this is the one you wear most."

"That works I'll swing by tomorrow with it."

"What about you Silver Shadow? Prince Bol-Ton?"

"Sure. If I'm going to live here with my brother I might as well make use of the facilities provided, right?"

"I think so." Sol concluded. "Prince Bol-Ton? What do you say?"

"Allow me to procure an extra set of clothing from my vessel and I will gladly make use of your clothing transporter."

40

Cap snapped his fingers, "Of course. He's right, it's a clothing transporter. That makes sense."

Sol grinned, "Yes it is Cap. It has almost limitless range, at least as far as I've used it. I don't think we could travel off world with it and make it work, but anywhere on the planet it should be fine."

"Fantastic and thank you."

"My pleasure."

Cap hesitated a moment then asked, "Can I get a word with you in private?"

"Sure, Dragonfly, why don't you show Silver Shadow and Creature to their rooms and the Captain and I can have a private chat."

"Okay Sol, whatever you want." Dragonfly turned to the brother and sister team, "Follow me you two. Starbolt, you an' Marcus might as well tag along. Your rooms will be down this way too."

The five people left, leaving Cap and Sol alone. Cap turned to his host for the last couple of hours and asked simply, "Why?"

"Hhhmm? What do you mean?"

"Why are you doing this? You open your home up and you have it set up for people to live in. Hell, I have no doubt you have a training facility in here as well, set up for a team and not just the two of you. What's really going on here? Were you really waiting for something like this to happen? Because that's exactly what it seems like."

Solaron smiled like a sly fox and replied, "Yes. I was waiting for this to happen. It was only a matter of time before some big catastrophe of one kind or another took place and several of the just bourgeoning breed of super-

41

heroes appeared to save the world, or stop the larger threat at least. I honestly had no idea it would happen on my almost doorstep. Let's take a walk to the hanger level, I want to check out their spaceship"

"I always figured something would happen somewhere around New York City, never really this far west of it. At the speeds we fly though we could be there in seconds at most." Cap added while standing up from the table

"That's right we can. Do you realize what an opportunity we have here? My God, with the power represented by this group, just about anything is possible."

"Yes it is," Cap agreed, "But I'm warning you now, and make no mistake it's a very friendly warning and not a threat, I don't know you really. I met you only a few short hours ago. From everything you say you have the best of intentions, and that's why I'm agreeing to all of this. I'm not interested in playing God and trying to take over anyone's lives. I'm not going to overthrow countries or fight nations' battles. That's what governments and armies are for. The way I see it is that people like you and I, and everyone else here for that matter, should never get involved in stuff like that. We should only fight the foes that normal men cannot. I don't consider myself smart enough to run anyone's life but my own, and that's all I'm interested in. No government overthrowing in any nation. If say North Korea or some middle-east despot comes up with their own super human and is threatening his neighbor that's fine, we'll take him down. If one of them sends a killer squad of super-beings to attack this country I'm the first in line to stop them. But I will not allow myself to be used against ordinary people, no matter how in the wrong they are."

"What if they killed a family member of yours would you feel the same way?"

"I hope I never have to find out. I believe in the rule of law myself, and the proper channels to go through. For me to wield this kind of power I have to put restrictions upon myself." Captain Power looked down at his open hands while speaking.

Solaron nodded, "I understand, and believe it or not I agree. We should not place it upon ourselves to make policy for our nation or the world. We should be the last line of defense against beings of power, like we ourselves are, and let me add something to this conversation, I feel we are not for hire, not by the government, not by anyone. We pick what we are going to do, who we are going to fight and how we are going to fight them."

Cap relaxed, "Good I'm glad we're at least on the same page for this so far." Cap extended his hand. Both men had now walked to the hanger where the alien spaceship dubbed the Stargrazer sat. Solaron took it and shook it firmly.

"I'll be back tomorrow with this costume repaired and ready to try your changer doohickey."

"That sounds good Cap. Try to realize that what I'm trying to build here is with the best of intentions."

"Just remember that old saying Solaron, 'The road to hell is paved with the best of intentions'."

"Samuel Johnson I believe?"

"Nope. Actually it's believed to be Saint Bernard of Clairvaux, circa 1150."

Sol nodded and smiled. "Captain, you do realize that overwhelmingly those of good intentions do good things? A much smaller percentage end up in self-made hells. I'll see you tomorrow."

Cap nodded, then turned and flew away out of the hanger deck door.

Chapter 3

I think I'm turning Japanese
I think I'm turning Japanese
I really think so...

Seven days later...

Silver Shadow was walking about Manhattan, enjoying the warm spring weather and the feel of the sun on her face. She was in street clothes. No one recognized her. At least she thought no one recognized her.

Exiting a store on 48th street she began to get the feeling something wasn't right.

'What is this? I'm always 'hearing' stray thoughts of those around me, but right now they seem dimmed or muffled. Is someone doing something to my powers? Or are they failing suddenly on their own?'

She looked about herself quickly, but in a hustling and bustling New York City day there are thousands of people on the street at once, perhaps millions across the island of Manhattan, the home to eight million people.

Silver looked up and down the street quickly, snapping her head from side to side but still saw nothing.

'I have to-I need a minute. This is just not right. I need a quiet spot, but in this city? Should I call Creature and the others' her mind raced, *'what should I do?'*
Finally she turned into an alleyway and walked halfway down it, stopping at its center.

'I've got to reach out with my powers-feel what is around me, and look for what isn't.' she stood between

the two brick walls of the alley, her hands at her sides and reached out with her mind, feeling the minds of those around her. Touching them individually, but not intruding on their thoughts.

But then she felt it, a blank spot. Someone was shielded from her somehow, and he was across the street from where she stood. He was hidden in the crowd and watching her. That she knew without reading his thoughts.

Immediately she touched a simple buckle on her decorative belt about her waist, and in a flash of light her bright red and silver costume appeared.

She looked up then as something caught her eye. Instantly a Ninja in all black dropped from the fire escape three stories up, swung on the railings of each fire escape below him and landed at her feet, sword drawn in a cat-like stance.

"Really?" Silver blurted out, "You're going to do this here and now?" She turned her head back toward the street, still keeping an eye on her opponent, "Mikuro, come out and face me like a man. Don't send your lap dogs after me. Face me yourself."

A powerful male voice reverberated throughout the alleyway in answer, "You are in no position to ask for anything, Steel Flower."

"My name is Silver Shadow, now and forever."

A sword clanged to her feet from above, clattering on the pavement.

"Pick it up Steel Flower." the same heavily accented voice ordered.

"I don't think so Mikuro. I'm done with that life."

"You will die here Steel Flower, if you do not pick up your weapon, and face your brothers and sisters in battle."

"I'll take my chances Mikuro."

"You shame me." the mystery voice declared.

"You shame yourself," Silver roared, "Leave this place and this city, and leave me alone. I won't be coming back to you. Not now, not ever. I am in charge of my life and destiny, not you Mikuro."

"Then I will have to kill you here. Is that worth your precious freedom?"

Now Silver stared at the Ninja still stretched out with his blade held before him. "Absolutely." she growled.

The ninja leaped to the attack, slicing the air with his blade in successive cuts, left, right, left, right. Silver danced across the alley, up walls and to the opposite side of wherever the ninja went. He was fast and incredibly skilled. She was better.

Silver floated upward, levitating over her opponents head and kicking him in the jaw as she sailed by. He dropped to the ground his blade noisily slapping the pavement.

Silver landed as lightly as a feather. Her enemy reached for his katana again, and she kicked it away.

"Uh, uh, uh cupcake. No more swords. Now it's just you and me."

Silver rushed toward him. Moving so fast she was a blur, the ninja threw a handful of shurikens' at her. The small throwing stars spread out and towards Silver Shadow. She leaped through the air, no flight, just pure body control, and dove between the stars feet first, avoiding them as she twisted her sinuous body about between the razor sharp blades.

Silver landed in a stance mirroring what the ninja had landed in when he had leapt down from above. Now she stood and went after her enemy.

"That shuriken trick was always a pain in the ass." she grunted.

The ninja stood his ground, silently, his eyes the only thing seen above the blackness of his uniform. Moving like greased lightning he attacked, his first move, a side thrust kick to her jaw. She sidestepped and parried, easily avoiding it.

Silver danced in, snapped a kick to his knee. She made light contact, nothing too damaging, but enough for him to stumble back a step.

Silver pressed her advantage; dancing in close, she chopped his extended arm down, and then jabbed at his eyes. He countered with a straight punch, catching her solidly in the jaw. Silver backed up a hair, but never lost her guard.

Silently they faced one another. No more words need be said between them.

"Kiyyyaaaai!" the ninja shouted. He streaked toward her, throwing kick after kick, trying to drive her backward.

Silver stood her ground, parried and ducked to her right of a palm blow her opponent threw and chopped at his neck, stunning him. She slid past and fired a rear thrust kick at her enemy, making solid contact to his left side kidney. He flung forward and fell into several garbage cans.

Silver spun in the tight confines of the alleyway, a roundhouse kick rocked her opponents jaw hard. She landed with a hiss of air.

The ninja shook his head, and wiped a spray of blood from his jaw.

Now anger got the better of him. He attacked Silver almost haphazardly. She simply stepped backward each time, avoiding his attacks easily.

"Go back to Mikuro and tell him you got your head handed to you by a girl, you over confident fool." Silver swept inside his line of attack and with her right hand, slashed at his throat, making him gag. Then she followed that up with a left cross to the nose. Now she was moving faster with each attack, and he slower.

Again, the ninja kicked at her this time with a right footed Thai kick. Silver levitated upward and summersaulted over his head, landing behind him, as he turned she threw a spinning wheel kick to his jaw, slamming him to the cold, hard, filthy pavement at her feet.

"Stay down. Next blow does permanent damage."

But the ninja did something curious then. He began to laugh. He continued to lie on the ground and laugh.

"What the hell? Did I rattle your brai-" Silver stumbled suddenly. She reached for the wall but it seemed so far away. Then her vision began to look like a funhouse mirror. "What the hell did you do to me?" she choked.

The mysterious ninja continued to laugh and pointed at her side. She reached down and her glove came away bloody. Her costume was slashed and when she looked behind her she realized one of the shuriken throwing stars lying on the ground was likewise covered in blood.

Silver stumbled now, "Poison." she mumbled, already feeling her throat tightening up. The ninja continued to laugh.

Silver concentrated, she wanted to fire one of her telepathic stun bolts, but nothing happened. She was too disoriented.

"Got to get out of here…"

Silver began to fly upward shakily and without her usual grace, when a hand reached out and pulled her back to the ground. It was the man she immediately recognized as Mikuro.

"You…bastard…what did you… do to…me?"

"A little diluted and augmented puffer fish poison, traitoress. You will be docile on the ride home."

Mikuro, an average height, non-descript Japanese man in all black with a single scar running down his face from forehead to jaw pointed at the sword that Silver had refused. By now ninja's were dropping down from above to land silently within the alley. A dozen black suited shadow warriors stood staring at the girl laying on the ground breathing heavily, her eyes glassy.

The ninja Silver had defeated regained his feet, retrieved the sword and handed it to Mikuro, who quickly and without a word decapitated the man who failed him.

"Take her out of here. We go home now. She has much to atone for. No one leaves the 'Brotherhood of the Blade' and lives."

***

50

Two minutes later Solaron, Captain Power and Creature flew into the alleyway from above.

"Where...is...she?" Creature growled in his barely discernable voice.

"She's not here, that's for certain." Sol replied, "I had her signal up until a minute or two ago, then it just... disappeared."

"She was though, look." Cap pointed.

"Blood. This alley has blood all over the walls and the ground." Sol commented.

Creature was beginning to growl audibly now. He pointed at a dumpster where the blood trail had led to.

Cap was the first to it. He tore the lid off and stepped back.

"It's not her."

Inside was the decapitated ninja.

"Where could they have taken her?" Sol asked Creature.

"Only...one...place...Japan."

"They can't have too much of a head start on us. They have to be going to an airport. I'll take JFK, Sol, you take Newark, Creature you go to LaGuardia."

Sol nodded in agreement; "I'm contacting Dragonfly and telling him to get the Stargrazer ready for flight just in case. Starbolt is with him."

Creature was already airborne; his massive leathern wings sprang from his back and bore him upward and out of sight in a heartbeat.

Cap and Sol streaked through the sky heading toward opposite airports, and were gone from sight immediately.

Solaron streaked through the sky toward Newark airport in New Jersey. Pulling up, he began to hover above the tower, scanning the field.

'I have no idea what I'm even looking for. Logically it has to be a private jet and a car or van with people holding her captive within. That must be like trying to hold down a tiger. I just don't get it. Her tracker I installed in her costume has gone dead. That was a waste of time and money. I wish I had Randy here. His spectroscopic vision would come in handy right now.' Solaron floated in mid-air, scanning all around him continuously.

Then, *'There. That black van pulling up to that Lear jet. That's got to be them, and someone's struggling getting out of it.'*

Solaron streaked toward the van and jet in question. Black suited ninja's emptied out of the van and ran toward the jet. Solaron began peppering the ground at the feet of those trying to get aboard the jet with blasts of solar heat, turning the tar to puddles about them.

"Hold it, nobody move." he ordered.

Sol floated in the air above them, his gold and white cape fluttering in the breeze.

One of the ninja's emerged from the van with a machine gun. Raising it up he shouted "Die gaijin!" He sprayed the air in Sol's direction, looking to perforate him where he floated. Sol didn't move, but he glowed brighter. The bullets melted before they ever reached the living star. Solaron dropped to the ground and walked toward his enemies. Several of them had taken up guns and were firing at him, "You idiots are just lucky that I'm melting everything your firing at me. If any innocents got hurt here today there'd be hell to pay. Now where is she? Where's Silver Shadow?"

The ninja's now ran screaming at him, several with raised swords.

"All right, if you want to play it this way…" Solaron fired solar blasts at the swords, melting them to slag instantly.

The ninja's did not reply, they merely continued to run at him with swords or fire guns at him.

"Enough of this already." he tapped his gauntlets and then fired. The thicker, heavier high density energy blasts leapt from his wrists, ramming his opponents over and to the ground. They lie on the tarmac runway moaning, partly burned, but mostly hurt from the sheer impact of the high density beams.

"You idiots are just lucky I turned down the heat so my beams didn't cut right through you."

Sol turned toward the van, and ripped the door open to find it, "Empty."

"That is right gaijin," a Japanese man standing on the steps of the plane shouted, "she is not here. He turned and entered the plane slamming the door behind him.

'I saw this guy drive up in the van, I know they didn't hustle her onto the plane, but they're not getting away this easily.' Solaron fired three blasts, one at each set of tires on the plane. "You're not going anywhere, whoever you are."

Cop cars raced up the runway behind Solaron, a burly lieutenant was out the door immediately and heading toward the hero, "You're that superhero guy who stopped those aliens last week? What's this now? Ninja's?"

"Yes, I'm him, one of them anyway. I'm called Solaron. Yes these are ninjas. They shot this place up. You'll find them all subdued. I have to go."

Without another word Sol streaked skyward, breaking the sound barrier almost instantly. He spoke into the jawbone mike embedded in his cowl, "Dragonfly where are you?"

"Coming up on your six right now."

Sol turned to the right and Dragonfly pulled up next to him.

"What's goin' on Sol? Did you find Silver?"

"No. They had a decoy car set up at Newark. Let's go to LaGuardia. That was Creatures destination."

"Great, he's probably tearing the place apart."

Both heroes streaked toward the nearby airport.

***

Several minutes earlier…

On a runway at the back of the airport near the private hangers, Creature was howling madly while fighting more ninja's who had arrived in a limousine. A dozen of the black garbed warriors attacked him, their swords bouncing off his suddenly rhinoceros hard skin. He slashed and cut at them with talons that grew from his fingertips. Several lie on the floor bleeding already. Then one emerged from the limo they were driving with a powerful machine gun and began spraying the air with it, trying to kill the hero.

Creature shape shifted and he became more feline, dodging back and forth, avoiding the deadly spray of bullets. Sure he could grow his armored hide thick enough to deflect a sword, but he had no illusions that it was tough enough to take multiple heavy ordinance hits. In short, Creature knew he wasn't bulletproof.

Behind the ninja's was another jet sitting there idling, ready for take-off.

Now another ninja had a second machine gun and both were peppering the ground and air where Creature was.

Creature looked at the limo that was between them and bounded for it. Once behind it he grabbed it and lifted, raising it up like a shield. He shifted the Limo in his powerful hands until the hood, roof and trunk was held out before him. He grasped it from underneath and ran forward growling madly while bullets ricocheted all about him. The multi-ton limo was now a shield taking all the damage.

Creature bowled over the ninja's who were left and not aboard the plane, flattening them. Now the plane began to taxi away, heading toward the runway. Without hesitation Creature hurled the limo at the plane, tearing out the rear set of wheels. Instantly the small jet slid to a stop.

"Sil-ver!" he bellowed, bounding across the air strip toward the downed plane. Leaping upward, his body constantly changing shape, he tore the side door off and tossed it to the runway below. Then he forced his way inside.

What he found stopped him dead in his tracks. Save for wounded and bleeding ninja's, the plane was empty.

Creature leaped to the runway and howled madly. Solaron and Dragonfly landed nearby him.

"She's not here." Solaron announced.

"J...F...K." Creature rumbled, again the great bat wings grew from his back and he shot skyward, this time with Solaron and Dragonfly beside him.

***

JFK airport. Captain Power approached from above and settled on the terminal roof.

'I don't see a thing here. Nothing's out of the ordinary at all. Where are they-there!" Caps attention was riveted toward a suburban racing across the tarmac toward a lone Lear jet idling on the runway.

Captain Power flew into the air, energy blasting out of his legs. He arced downward toward a blacked out suburban with tinted windows, holding his position a moment above it. The vehicle stopped opposite the jet and the door burst open on the suburban. Half a dozen ninjas ran out. "This is just stupid." Cap muttered.

Slicing down, he slammed into all the ninja's at once, scooping them up and heaving them against the side of the jet in a heap. None of them was even able to draw a breath, let alone a sword.

"Where is she? I'm asking this only once."

"Not...here." one of the ninja's spoke.

"Where then? Where is she? Tell me now before I get angry."

Captain Power grasped the man by the front of his uniform and pulled him close. He could feel the supposedly fearless ninja trembling in his grasp.

"W-what are you?" the man stammered.

"I'm Captain Power, that's all you need to know."

"You will die now, Captain Power. The girl is ours, and will remain that way." A voice shouted from beneath the jet on the runway. Cap turned toward it and saw a black suited Japanese man with sunglasses aiming a rocket launcher at him.

"Are you kidding me?" Cap blurted out.

The sunglass wearing man fired, and the rocket exploded the instant it hit Cap and the ninja he was holding. The suburban also exploded, showering the front of the hanger area with flaming metal and plastic. The rocket launcher bearing man grinned evilly while he stared into the heart of that inferno. He began to ascend the steps leading to the planes door when he stopped and removed the sunglasses, staring hard in disbelief at what he saw. "It cannot be." he murmured.

Out of the roaring flames a powerful figure strode purposefully toward the jet that 'Sunglasses' was about to enter. "Captain Power lives?" Sunglasses cried.

"Damned straight I do." Cap rocketed through the air at the man, landing in front of him on the rolling staircase instantly. Cap grasped the rocket launcher and tore it from his foes grasp. Then blocking the railing so Sunglasses could not escape, Cap crushed the rocket launcher, being careful not to explode the remaining rockets. Tossing it down to the ground he heaved the man upward in his grip and flew to the tarmac, dumping him unceremoniously next to the ruined rocket launcher.

"Now tell me where she is." Cap ordered.

"I-I." The man suddenly set his jaw firmly, seemingly biting down on something. Foam began to spill out of his mouth. Simultaneously he began to shake uncontrollably, and then seemed to melt away to dust in Cap's grip.

"What the heck was that?" A familiar youthful voice inquired.

Cap looked up at where the voice came from and saw Dragonfly, Creature and Solaron descending toward him.

"I don't know Dragonfly. Whatever these ninja's are they seem to have limitless resources. This one who turned to dust in my hands by biting down on something shot at me with a rocket launcher."

Creature landed on the boarding staircase and tore the door off the plane with one powerful yank of his clawed hand.

He was back outside an instant later.

"Empty." he growled.

"I'm not surprised." Solaron replied.

"All of this was a ruse. They wanted our attention. They wanted us running around where they could get her out of the country some other way." Cap postulated.

"It has to be another airport. There's no other way." Solaron said.

Creature walked around the plane and the burning wreckage. By now police and fire had arrived. Within minutes the burning wreckage was put out. Creature stood by the jet and howled madly like a forlorn beast, roaring his rage to the heavens.

"What do we do?" Dragonfly asked.

"We have to go after them." Cap said, "But Japan's a big place. We need a hook, something to help us find her." He turned toward the pile of ninja's he had knocked unconscious and grabbed one that was beginning to come to. "You, wake up." Cap shook him and the man stirred.

"Wh-oh! You! L-let me go I-"

Cap grabbed his jaw, making sure the ninja could not clamp his teeth shut. "I'll pull every tooth out of your mouth if I have to. You are not going to activate whatever the hell your partner used to turn himself to dust. What you are going to do is tell me where they took Silver Shadow. Otherwise I'm not going to be as gentle as I am now. Comprende?"

Cap held the ninja's jaw firmly in a rock hard grip. Slowly the ninja began to nod. Cap tore the head covering the ninja wore off and exclaimed in surprise, "It's a girl!"

She looked at him with vehemence in her eyes. Still he shook her once again roughly. "Where is Silver?" he asked again, "What have you done with her?"

She looked back and forth between the eyes of the men circling her. Creature let loose a low growl. The female ninja met his eyes and narrowed her own fearlessly.

Undeterred, Creature brought his face up close to hers and rumbled, "Where...is...she?"

The ninja tried to look away but couldn't. Finally in heavily accented English she said "Westchester, an airport there."

Solaron tapped his right gauntlet and fired a blast at her. But instead of hitting her the blast enveloped her in a globe of solar energy. "I'm taking her with us. Let's go." The four heroes rocketed skyward heading toward Westchester.

"We'll be there in a few minutes, at most." Solaron advised.

They landed two minutes later, near a nondescript beat up white truck with its driver's door left open. Their captive had pointed to the truck and Solaron put her down near there.

"Where are they?" Solaron demanded.

The ninja smiled, "They are gone. You have failed." she spat disdainfully.

Creature roared, his bellowing rage shocking his three teammates. He had the female ninja in his hands instantly, "Where …is…she?"

"J-japan. They are going to Japan." she stammered, looking away from his ferocious countenance.

An instant later the Stargrazer landed at the airport vertically, setting down lightly. Starbolt was at the controls.

Solaron turned to the young silver clad hero, "Japan. We have to get to Japan. Once there, our guest is going to show us where they've taken Silver Shadow."

Creature gripped the young woman's arm and shoved her roughly aboard the spacecraft. His claws bit into her arm through her warriors' garb. She knew she was immediately bleeding without looking.

Solaron leaned over the back of Starbolt's pilots' chair, "Can you get us to Japan?"

Starbolt looked at Solaron very seriously and said, "Yes. This *is* a spaceship you know?"

Solaron grinned for an instant and then answered, "I know what it is Prince Bol-Ton. I meant, and I realize I should have spoken clearer, do you know where Japan is?"

Starbolt nodded, "I am tying into your GPS satellites and we will head there directly. I will be taking us into space momentarily and flying an arc that will have us in Japan in a minute or two; allowing for air currents and weather displacement of course."

Solaron nodded and grinned, "Of course."

"You had better take a seat Solaron. The acceleration can be quite…jarring."

Solaron nodded, "Understood Starbolt."

Sol buckled in to the seat next to Starbolt's and the Stargrazer angled up toward space, disappearing so quickly those below questioned if it had even been there.

The small, sleek craft rocketed upward and performed a parabolic arc, dropping back down to earth on a direct line with Japan. Within two minutes they were hidden in clouds above the city of Tokyo.

"Where should I land?

"I don't know yet. She said they were taking Silver to Tokyo, but who knows where actually?"

"I think we should ask her, or maybe have Creature do it."

Sol nodded at Starbolt, with a new appreciation of his savvy.

Sol unbuckled and walked toward the back of the small ship, "Cap, Creature, we need our guest to tell us where to land."

Cap and Creature both nodded affirmatively and followed Solaron toward their captive.

"What do we call you?" Sol asked.

"Death…" was her straight faced reply.

"Really? You're going to play that game with us?" Cap asked, almost guffawing.

"Where…is…Silver?" Creature growled, his fangs mere inches from the face of the female ninja. She stared at him eye to eye, but after a moment seemed to melt under his glare.

"A-at the mansion of the master. I-I can show you. But there will be an army awaiting you there."

Sol laughed, "Lady we're about ten hours ahead of them at this point. What airport are they going to land at?"

"Haneda international airport."

"Is it going to be at a private terminal? Do you know exactly where?" Cap asked.

"Y-yes. J-just keep the monster away from me." She stammered again. This time all of her resolve and show of strength was gone. Creature's ferocity washed over her with each breath he took.

"Does this ship have any kind of cloaking device?" Sol asked.

"It does." replied Starbolt.

"Activate it and take us to a point hovering above the private terminal our guest points out."

Starbolt nodded, and turned toward the captive ninja, who could not keep her eyes off of Creature. There was good reason for that though, he kept staring at her and growling in a low rumble.

Cap stood near Sol and said, "She probably thinks he's going to take a bite out of her."

"At this point I wouldn't be surprised if he did. Look at him; he's a man at his wits end."

Cap nodded in agreement, "He loves her."

"Well, we know it's his sister."

"Yes we do, and I have to think he lost her once before and never wants to again from this reaction. He wants to guard her with his life." Cap watched Creature who was hovering around the ninja, watching her intently. His face was a contorted mass of fur and teeth. His claws grew and receded from his fingertips repeatedly.

He wanted to tear the ninja apart; it was evident in everything about him right now, even the way he breathed when staring at the woman.

"We're going to have to watch him like this for the next ten hours?" Dragonfly came up behind them and asked.

"No. We're going to ask our guest and Creature some questions." Solaron replied.

Sol walked up to Creature and their captive and placed himself between them. Captain Power placed himself behind the woman with his arms crossed upon his massive chest.

"Creature, what does this ninja master want with Silver Shadow? Why did they kidnap her?"

Creature snorted derisively, "Silver…she trained…with…them…for years. They…separated us both…took Silver…from me. I searched…for years. Finally…she came…back to…me. She…told me…she had…escaped. It…looked…like she…did."

"How long ago did she come back to you?" Cap asked.

"A year…ago."

"You two are twins ain'tcha?" Dragonfly asked.

"How…did you…know?"

"I just had a hunch. I know some twins in school. They act like you two do. Like slightly more than just brothers and sisters. So how'd you guys get your powers?"

Creature shrugged and walked away from the captive female ninja. He walked over toward Dragonfly and looked him in the eyes, "We…were…born with…them."

"So you two are genetic mutants then?" Solaron asked, his scientific curiosity piqued.

"We…have been…called…that."

Sol looked at Creature, tilting his head slightly to the right, "How old were you when your abilities appeared?"

"We were…mid-teens."

"Creature, I'm not trying to pry so please forgive me for asking, but were you born looking like this? Or did your features change when you…came of age?"

Creature seemed to sag inwardly before answering that question. He sat in a seat and held his face in his fur covered hands. After a moment he finally spoke, "I looked…as normal as…any of…you. But…eight years ago… I…fell asleep…looking like…any normal…fifteen…year old…boy, and…awoke…looking like…this." He held his hands out before his face staring at them.

The silence within the Stargrazer was palpable. Finally Captain Power cleared his throat and broke everyone's silent reverie.

Solaron placed a hand on Creatures shoulder, "I apologize if I dug too deeply. I did not mean to open any old wounds, or to cause you any new ones."

Creature sighed, his massive frame and black fur shook up and down as he did. "You…did no…wrong.

You...have...all been...most kind...to my...sister...and I. We...must...trust each...other.
We...are...Hyperforce...now. That...will...mean something...to the...world...someday. It must...mean more...to us...all, now."

Silently the rest of the team stood there and processed what Creature had said; a man who until now had spoken barely more than a few words between grunts.

Finally, after many hours of watching alien gauges that approximated radar as well as a few other means of tracking that were unknown to everyone, including Solaron, a new blip appeared on all the indicators.

"It's probably another passenger jet." Dragonfly offered.

"No, it is too small." Starbolt replied.

"Visual?" asked Solaron.

"Of course." Starbolt answered.

He tapped a control and an image of the oncoming plane instantly appeared on his console.

"Can you magnify that?" Sol requested.

Starbolt nodded and the he touched another control instantly the image zoomed way in.

"How far out is this?" Sol again asked.

"Twenty five of your miles. It will be here in a few minutes."

"Okay, keep us cloaked, and Starbolt?"

Starbolt swiveled his chair to face Sol, "Yes?"

"Good job."

The young hero smiled and turned back toward the control panel.

"Put us down directly in front of that plane when it lands."

"Yes Solaron."

"Relax Prince Bol-Ton, we have enough fire power here between us to take out half the nations on the planet. A few ninja's won't be any problem."

"That is exactly what I am concerned with, Solaron. Something is not right about all of this. Why would these 'ninja's' as you call them attack us when we are so powerful a group? We are not well known, but the battle with General Zaring has spread around your internet like a fire that is wild."

"You mean a wildfire, kid." Cap offered.

"That is what I have said is it not?"

"I guess it is." Cap chuckled.

"Heads up," Solaron ordered, "here they come. The minute we see Silver come out of the jet, we put down in front of it and we put them down. You all know the rules, we do not kill. You got that Creature?"

The man-beast nodded his head and growled, his claws popping in and out of his fingertips while he stared at the landing plane.

"It's coming to a stop," Dragonfly commented, "but I don't see-, oh wait, there she is."

"Let's say hello." Solaron said.

The Stargrazer touched down in front of the jet and immediately de-cloaked.

Ninja's exploded from the Lear jet, swords drawn. The doors on the hanger the plane had stopped in front of suddenly opened and a veritable river of black suited ninja's erupted from its doors.

Starbolt and Dragonfly immediately flew to confront the group coming out of the hanger.

"Come an' get some, jerks!" Dragonfly shouted, spraying them with his electron power bursts, or as he called them, his 'Dragonblasters'. The rows of ninjas dropped instantly to the ground and lie there spasming.

Meanwhile Starbolt hovered above another group, who were now aiming automatic weapons at him. He shouted, "Heavy mass beam." Energy leapt from his fingertips and sprayed all over the ninja's in this group. To a man they all dropped to the ground and lie there struggling to get up. But they could not, it was as if they were pinned to the ground by their own bodies, which in truth they were.

"Nice job." Solaron told him over his micro-communicator that he had installed in Starbolt's costume.

Creature dove from the Stargrazer, lifting into the air immediately as the massive wings grew out of his back once more. He aimed directly for the man called 'Mikuro' with outstretched claws and a roar on his lips that shocked friend and foe alike.

But as fast as lightning, Mikuro drew his sword and slashed at Creature, knocking him from the air. The hairy hero slid across the pavement, sliding to a stop near the wheels of the jet.

Almost instantly though, he was back on his feet. Blood flowed from his shoulder, and he grasped it while growling angrily.

Undaunted Sol floated down toward the ninja master, "We're here for our teammate. We're not leaving without her, even if we have to raze this airport to the ground around you."

Mikuro met his gaze and sneered, "The girl is mine I own her body and soul. The Brotherhood of the Blade claims her life."

"So I'm guessing you didn't see how we just took your ninja's out in zero seconds flat?" Dragonfly chided.

"Foolish boy. Those men pledge their lives to me, and those you downed were only neophytes, not fully trained warriors. The Brotherhood of the Blade is feared throughout the world. We have warriors hidden everywhere." Mikuro turned and waved his sword at Solaron and Dragonfly and shouted "Kill them all!"

Instantly waves of blood red garbed ninja's seemed to grow out of thin air. Literally hundreds attacking at once.

But Hyperforce did not pause, instead they charged forward to the attack.

Creature, still bleeding bellowed horrifically and then jumped into the midst of the fray. His fur receded immediately and an armor-like skin took its place. Now his claws grew to great lengths from his fingertips and he began slashing at the red garbed warriors. His ferocious strength and power protected him as much as his armored skin did. Bodies were flying everywhere from his attacks.

Meanwhile Dragonfly was rotating between firing his explosive fletchettes and his dragon blasts.

Solaron went straight for Mikuro. The ninja master attacked with a screaming "Kiii-Yai!" slashing at Sol repeatedly.

But Solaron's ever-present solar field blunted the attacks.

"This is not possible," Mikuro roared, "this sword can cut steel itself. Nothing can stop its attack."

"Well I guess something has finally, me." Sol replied.

The ninja master charged Solaron with his sword held above his head. Solaron fired his right gauntlet, set in the high density position. Mikuro flew away from Solaron as if shot out of a cannon. He landed twenty feet away, his clothing smoldering.

Nearby Cap slammed his hands into the pavement and ripped upward and out from under their enemies. He shook the tarmac in his hands like it was a carpet. More ninjas continued to appear, encircling them again and again.

Starbolt dropped down in the midst of the ninjas and shouted "Explosive wave!" energy flared from his body, smashing the red suited ninjas away from them all.

"We've gained a respite but who knows how long this is for?" Cap announced.

"Where's Silver?" Dragonfly asked.

"Over there." pointed Starbolt.

Everyone turned to see what he was pointing at and they immediately recognized Silver Shadow being dragged toward a door in the hanger by several of the ninjas'.

"She's hurt." Dragonfly shouted to the rest of the team. He aimed his gauntlets and unleashed his Dragonblasts, stunning the two ninja's who were holding onto Silver Shadow. She fell away, and her former captors crumpled to the dirt, unconscious.

Immediately Creature was at her side, steadying and holding her. She was barely conscious, "Creature...Billy, Thank you." she mumbled while holding on to his neck, "You came for me...you *all* did." Silver Shadow looked around at all of the team. Her brother picked her up and carried her back toward the awaiting Stargrazer.

"How do you want to play this?" Cap asked Sol, "We could wipe the street with these guys but we'd end up killing lots of them if we did."

"I'm not sure we have a choice. If we just left they'd come after Silver again when she least expected it, and she can't live her life looking over her shoulder. That's no way to live."

"So what are you thinking?"

Sol turned and looked where he had blasted Mikuro, "He's gone."

"Who is?"

"Their leader the ninja master. I blasted him up against those hanger doors over there, but he's gone now. We have to find him. This won't be over until we do."

"Wonderful." Cap added.

A voice blared across a PA system all around them, "You gaijin fools will never leave Nippon alive. I will see to that."

"That's the leader; Mikuro is his name I think." Dragonfly announced as he touched down next to Solaron and Captain Power.

"Yes, correct on all accounts Dragonfly." Sol replied.

"So what do we do? I mean we could probably take out this entire army of ninja's alone, I mean the four of us could at least." Dragonfly included the just arrived Starbolt.

"Are you okay? You don't look as wiped out as you did last time you pulled that stunt." Cap questioned.

"I have never done that before. You confuse my Starbolt with the energy wave. One is simply a very pale reflection of the other. The Starbolt would have wiped out this airport and everything in it. The energy wave I created merely pushed back a small area about us."

"Okay good, so you're up to power then?" Sol asked.

The youth nodded, "I am."

"Good we're going to need it I think."

"Look at that!" Dragonfly shouted.

Out of the sky something was streaming rocket trails and heading right for them, and it was something enormous. A monstrous metallic figure landed a few hundred feet away and roared its rage at the heroes.

"What the hell? It looks like a giant ninja robot or something." Dragonfly commented.

"That's exactly what it looks like." Sol replied.

Mikuro's voice blared at them from the speakers again, "Did you fools not realize the vast resources of my organization? Did you think me simply attached to the old ways? I am more than that, much more! I will now be all your deaths as well."

"This guy talks too much." Dragonfly remarked.

"You're right," Cap replied, "I'm going to take on the metal Godzilla over there. But we still have the ninja's running around here to worry about, even though most of them scattered when that thing showed up."

"We…will…handle…them."

They all turned to see Creature and Silver Shadow standing there beside them, having just emerged from the Stargrazer.

"Are you all right?" Cap asked Silver.

"Better. Not perfect, but better."

"Are you up to this?" Sol asked.

Silver Shadow nodded in the affirmative, "I'm fine. I got some food in me from the ships stores and some anti-venom medication.

"It's a good thing you insisted on all of that going into the Stargrazer." Starbolt commented to Solaron.

Sol nodded, "I'm glad you agreed to allow it. This is your ship after all.

"What do we do with this monster?" Dragonfly pointed with his chin at the towering behemoth standing amidst the runways bellowing at them.

"We take it down." Sol answered," Creature, you and Silver stay back and take care of any ninja's you find straggling around. The rest of us are going to send this thing back to the scrap heap."

Dragonfly leapt into the air, his boot rockets flaring, "Hyperforce go!" he shouted.

"Oh, that sounded terrible." Cap responded before rocketing away, directly toward the towering metal titan.

Cap flew with both fists forward and plowed into the three hundred foot tall robot in the middle of its chest. The impact was so great it sounded like a bomb went off, and the shockwave caused by his impact knocked down people and shattered airport windows hundreds of feet away.

The robot tottered then fell over with another thunderous crash.

Solaron circled above it. Setting his gauntlets on the middle density setting he unleashed his blistering solar blasts on the robots neck, seeking to sever its head.

But its eyes flashed and energy beams flew from them, knocking Sol from the sky to land in a heap. With surprising speed the gigantic robot was back on its feet

"Solaron!" Dragonfly shouted.

He turned his attention to the robot and began firing his explosive fletchettes. Hundreds of miniature explosions covered the robots face and upper torso.

Again its eyes flashed and it shot its deadly energy beams from its eyes directly at Dragonfly.

"Not so fast, Tin Kong." Dragonfly shouted, raising his right side wing up to absorb and deflect the attack.

Dragonfly flew over the robots head, and fired his Dragonblasts repeatedly, but to little affect.

Cap suddenly shot up from the ground, where he had landed after his devastating attack. Like a missile he struck the towering monster under its jaw, lifting it upward and over. It landed with a reverberating crash that shook the ground like an earthquake.

Starbolt flew above the metal monster now and shouted "Disintegration beam!"

His beam disintegrated part of the chest, at least the upper layer of mechanics. But before he could finish it off, its arm flailed upward and knocked Starbolt from the sky.

"No!" yelled Solaron, he fired beams that encased Starbolt in a bubble of solar energy. Softly he lowered him to the ground.

Sol ran to Starbolt's side and quickly looked him over. He turned and spoke into his comm unit, "He's okay, just stunned."

"Okay this is getting stupid. We have to put this thing down." Cap replied.

"You're right. We can't drag this out any longer. If this thing leaves the airport and heads into the city the loss of life will be catastrophic."

"I don't think it's going to, Sol. I think it only wants us. That's what its master sent it to do. Kill us."

"So let's destroy this thing then." Sol confirmed. He turned back to Starbolt, "We're going to need you I think."

"I-I just need a minute."

"I'll get it for you, but no more. This thing has got to go."

Starbolt nodded weakly.

Solaron streaked into the sky and began hammering the robot with his high density blasts. Captain Power likewise unleashed his force bolts. Again and again the robot flailed about and staggered now. Dragonfly zipped by and peppered it over its opened chest cavity with Dragonblasts and explosive fletchettes.

Cap circled back around and rocketed in for another strike to the towering robots head, but instead it batted him away as he drew close. Cap sailed across the horizon, disappearing into the distance.

But now Dragonfly streaked in fists first, to slam madly into the giant metal head with a deafening 'splang'. The robot staggered slightly, but Dragonfly's strength was decidedly less than Captain Powers. Still it was enough to get the robots attention. It swiveled its head and fired its eye beams. Deftly Dragonfly flew around them, "Try again too tall. I'm not that easy to catch."

Solaron hovered a few feet away and unleashed blistering solar blast after solar blast. "Keep its attention Dragonfly. Cap's not back yet and Starbolt is still out of it."

"Trying to, boss."

Solaron used his blasts like lasers, cutting away at the neck. But the robot moved deceptively fast, its hand swung up and batted Solaron away.

"Ugggh!" shouted the solar superhero, as he careened across the night black sky to land in a heap across the field.

Starbolt looked on in horror, *'Everyone but Dragonfly is down. I have to stop this monsters rampage or we will all be dead.'*

Fighting his way painfully to his feet Starbolt raised his hands up, aimed at the metal juggernaut before him and shouted "Zero mass beam, anti-gravity effect, acceleration ray!"

Instantly the robot shot up from the earth, disappearing into the star speckled night sky, and away from the planet.

Dragonfly landed next to Starbolt and said "Dude, what'd you do? That was incredible!"

Starbolt's gaze followed the disappearing robot before he answered, "I shot it into space. As far away as I could." he turned back toward Dragonfly and admitted, "I wasn't sure that was even going to work."

"Well I'm glad it did at least. Without Sol and Cap here I don't think we would have lasted much longer.

Solaron and Captain Power landed next to the two younger heroes, "Is everyone all right?" Cap asked.

"Yeah, we are. How about you two?" Dragonfly replied.

"I'm banged up, but my solar field protected me, at least enough so that I'm still here to talk about it." Sol replied.

"You okay Cap?" Dragonfly asked.

"Yes, I'm fine. That thing smacked me miles away, but I landed in car lot. I hated to do it, but I absorbed a couple of the cars I destroyed with my crash landing. I hope those folks have insurance."

"Let's go find Creature and Silver Shadow." Sol offered.

They flew across the field and landed by the Stargrazer. Unconscious ninja's were strewn about, police were everywhere. Creature sat on the steps that led up to the Stargrazer's hatch growling loudly every time a police officer approached him. Silver Shadow sat inside the ship; her head leaned back with an ice pack on her forehead.

Sol entered the ship first. Silver saw him and smiled, "He escaped."

"Who did?"

"Mikuro. He got away in all the madness that went on here."

Sol smirked, "I wouldn't worry about it Silver. He's not going to bother you again. We embarrassed him and tore through his forces, including his giant robot which had to cost him hundreds of millions, perhaps billions of dollars. He's not going to recover from that so easily. C'mon lets go home."

"Everyone settled in?" Cap asked two minutes later."

Everyone nodded in the affirmative. The Stargrazer lifted upward and streaked away into the night time sky toward home.

***

Far away a mysterious red cloaked figure with bright metallic gloves and a matching helmet watched the Stargrazer fly away on the security camera's from the airfield. He shut the feed off and his room full of monitors went blank.

He shook his head side to side and smiled, for only his mouth and jaw were visible below his helmet line, "Soon." was all he said.

Ralph L. Angelo Jr.

Chapter 4

Mayhem in Manhattan!

The Stargrazer sat cooling in the landing bay beneath the solar observatory. The team sat in the meeting room while they debriefed about the mission.

"Is all of this really necessary?" Dragonfly asked.

Solaron nodded affirmatively, "Yes it is. We need to build a database of these enemies for the next time we have to battle them. We have no idea when that may be, but the 'Brotherhood of the Blade' obviously has unlimited resources, and that means even though we devastated them, they could be back."

"C'mon, we trashed their robot; beat their pajama wearin' guys into the ground. How much more thoroughly could we embarrass them?"

"Dragonfly, you're just not getting it. That was one robot today. What if they had two? Or ten? Or thirty? How would we have won then? Heck, one robot almost killed us all. Cap and I were out of it, at least temporarily. My energy field can only absorb so much. I maxed it out as it was. If Starbolt hadn't have pulled that last minute save we'd probably all be dead right now. Or at least some of us would have."

Dragonfly's eyes went wide, "What you don't think I can handle myself?"

"I didn't say that Dragonfly. I said we could have had some casualties. I wasn't pointing a finger at you or at anyone actually. But that was a bad situation. Starbolt saved our bacon. Look, I'm just asking everyone to enter what you thought was any pertinent info you noticed in the battle into the pad I just gave each of you. I'll collate it all in the database tonight. This is a must do after each and every battle."

"Okay I got it. Sorry boss." Dragonfly sat back in his seat and continued entering what he remembered.

"Silver," Captain Power began, "can you tell us anything else about how they abducted you?"

"Like I already said, they drugged me. Once they did I couldn't fire my psychic stun beam. Then they just threw me into a dilapidated van. At that point I passed out completely from whatever they gave me. The next thing I knew I was in the air over the pacific."

"That's what I thought."

"Solaron, my Prince," Mar-Cus appeared at the door of the conference room looking agitated, "You all must see what is on the TV. Hurry."

He ran into the room, picked up the remote on the table and turned the flat panel on the wall on, immediately turning on a local news feed.

"What the hell?" Cap asked.

On the screen, a man in a black and yellow costume was battling another man wearing a brightly polished steel helmet with matching gauntlets. He had on a black bodysuit with a stylized 'M M' emblazoned across it with a red cape upon his back. This was all taking place in Times Square.

"The guy in black an' yellow is getting his tail whupped." Dragonfly observed.

"Yes he is. But he seems powerful." Sol added, "Look how fast he moves. He has some sort of instant acceleration power. He seems to almost disappear for an instant every time he flies out of his enemy's way."

"He's strong too." Cap added. He just picked up a truck and threw it without considerable effort."

"Whoa, he fires energy too." Silver observed.

"Yes, looks like some kind of explosive blasts. But 'Mashed Potato Man' seems to have some sort or psychic force field. Look at that energy erupt out of that jewel on his helmet.

"I think his name must be 'Mustard Man' myself." Dragonfly muttered.

"Why's that?" Cap asked.

"Cause he's beating the condiments out of the other guy in the black and yellow suit."

"Look at that, he caught the truck in an energy field from his mind somehow. That's amazing." Sol commented.

"How do we know who the good guy is?" Silver asked.

"I think we just found out." Cap replied.

On the screen they watched as 'M M' had caught the box truck the black and yellow suited super being threw at him in a globe of mental energy, then he turned it around and tossed it at some civilians hiding near his foe. He laughed as he did it. The black and yellow suited man flew through the air, landing in front of the endangered people and shouted, "Run!" before he caught the impact of the truck and saved them from a very crushing death.

But he himself was crushed to the pavement by the massive box truck.

The obvious villain shoved a reporter out of the way telekinetically, and had his microphone floating in the air before himself, which was the first thing the team heard clearly because of all the sounds of battle that had been going on.

"Tell Hyperforce that Mind Master awaits them in Manhattan. Tell them I will kill this fool," the limp body of the black and yellow suited man floated out of the wreckage and over to Mind Master, "If they do not come to Times Square and swear subservience to me."

The screen went to static for a moment until the feed was picked up again by the newsroom crew.

"Dragonfly, ammo up and recharge your suit right now."

"On my way, Sol."

"Cap, you and Starbolt get there immediately. Creature are you okay with your wounded arm? Do you want to sit this one out?"

"No…Solaron… I am…fine…to do…battle."

"Okay but keep that bandage I wrapped you with clean if you can. It may be weeks before you heal properly."

"No, not…weeks. Days…I heal…slightly faster…than normal…people. Part…of…my…shapshifting…ability."

"Okay good, but still take it easy. Silver, you should sit this one out. Those ninja's pumped you full of drugs"

"No, uh uh. I'm fine, and I'm going with you. No buts about it."

82

"Okay lady ninja, you've got it. I'm not going to waste my breath arguing with you."

"We're on our way Sol." Cap advised.

He and Starbolt shot out of the hanger underneath the observatory and disappeared into the mid-day sky.

Within minutes they landed in Times Square, where they found the black and yellow suited man hanging from the Times Square large screens in effigy.

"This is nuts." Cap whispered.

"Watch my back kid, I'm getting him down."

Cap flew over to the imprisoned man, who was hanging there by steel rods bent around his arms and legs jammed into the sign itself, which now streamed static behind the unconscious super-hero.

Cap pulled the steel bars apart, bending them easily open. Taking hold of the defeated super-hero, he flew to the ground and placed the man out of the way behind a police barricade.

"See to this man, he needs help." Cap ordered.

Cap turned and walked back out into the street, his cape fluttering in the breeze behind him majestically while he looked for Mind Master. Above Starbolt floated in the air scanning the street.

"I don't see him anywhere." Starbolt offered, "Maybe he left?"

"I wouldn't count on it. No one makes that big a stink to just disappear a couple of minutes later."

Cap looked around; the center of Times Square was in ruin. Cars were laying on their sides or roofs. A fire hydrant shot a geyser of water thirty feet into the air. Windows were smashed in storefronts and store alarms' blared continuously.

"This is madness. Where could this guy have gone?"

A blast of energy enveloped Captain Power and drove him to his knees. Starbolt began to fly to his aid, when he was seemingly gripped by an invisible hand and slammed to the pavement.

Mind Master appeared, seemingly stepping from invisibility into visibility. He walked up to Cap who was struggling trying to stand. Energy arced all about him as he fought to regain his feet.

"My, you are strong. Stronger even than poor Stryker over there." Mind Master gestured towards the man in black and yellow who was being tended to by ambulance personnel.

"Not that it matters. I am Mind Master. I am going to reshape this world. I will allow nothing and no one to stand in my way. You and your friends appeared at a bad time you see. I can't have you interfering in my plans. Soon I will do away with all strife, all hunger, all want. I will rule this world completely and with an iron fist, but those that obey will be well provided for. Everyone will have a role to play. You and your friends, if you decide you want to continue to live, will have the role of being my enforcers. What do you think? Will you all be interested?"

A blast of burning golden energy slammed into Mind Master, hurling him across the pavement. He slid to the opposite curb and into a storefront shattering the entire front of the store, glass and steel rained down to the pavement, burying Mind Master within.

"Are you all right?" Solaron asked. He landed next to Cap who stood immediately and growled much like Creature would have.

84

Across the square the Stargrazer was settling down. Out flew Silver Shadow and Creature.

Dragonfly was hovering above Sol and Cap and had been since Solaron arrived.

"Let's get him." Cap rumbled.

The front of the store exploded outward, glass and steel showered the team.

Mind Master stood straight up and floated out of the store toward them all.

"Greetings Solaron. I am Mind Master. I am pleased you chose to appear. As I so graciously offered your subordinate here, I will reiterate with you. Join me. Work as my lieutenants and I will not have to kill you all. What say you?"

"How about take a hike?" Dragonfly answered. He fired his explosive fletchettes at the floating villain. But they exploded short of him against an impenetrable shield of mental energy.

Creature growled madly and attacked, hurling himself at his enemy. His claws extending, he slashed at the barrier separating him from Mind Master.

"Foolish, ignorant brute. Sleep."

Like a puppet with its strings cut, Creature dropped to the ground.

Seeing her brother taken out so quickly Silver Shadow did not hesitate but began unleashing her mental stun bolt at Mind Master.

"Wh-what?" he stammered, surprised by her attack. He took several steps backward under her assault.

Cap did not hesitate. He flew in and hammered at the shield with punches that could bring down mountains. The mental shield shattered instantly.

Solaron attacked again, throwing blistering solar blasts again and again at their foe, haranguing him.

"Th-this is not possible." the embattled villain moaned.

"Yeah it is, you clown." Dragonfly flew down from above and pounded Mind Master across the jaw, knocking him fifty feet, and into the side of a hastily abandoned newspaper truck.

Now the entire team including a just revived but still groggy Starbolt and Creature approached their enemy, looking to finish the battle.

Mind Master stood again, but this time on unsteady feet. He looked at the powerful enemies he had made approaching him with blood in their eyes, "It seems I underestimated you all. I won't make the same mistake twice." Then he winked out of existence, as if he had never been there.

"Dragonfly!" Sol shouted.

"I'm on it." Dragonfly answered. He squinted and began scanning the area with his spectroscopic vision. "If he was here he's gone. I can't find any trace of him."

Solaron ground his teeth in frustration, "What just happened here? This 'Mind Master' appears out of nowhere and challenges us, then disappears the moment we begin to get the better of him? Something's not right. He gave up too easily."

Dragonfly shrugged, "He's a coward maybe? Aren't all villains a cowardly lot or something like that?"

"That's what they say. I'm not sure I agree with that assessment though." Cap replied.

"Let's see how the guy is doing who was fighting him."

They all walked over behind the police barricades where the black and yellow suited man was sitting up on the back of an ambulance. His mask covered most of his face, but like Sols and Dragonfly's the mouth and part of the face was left open. His eyes were covered by yellow lenses.

"Oye! Thanks for savin' me bacon there. Me name's Stryker with a 'Y', pleased ta make yer acquaintance." He shoved his hand out towards Solaron with a grin spread across his bruised face. His blonde van dyke quivered when he smiled.

"I'm called Solaron, and this is the rest of Hyperforce. Is that an Australian accent I hear?"

"Aye mate it tis."

"We'd like to talk to you about what happened here. It appeared you were trying to save the bystanders caught in the crossfire."

Stryker smiled again, "Oh yeah mate, you got it, you got it. That dingo was goin' ta kill some innocents an' I couldn't a had that on me conscience, could I?"

"No," Sol replied, "you couldn't. I know I couldn't."

"Yeah mate, it's not what heroes do." he grinned. Then he noticed Silver Shadow, "Well 'ello gorgeous. Come to me rescue didya? I haveta say I am one lucky Aussie, then." Stryker grinned a charming smile. He stood up and continued to beam at Silver. He was tall, perhaps six foot four. Taller than Solaron by two inches and shorter than Captain Power by four. His body was broad and strong, as evidenced by the skin tight black and yellow leather body stocking he wore.

"Whoa, me heads still a little bi' wobbly, it is." he grasped his head and the EMS techs helped him back down. "I just need another minute boys I'll be fine." he grinned that defense breaking grin.

"How'd you happen to be here when this 'Mind Master' appeared?" Cap asked.

"I was on holiday, mate. Seein' th' sights o' old New York."

"Right…" Cap nodded emotionlessly.

"All right, Stryker. If you need anything, or if you run into Mind Master again, contact us." Solaron held out his hand and in it was a small communicator that adhered to the neck with a small bit of skin adhesive, "Place this against your neck, under your cowl. You tap it once if you want to contact us. It will route through my own communications rig directly to us."

"Thanks mate. I appreciate the help. I hope to meet you all again." Stryker turned and smiled at Silver Shadow. She turned away and blushed slightly.

Dragonfly looked at Starbolt, "Did you see that? She blushed. She's buying the stuff this guy's sellin'. I don't get it."

"You are older than me my friend. If you do not understand females, I certainly do not."

"Yeah, but you're a prince. Don't you got a harem or something?"

"I am sorry Dragonfly. I am unfamiliar with that term."

"Ah, to heck with it. She's too old for me anyway." Dragonfly waved his hand in disgust.

"Let's head back to headquarters." Solaron ordered.

"Sounds like a good idea." Cap replied. They all began to walk toward the Stargrazer, but Cap glanced back at Stryker one more time. The other man saw, smiled and nodded.

Cap nodded in return, without the smile.

Solaron caught the whole exchange. Once they all walked back onto the ship Solaron turned toward the Captain, "What just happened between you and our new found friend?"

Cap turned and looked Sol in the eyes, "Something's not right with that guy. I may be wrong, but I don't trust him."

Sol tilted his head, "He seemed pretty honest to me. It looked like he was really trying to save those people."

"I agree. But…Ah, forget I said anything. Maybe it's just the guy thing where I don't trust anybody that smooth."

"You mean the way he had Silver's heart all aflutter?"

"What else? Forget I said anything. I think we have to go over the information about this new threat. That guy 'Mind Master' seemed evil and brilliant. He had that haughty 'I'm smarter and more powerful than you attitude.' that villains do, the good ones at least."

"Good ones?"

"Really, really bad ones. You know what I mean."

"Unfortunately I do. This guy may be our first big league threat."

"You think he's bigger league than the General?"

Sol nodded slowly, "At least he's a homegrown one in Zaring's league. Let me put it that way."

"Whatever happened today, this is someone we have to keep a lookout for."

Sol squinted slightly, "Mind Master or Stryker?"

Captain Power locked eyes with Solaron and answered grimly, "Honestly Solaron? Maybe both. Or maybe I'm just being paranoid."

The Stargrazer hovered upward with Starbolt at the controls and then disappeared into the horizon, heading toward home.

Chapter 5

The Fire This Time

Two weeks later...

Solaron was sitting at his monitor station in the main lab of the Solar Energy Research Facility, working on an experiment.

Dragonfly walked into the room with his cowl pulled off and hanging on his back. He was an average looking kid with short brown hair and a big smile.

He walked up next to Ronald Anderson and began fiddling with some tools on the workbench in front of him.

"What are you doing Randy? And why is your mask off?"

"C'mon Uncle Ron, you have the new guys living here for three weeks now. I think we can all be friends. I mean I don't think I have to worry about trusting them."

"Randy, when I want your opinion on how to run things I'll let you know. For now, any risks I take like revealing my identity to our new friends is something I'm willing to do because I'm an adult and willing to make my own decisions and take my own chances."

"Oh, but having a sixteen year old boy with you in a fight with super-villains is okay with you?"

Solaron turned to him and frowned, "Are you kidding me? How long did I fight with you about not being involved in all of this? I tried for weeks to keep you out of it all. But you insisted that you would follow my lead and that you would only go into action when we were together."

"And I've followed the rules, exactly as I promised, haven't I Uncle Ron? I've been a good little boy, sorry I mean soldier, or is it super-hero?"

"Randy, you're getting this close to me shutting down your suit and shutting you down."

"Hey Uncle Ron, I know-"

"That's just it, Randy. You don't know. Every time you want to say the words 'I know' stop yourself and realize you don't know. Not at all. You know nothing right now. In five years you might start to get a clue. For now you know nothing. I don't want you making an uninformed or rash decision and getting killed because of it. How am I supposed to tell your parents that you were really a super-hero and that you died in the line of duty, fighting what? Aliens? Robot monsters? Ninja's? Super-Villains? Do you know what a hard time I'm having with you going out there at my side every single time we get into a fight with some nut job?"

"Uncle Ron, I can take care of myself. I'm strong and fast, and I got this suit that's keyed up to only me-"

"That's right, a suit I designed. It was a prototype for the military that you happened to be wearing when some international spy organization broke in here trying to steal it. You happened to be messing with it at the wrong time, when they were shooting the hell out of this place, and the only way you could save your skin was to activate the suit. It imprinted itself with your DNA and became *your* suit. Then of course we had the fateful explosion of the solar energy storage facility and that one lone dragonfly that was flitting around of course got its DNA mixed up with yours when the radiation was all over the place in here."

Randy added in a low voice, "Radiation you absorbed. At least most of it."

"That's right Dragonfly. While you got super-strength, agility, dexterity and spectroscopic vision, I was lucky enough to become a walking star. If not for these items like my watch, pen and ring that I designed to bleed solar rad off of me all the time I could have exploded and taken out a quarter of northern New Jersey."

"Aren't you being a little hard on the boy?" a new voice intervened.

Both men turned and realized Captain Power was standing in the room with them, leaning against the wall with his arms crossed upon his chest.

Solaron guffawed, "Where've you been? I haven't seen you in two weeks, since the Mind Master attack."

"I've been busy, Ron. Whether you realize it or not I take on solo missions from time to time as well. But if you called I would have been here."

Solaron sighed and placed his hands on the meeting table, staring at its blank surface, as if seeking the knowledge of the ages hidden there.

Captain Power continued, "You're still being a little hard on your nephew. Look, seriously, I don't want to get involved in your little family dynamic you have going on here, but Randy or Dragonfly or whatever you want to call him is right. He's been in some heavy duty stuff since we've been together, and I have no idea how many times you two have taken on who knows what outside of the team."

"That's right, you don't. You don't know anything about us, other than what I've told you. But the problem is I told you quite a lot, and we still don't even know your real name."

"Weren't you the one who told me it was fine and you didn't care what my real name was?"

"Yes, but that was before you heard my nephews name."

Now it was Captain Power's turn to sigh, "My name is Tom. Thomas Jackson. I'm a college student in Manhattan."

"Looking like that?" Randy blurted out.

"Uhh, no. I told you all once before you wouldn't recognize me. There's a reason for it. I can change back to my regular form."

"What do you mean 'change'?" Solaron asked.

"You've seen me absorb matter to power my strength and durability. Usually about two tons of matter brings me up to full power. It takes a lot for me to burn through that. A powerful foe like General Zaring, or the giant robot in Japan. Otherwise I'm good for hours."

"How do you change when you want to?" Dragonfly asked.

Cap shrugged, "I can shunt off the remaining energy that powers me up. It disperses into the atmosphere and I change shape into my 'regular me' form."

"Show us!" Dragonfly beamed.

"This ain't a circus, kid. It's not something I like doing at a whim. I'm not on display here. Besides, what would I absorb to change back to Cap? So no, I'm not going to change."

Sol smiled, "I can't say that I blame you, Cap. And I'm sorry I came off like jerk a few minutes ago. Randy gets under my collar at times. He's got that 'I know it all' thing going on that all teenagers get."

"Hey!" Dragonfly shouted.

"Hey what?" Cap replied, "I understand what your uncle is saying. I also know that you're still going to run off and do what you want, when you want, because you're a kid."

"Him running off is not really the problem here," Sol interrupted, "he has been good about only using the suit when we were together."

Cap turned back to Sol and furrowed his brow, "Then what is? I'd have to think that would be your biggest concern."

"I just don't want him doing something foolish that gets him in over his head."

"So you're parenting him. I can understand that. He's your nephew and you care about him, I get it. It's not a problem. I shouldn't even be involved in this conversation, I'm sorry guys."

"Actually I'm glad you were here. You probably stopped me from saying something I'd end up regretting a minute later."

"Yeah I can understand that. Not to change the subject, even though I really want to, but where is everyone else?"

"They're all around here somewhere. Creature spends a lot of time in the rec room. When he's not playing video games or watching TV he's reading. He's ordered a lot of books on my amazon account."

"Wait, where's he getting the money from?"

"It's me. I'm allowing him to buy whatever he wants." Sol answered with a slight grin.

"You better hope he doesn't pull up here in an Escalade any time soon."

"I'd be okay with that."

"You're kidding right?"

"Not really Cap. You have no idea how much money I really have do you?"

"It was none of my business so I never questioned it."

Remember when I said I had a few scientific breakthroughs patented? Well those things are worth nine very large figures to me."

"You're kidding?" Cap asked, wide eyed.

"No my friend, not at all."

"What about Silver and our resident aliens?"

Silver is probably back in the city again, looking at spending money on things girls do, while Bol-Ton and Mar-Cus are probably training in the gym."

"They do that a lot?"

"About six hours a day, every day."

"That's kind of intense isn't it?"

"I think Mar-Cus wants Bol-Ton to be the best he can be to be ready for Zaring's return if he does happen to come back."

"Makes sense and I can't fault them for having the right attitude. Mar-Cus wants the kid absolutely ready to take on this madman that already chased him across half the galaxy."

"Yes, you are right, Cap. Starbolt has a lot of weight on his shoulders, more than any fifteen year old should have to bear."

A red light started to blink on the control panel where Solaron had been sitting and it beeped annoyingly as well.

"What's that?" Cap asked.

"A warning, something's going on we may be needed for."

"How'd you rig that up?"

"Oh that?" Sol shrugged, "It's easy enough, Randy-, I mean Dragonfly actually did it. He setup a computer to monitor RSS feeds from every news organization around the world. Then they all get sorted through until something that screams 'Hyperforce' is found and we get notified."

"So what could be screaming 'Hyperforce' at the moment?"

Sol spun the monitor he had been watching around and showed it to Cap, "That."

On the screen was a man flying through Manhattan with wings that stretched from his wrists to his ankles. But that wasn't the strangest part.

"Holy cow! He's on fire!" bellowed Dragonfly.

"And so are half a dozen store fronts below him. He's trying to rob the diamond district."

"That's amazing, the flames are hiding his face like a mask." Solaron commented.

"He's on fire head to toe. I wonder what this pyromaniac calls himself?"

"Firefox." Sol replied.

"You're kiddin'?" Dragonfly queried.

"No I'm not Randy. The feeds are saying that's his name. Local news is also saying there are already casualties and wounded." Solaron turned his face up from the computer and looked at his teammates, "This guy's already a killer."

"I'm heading there pronto, his flames can't hurt me." Cap said.

"I'm coming with you." Dragonfly began following Captain Power out the door when he turned back to Solaron, "As long as that's okay with you, Uncle Ron."

Dragonfly, you're about to go into battle. It's Solaron, not Uncle Ron."

Randy Anderson nodded and smiled. He pulled his cowl back over his face and the three men exited the observatory, flying into the sky from the landing bay.

Minutes later they rocketed into Manhattan, heading directly toward the diamond district.

"There he is." Dragonfly pointed.

Below, the three heroes could see the flaming man throwing blasts of fire around carelessly, burning buildings and vehicles without any restraint.

"What is this guy doing?" breathed Cap.

"Let's go and find out. Dragonfly, you're the only one of us who can actually be burned, so be careful."

"Okay, Solaron." Dragonfly replied.

The three heroes floated above their foe. It was obvious even though he was burning that he wore a costume underneath the raging flames. The mask he wore was that of a stylized fox, and it burned.

Dragonfly spoke first, "All right flame guy or whatever the heck you're calling yourself, time to give it up. You're surrounded by three real life super-heroes. This can only go badly for you, so you should do the cool thing and give up. Or resist. Please resist." Dragonfly smiled.

The flaming man smiled and started to laugh, "You three jerks think you're gonna stop me? An' who told you idiots I was alone?"

Smashing out of the buildings below three new figures joined the strange tableau.

"So you brought playmates?" Captain Power grunted.

"This doesn't change a thing", Solaron added, "You all have a chance to stand down, before this gets messy."

"For who? You?" one of the newcomers asked. He was a black man wearing a one piece suit of shiny material in dark blue with twin gold colored lightning bolts running from his shoulders on an angle to the middle of his waist.

"Oh yeah Stormsurge, definitely for them." the second of the three replied. A big, tough looking man with a short blonde crew cut wearing a domino style face mask, stood with his hands on his hips grinning, staring up at the three Hyperforce members.

"Why dontcha go say hello to these guys, Ground Pounder?" The final member of this quadruple threat asked. It was a woman in a skintight red and blue bodysuit with long blonde hair. She wore a small mask that covered only her eyes.

The brutish man turned and smiled a lopsided grin at the woman, "I think I will Skyrocket, why not?"

Instantly the man named 'Ground Pounder' grew to fantastic size and knocked a stunned Captain Power out of the sky with one punch.

"Here we go." grinned Dragonfly. He dove down toward the man called Stormsurge, when the woman

called Skyrocket rocketed upward toward him, knocking
him out of the way with a powerful right.

"Whoa!" Dragonfly grunted as he spun about in mid-
air. The woman smiled maliciously and streaked toward
him again, her left fist forward and her right cocked back
along her side.

Solaron raised his hands aimed and fired solar beams
blindingly fast, knocking both Stormsurge and Firefox
backward and on their rear ends.

"That was a love tap. Don't get up and I won't burn
holes through you both."

"As if you could…" Stormsurge laughed. He waved
his hand upward and out of the sewers lining the streets
cascaded a tidal wave of dirty, filthy sewer water,
engulfing Solaron and pulling him down to the
pavement.

"Hold him there 'Surge, I'm gonna fry him like a big
ol' piece o' fish." Firefox shot blazing flames at Solaron
while the strange waters held him tight in a vice-like
grip.

Above, Dragonfly streaked through the sky; while
the woman called Skyrocket batted him about repeatedly
left, right, left, right.

"You're not that fast sweetie, at least not as fast as I
am. That's a shame. I thought you'd be more fun than
this." She threw another left punch, but this time
Dragonfly caught it in his right fist. Her eyes went wide
with surprise.

"Gotcha." He dragged her in by her fist and kissed
her on the lips.

Skyrocket's eyes remained wide, then she kicked
him in the chest with all her strength, breaking free of his

grip, "You little sunova-I'm gonna slap that face! Who do you think you are?"

Dragonfly spun around her and slapped her on her rump while he sped past, "Hahahaha, c'mon an' catch me blondie, if you can."

Dragonfly rocketed away into the sky.

"I'm going to kick your ass." the woman called after him, racing away in pursuit.

The two blazed across the Manhattan skyline, Dragonfly staying just out of reach of Skyrockets punching, flailing hands, laughing to himself the whole way.

"Gotcha!" She yelled, grasping his boot, and avoiding the jet thrust coming out of it. She heaved him toward the ground. But the young hero simply righted himself and landed softly in a barren lot where a building had only but recently stood.

Skyrocket streaked right at him, both fists thrust outward.

Dragonfly fell on his back as she blazed past; he kicked upward with both feet and carried her over to smash face first into the ground. He was on his feet in a blur.

"Hey babe, give up now an' I promise not to hurt you." he grinned at her, which was even more infuriating.

"I'm going to tear you apart you little punk." She ran toward him.

"Hey lady, I'm taller than you." he ducked her roundhouse right punch and slapped her in the back of head as she stumbled past.

"I'll kill you!" she roared now, kicking at him with her right foot and catching Dragonfly under the chin just as he was walking in toward her. Her kick lifted him off the ground.

But he sumersaulted in mid-air and landed deftly on his feet.

The two combatants circled each other.

"Wow lady, you are strong, maybe even stronger than me. I'll give you that."

She rubbed her lips with her right fist, "I am stronger than you, twerp. I can tell. I'm going to grab your arms and break you like a wishbone."

"Well that's just not a nice image to consider is it sweetums?"

She charged at him, hands outstretched, Dragonfly jumped up and leap frogged her. She passed underneath, her hands grasping empty air.

"Arrrgghh!" she shouted spinning and charging him again.

This time Dragonfly dropped low and swept her legs out from under her, snapping her to the ground.

"You little punk!"

Skyrocket grabbed at him and caught his right leg, she pulled him down, and then, climbing atop Dragonfly, she punched him in the face once, twice, thrice.

"Enough of you lady."

Dragonfly's boot jets activated and he sped out from under her streaking skyward. Instantly she was flying after him. Dragonfly was no longer smiling. He spun backward in mid-air so he was facing her. She raced after him and he side stepped in flight, lashing out with his left wing, with a resounding bang he slammed the flat of his wing against her head. She tumbled and fell out of the sky, stunned. She impacted the ground and groggily fought her way to her feet.

"I'm gonna kill you, you little punk."

"Yeah you played that tune already babe." Dragonfly was no longer playing around; she turned and stared at him, then flew upward. He matched her in a descent. They slammed together and began hammering away at each other in mid-air. She threw a right; he blocked it with his left wing. Then he threw a right, and caught her full in the jaw.

Her head snapped back. Now he was no longer hesitating. Dragonfly kicked her in the stomach, hard. She shrugged it off and back handed him, sending him hurtling toward the ground. Now it was his turn to impact hard.

She landed with twenty feet separating them as he got to his feet, "What's the matter squirt? Nothing witty to say anymore?"

"Naah babe, I'm just bored with you. You're just not as much fun as I thought.

"Aww, poor baby. Here let me tuck you in for the night." she charged him again.

But now, Dragonfly raised both hands and shot his Dragonblasts stunning her in mid-step. She arched her back painfully as a cry of agony escaped her lips.

"Y-you little Sonuva- I'm gonna tear you apart!"

"Yeah babe, I don't think so." He fired the Dragonblasts again, and kept firing them this time. Skyrocket continued to struggle to get to him, but after a few seconds more of having her electrons scrambled she passed out from the pain falling face first into the dirt at her feet.

Dragonfly removed some cable from within a compartment on his wings and wrapped her wrists in it, tying her up tight. "You're not going anywhere babe." then as an afterthought said aloud. "I wonder how the others are doing?" he asked no one in particular. Throwing her unconscious body over his shoulder, Dragonfly rocketed away toward where he had left the rest of the team.

Boom! Boom! Boom! The giant called Groundpounder had Captain Power in one giant fist and was pounding him into the concrete at their feet repeatedly.

Suddenly Caps boots shot thrust out of them and both Cap and Groundpounder, who was still holding him, streaked toward the sky.

"Wha-what are you doin'?"

"We're going for a ride in the sky, big guy." Cap replied.

"N-no!" Groundpounder opened his hand and Cap shot away, but immediately Groundpounder started to fall back to the earth as soon as his upward momentum waned and disappeared. He tumbled through the sky and slammed into the street from three hundred feet up. The pavement buckled and heaved when he careened into it. Cars were thrown into the air and came crashing down again.

Groundpounder struggled to his feet holding his head, "Oohhh that hurt."

"Then surrender. We'll get you checked out faster than if you keep fighting."

Groundpounder took his head out of his hands and
sneered at Captain Power who was standing on the
ground in front of him with his arms crossed over his
chest.

"I'll crush you!" Groundpounder lifted his boot up to
step on Cap, but Cap rocketed into the air and uncorked
a bone crushing right to Groundpounder's jaw. The
crack of fist impacting jaw was like thunder.
Groundpounder fell like a tree cut down in the forest.
When his unconscious form hit the ground it was akin to
an earthquake.

"No, I don't think you will." Cap replied.

Several blocks away from where Groundpounder had
fallen, Solaron was still being drowned and burned
simultaneously by Firefox and Stormsurge.

"You think he's dead yet?" Stormsurge asked.

"I don't know, why don't you ask him? I don't
understand why he ain't burnin' though."

Solaron began to glow, so brightly that both men had
to step back and cover their eyes. The hard water
shackles at his wrists and ankles steamed away to vapor.
Solaron flew upward and hovered back above his two
foes.

"Last offer you two idiots, surrender now."

"Yeah I don't think so." Firefox replied, before he
unleashed streaming flame at Solaron again.

Sol threw his hands forward and shot twin high
density blasts at both men, sending them careening
painfully across the street and into the brick buildings
behind them.

"This ain't fun anymore." Stormsurge said.

"No kidding Storm, you think?" Firefox replied.

Sol began firing blast after blast at the two villains, driving them both away from the buildings and toward the center of the street.

"This guy's missing us on purpose." Stormsurge barked.

"Yeah, yeah I see that. I'm goin' ta get his attention. There's a hydrant over there, take it out.

"You got it, and somethin' else is happening too, man. The sky is cloudin' up. I think our luck with this clown is about to change."

"I'm gonna burn you where you stand!" Firefox threatened. He flew into the air after Solaron and blasted him with a barrage of flame. Sol put up a shield of solar energy, blocking the attack.

"Sol, are you all right?" Dragonfly's voice shouted through Sol's cowl communicator.

"Yes, Dragonfly, I'm fine, just finishing up with these two. Are you all okay?"

"I'm okay boss-man. I have that chick in tow. I'm on my way back now."

Sol didn't answer; below, Stormsurge pointed at a fire hydrant, and at his command the water within it burst the hydrant, building up tons of pressure in a heartbeat.

"Ha! Gotcha!" Stormsurge shouted and then grinned maniacally.

He aimed at Solaron now and the water that was running at tons of pressure turned in mid-air and slammed into Solaron at Stormsurge's command. Instantly and completely surprised, Solaron was knocked from the sky to the pavement below.

"An' now for the coup de gras." Stormsurge raised his arms up high, then brought them slashing down toward Solaron. Lightning blasted from the darkened sky and impaled the hero repeatedly.

Solaron screamed painfully and collapsed to the pavement.

"You're still alive? You're a tough hombre I'll give ya that." Stormsurge admitted.

Stunned and disbelieving Solaron shook his head trying to cut the cobwebs out of his mind when he saw a new figure hurtling through the sky at Stormsurge. With a tremendous crash the black and yellow clad Stryker appeared, and unleashed a powerful left haymaker at Stormsurge, knocking him across the street and unconscious with one punch. Stormsurge slammed into the side of a panel truck and limply slid to the ground.

Sol nodded at his benefactor and aimed both fists at Firefox who was now trying to streak away. Solaron fired twin medium density beams at Firefox, The man was rocked in mid-flight, his arms went up above his head and his back arched. He let out a painful howl and dropped out of control toward the ground.

Out of seemingly nowhere Captain Power appeared and caught Firefox before he could possibly fall to his doom.

Cap landed with both Firefox and Groundpounder in his hands, holding both men by their collars.

"Where's Dragonfly?" Cap asked the instant he set down.

"I'm here." the young hero answered, touching down with the curvaceous blonde lying limply in his arms.

"I see you took care of Skyrocket. She give you any trouble?" Sol asked.

"Naah, none at all. Piece o' cake really."

Sol turned toward the grinning Stryker and extended his hand, "Thanks for the save."

"My pleasure mate; just tryin' to repay the favor. Pleasure to be helpin' ya out."

Sol nodded before continuing, "I thought you'd be going home by now. I'm surprised you're still here."

"Ah you know how it is mate, a new exciting place, an' I can't get enough o' this town. Anything back in Oz is just plain borin' compared to the bright lights o' the big city."

"If you say so, Stryker. Look, this is twice we ran into each other, and by the way, how'd you know we were fighting these guys anyway?"

"It's all over the bloomin' news mate it is!"

"Ah that figures. Listen Stryker, since you're going to be around for a while yet, how'd you feel about joining us, at least until you head home. You look like a man of great power, and you heart seems to be in the right place, so I'm going to extend an invitation to join Hyperforce, at least on a temporary basis."

"Aw mate, I'd be happy too. Thanks greatly!" He shook Sol's hand once again and then Dragonfly's. Finally he reached out to Captain Power, who hesitated a second and then took the man's hand and shook it. Cap locked eyes with Stryker and nodded solemnly. He let go of Stryker's hand allowing the man to turn away from him and back toward Solaron.

But Cap kept his eyes on their newest teammate, and would for the foreseeable future.

Chapter 6

Everything is fine…

" 'Ello me lovely!"

Startled, Silver Shadow tried to hide a smile from the big Australian but couldn't suppress the grin that forced its way onto her face, finally she relented and looked up, her cheeks flush, "Hello Mr.…um, Stryker was it?"

"Aw ya wound me! I guess I din't leave enough of an impression on ya last time we met."

Silver almost giggled, but controlled herself. Stryker leaned forward and took her hand and kissed it, "There missy. Are ya gonna forget ol' Stryker now?"

"Oh I don't think I will Mr. Stryker. Not after that show." Silver blushed completely now. Creature began to growl. He was seated next to Dragonfly at the conference table. He turned and looked at Dragonfly to see if his teammate had any reaction to what they had both seen. But if anything Dragonfly seemed to be taking it all in. He had a surprised grin plastered all over his face. Stryker walked past them both and winked knowingly at the boy.

Solaron stood at the head of the table, Captain Power at the other end facing him. To Sol's right sat Dragonfly, then Creature and then Silver Shadow, who had just taken her seat. To Sol's left sat Starbolt and Mar-Cus. Stryker jovially took the empty seat between Mar-Cus and Captain Power.

"Thank you all for coming, it's been little over a week since our battle against that unnamed group of super-villains in Manhattan trying to rob the diamond district."

"A battle you should have called us in on." Silver Shadow scolded.

"You're right Silver, I should have. But we thought it was simply one villain causing all the mayhem and between the three of us, we were sure we had it wrapped up."

"Don't…leave us…behind…again" Creature rumbled.

"Agreed, we won't. To be honest we thought you three were busy here. I promise to give everyone the option to join us from now on, even on missions that appear to be easy or light duty missions."

"Good." Creature added.

Sol turned toward Starbolt and prodded him, "What about you Starbolt? Nothing to add to the conversation?"

The boy shrugged, "I was fine with your decision. Mar-Cus and I were training. I felt that if you needed me you would have called upon me."

Sol nodded and smiled, "Okay that makes sense. Anyway, there are several orders of business to be discussed today. First is the eight hundred pound gorilla in the room-"

" 'Ey! I ain't no bleedin' ape!" Stryker interrupted while standing up.

"Relax Stryker, it's metaphorical. Meaning everyone is wondering what you are doing here, at least those of us who weren't involved in the battle last week."

"Okay as long as you ain't callin' me a gorilla."

Sol cast a glance at Captain Power who looked away, out the windows lining the far wall of the conference room. Sol sighed quietly and returned to the matter at hand.

"I just want you all to know that we're making this up as we go along. This is all unfounded territory for me. So there are a few changes. As of today we have an addition to the team; you all know Stryker. He's going to be joining us at least temporarily, until he decides if he's going back to Australia or not anytime soon."

Stryker sat there grinning at everyone. Mostly everyone grinned back save for Captain Power and Mar-Cus who merely nodded at the newcomer.

"Also," Sol continued, "Marcus has agreed to be our mission coordinator. Meaning while we are out on a mission he will man the communications console and keep us apprised of any issues or be able to call in any teammates that are not currently engaged if a situation like last week's rises again. It will amount to us being able to contact the base in time of crisis and being able to get additional members of the squad in action to wherever we are."

"What about if we're halfway around the world? Like Japan again?" Dragonfly asked.

"Good point D-Fly. We're working on that. At least five people here can fly supersonic or better. The rest we'll have an answer for shortly."

"What kind of an answer?" Silver Shadow questioned.

Solaron smiled, "It's something Marcus and I are working on together. It should aid us greatly in case we have to get someone somewhere fast."

Sol continued to stand and looked about the room at everyone's faces, then said "If there's nothing else, let's all welcome Stryker to the team." Solaron began to clap and the rest followed, even Captain Power and Mar-Cus who exchanged uneasy glances.

Everyone left the room and headed to the cafeteria, save for Cap, Sol and Mar-Cus.

"Okay Cap, let me hear it." Sol began.

"What's to hear? You know I don't trust this man. He was conveniently in two places at just the right time."

"So? The first time he was battling a villain, who may be the greatest threat we've ever seen yet. That was when *we* appeared and bailed him out. The second he saved *my* skin. My protective energy field was all but depleted because I was barely conscious. Another moment and those guys could have done me in."

"Really? How?"

"W-what do you mean how? They were going to drown me or burn me alive."

"Except you're, in your own words, 'a living star'. So I doubt the flames could do more than get annoying. I saw you fly into space, so I know you don't have to breathe and can just draw straight nourishment from solar energy that you emit. You're still flesh and blood, but that ever present energy field of yours deflects everything but the most powerful of attacks, then you throw up a full-fledged solar shield for the more powerful stuff."

"I know you're observant Cap, but what does this have to do with our new inductee?"

"I don't trust him, period. He's a little too flip, a little too congenial. He's already got Silver Shadow wrapped around his finger and your nephew is starting to look up to him."

"What? Randy? That's preposterous."

Cap tilted his head slightly and grimaced, "If you say so, Sol. Just remember I warned you."

Solaron turned to Mar-Cus, "Marcus, what's your opinion about all of this?"

Mar-Cus shrugged, "The Captain is correct Solaron. I noticed these things as well. That does not mean Captain Power is correct about everything. The man may *not* be the threat the Captain perceives him to be."

"Or I could be spot on right." Cap completed.

"What do you want me to do Cap? Toss him out on his ear?"

"No, not at all. That's not what I'm telling you. All I'm saying is keep an eye on him, and maybe keep a tighter rein on the super-hero in training, just in case."

"Randy is already his own man. In case you didn't realize it, he had his opponent knocked out and wrapped up faster than either of us last week."

Cap nodded, "That didn't escape me, Sol. But that also doesn't necessarily mean he's the fastest gun in the west either. The kid likes to play it on the edge. He's a good kid, no doubt, but he's also a little power drunk right now. He kicks ass and can take a beating too. He's got a ton of confidence."

"Do you think he's overconfident?"

"Yeah a little bit. But he's good and a bit lucky too. Let's face it the kids a player. The problem is he's more like our new found friend than you are willing to admit. That could lead to trouble especially when and if he starts following Stryker's lead, or he decides that

Stryker's a bit cooler than you are, which he probably will very soon."

"You said you were in college, what are you studying?" Sol asked through squinted eyes.

Cap chuckled, "Majoring in law, minoring in psychology."

"Ahh, I knew it."

"I'm just trying to warn you Sol. Keep an eye on the new guy; I know I will."

Solaron nodded, "Agreed. C'mon let's all join the others, and Cap, I am taking this seriously, but right now everything is fine."

The three men entered the recreation room. Cap nodded at both Mar-Cus and Solaron and continued inside, leaving the other two at the doorways entrance.

Dragonfly and Creature were playing a video game together, while Starbolt stood watching over their shoulders with a huge grin on his face, almost begging for a chance to try the game.

Sol leaned over to Mar-Cus, "Look at that Marcus, your charge is actually smiling. I think that's the first time since you've been here."

Mar-Cus nodded, "That is indeed true Solaron, and it is painful to see him so grim; he was at one time a very happy boy."

"He will be again; it's just going to take some time and planning to defeat General Zaring."

Mar-Cus nodded, "I know that my friend." Both men continued on into the rec room.

The first thing Solaron noticed when he looked into the room was that Silver Shadow was leaning against a wall with her hands clasped behind her back and Stryker was standing over her, leaning against the same wall with his right hand, towering over her. Both were laughing congenially and were drinking something Sol assumed was soda, because he didn't allow any alcohol on premises. Not that Sol was anti-liquor, he wasn't. But the last thing he needed was drunk super-heroes chasing bad guys through the streets of Manhattan or wherever. *'That would end this little glee club really quickly.'* he thought.

"You are still troubled." Solaron turned toward the sound of the now familiar voice and found Mar-Cus standing behind him.

"Yes I am Marcus. I want this to work so badly. Did I make a mistake inviting this man to join us? You and Cap seem to think so or at least to be slightly unsupportive of the action, though him more so than you. So far this has all worked very well with the group we have, and we know each other all of a month."

"Yes, and Prince Bol-Ton and I are decidedly *not* from around here."

"Correct there is that too. I took a huge risk inviting both of you in here to my home. For all I knew you were both alien spies sent to observe our weaknesses for a coming invasion."

"Ronald, my friend. You have no weaknesses. While your race may not be as advanced as others you are more than capable of dealing with any threats, especially with men like yourself and the Captain on this world."

"Yes. True. I do understand what you are saying Marcus, but I'm not seeing anything negative about our new found friend. Oh sure he's bombastic and larger than life, but those seem to be his worst traits. If that's

115

the case, I can live with a powerhouse like him on the team."

"I agree. But I also agree with Captain Power. Until he proves himself he'll bear close watching."

Sol nodded in agreement and said, "Come on, let's join the rest of the team."

The two men entered the room; Solaron was doing his best to relax and failing miserably.

Dragonfly walked up to his uncle, "What's the matter Uncle Ron? You don't look so thrilled."

"Is it that obvious Randy?"

"Uh duh, yeah."

Solaron led Dragonfly over to a quiet corner of the room, "Randy, what do you think of the new guy?"

Dragonfly shrugged, "He seems cool, why?"

"Do you trust him?"

"Yeah, I guess."

"Wrong answer. I'm looking for something a bit more definitive."

"I don't understand." The youth trailed off.

"I want to hear you say vehemently that you trust this man with your life, and that you have total faith and trust in him."

"Sol, you're the only guy I have that much faith in."

Sol nodded slowly, "All right lets go enjoy ourselves I think Cap's just a bit too cautious."

The team and its new member sat around chatting until late in to the evening. After the impromptu party broke up, everyone headed home or to bed.

Cap and Dragonfly flew into the sky.

"So what are you doing the rest of the night?" the younger hero asked Cap.

"Hhmm? Me? Oh probably going to go home and study a few hours. It may be Saturday night, but I still have classes on Monday."

"Don't you ever just go out when you're not on missions or patrolling?"

"No, not really. I was never much of a party person, to be honest. I care about my grades because I realize that's where my future lies."

"Okay I get that, but what if it's not?"

Captain Power looked at Dragonfly and grimaced, "What are you talking about D-fly?"

"What if your future is this, right here, right now?"

"You mean being a hero? I hate to tell you Dragonfly, but this doesn't pay, at all. Being a super-hero is never going to put food on the table and a roof over your head."

"It doesn't matter. What if you had to sacrifice everything else to be the world's protector or something?"

Cap looked away, "I'd have to stop being Captain Power then."

"Could you? I mean really, could you do that?"

"If I had to make a choice, yes. I really just want a nice normal life. When that golden lightning bolt hit me and transformed me into this I was as surprised as anyone."

"Wait, what golden lightning bolt?"

Cap sighed, "I let that slip. I never told you guys how I gained these powers, did I?"

"No, not yet."

"Okay this is going to take a while. Let's go find a roof to sit on somewhere near a coffee shop. I'm going to grab a cup before we start. Do you want anything?"

"Umm, I guess a hot chocolate an' a donut."

"Okay sounds good wait up here." Dragonfly sat on the flat roof of the donut shop with his legs dangling over the side while Captain Power disappeared inside.

Two minutes later Cap returned, and sat next to the young hero, "Here you go." He handed Dragonfly his hot chocolate and donut, took a few bites out of his own, washed it down with a gulp of coffee, and began to talk.

"About a year ago I was heading to the campus, and I was late for my class. What else is new right?"

Dragonfly smiled at that.

Anyway I'm walking along rushing with my books in hand, when out of a clear blue sky a bolt of lightning hits me. But it wasn't a regular crazy looking bolt of lightning. This thing had shape and was bright gold. I actually saw it coming. I remember being hit by it, then the next thing I remember was this kid shaking me saying...

***

"Hey mister, are you okay?" Tom Jackson looked around uncomprehendingly.

"Wh-where am I? What happened?"

"You got struck by lightning, man!" a young black boy was standing over him with equal parts concern and amazement written all over his face.

"What? Lightning? There's not a cloud in the sky. How can that be?" Tom looked at his hands and realized his clothes were ruined, burned and in tatters. He tried to stand and surprisingly found he could.

"Are you okay Mister?" the smiling boy asked again.

"I think I am my friend, I think I am."

Tom stretched his thin body this way and that. Besides a minor stiffness in his joints he felt fine.

"Either that was the lamest lightning bolt ever or I got very lucky."

"I think you got lucky too." the boy replied earnestly.

Tom Jackson looked down at his thin legs and arms. Looking for burn marks where the lightning had hit him and found nothing.

"This is crazy." he breathed aloud.

"Sure is mister." the boy added, still staring in wide eyed disbelief.

"Okay I'm going to have to run home and change. Looks like I'm not going to make Mrs. Keirney's one fifteen class after all. Sorry Mrs. Keirney." Tom turned toward the boy and said, "Thanks for helping me out kid."

The boy smiled a toothy grin and hopped off back to play. Tom watched him go and shook his head again.

'I wonder if I should go to the hospital? I feel fine. Heck, I feel great actually.'

Tom ran across the Manhattan street toward the room he shared with another student named Jake Townsend.

'Man, Jake is never going to let me hear the end of this one.'

Tom ran down the block and turned into an alleyway that was a short cut to his apartment near the college. He turned a corner in the alley and ran smack dab into trouble.

Five punks were in the alley smoking something and were immediately startled by Toms appearance.

"Where d'ya think you're goin', cupcake?" the nearest thug asked. He was a good head taller than Tom's five foot nine, and more heavily muscled. Tattoos covered their bodies. Instantly the rest of the group were on their feet and off of the stacked milk crates they had been sitting on.

Tom stopped short and raised his hands in front of himself, palms outward, "Relax guys I was just cutting through. I'm not looking for any trouble."

"Yeah well that's real funny, 'cause trouble just found you." another thug replied. He took a swing at Tom, knocking him down with the first punch.

"Ha! Lookit this guy will ya? He can't even take a punch." A third member of the alley way gang with a shaved head, sunglasses and goatee added.

"You jerks better leave here now." Tom ordered, not even sure why he did after he had said it.

"Oh yeah? Why's that scrawny? What're ya gonna do? Cry on us?"

Tom tried to stand, anger and embarrassment fueling his body, when another of the thugs kicked him in the chest before he could get off the ground.

"Haw haw! Lookit this Rickey, you were right, this guy can't take a punch."

Tom had noisily fallen between a stack of garbage cans and was fighting to extricate himself.

"Will ya look at this guy? He doesn't know when ta stay down," another gangbanger commented.

"Ya know what? I got just the thing fer that." another bald headed gang member with neck tattoos said. He pulled a long handled sledge hammer out from beside him, where he had been leaning on the handle lazily.

Neck tattoos walked over to where the downed Tom was lying between the garbage pails and raised his hammer up, swinging it around a few times to test it. Then he brought it down hard toward Tom's head. Only a hand shot up and caught the sledge hammer by its head.

"What the hell?" the hammer wielding braggadocio exclaimed.

The hand holding the hammer glowed then, and the hammer seemed to disappear, as if it became dust. Tom Jackson grabbed the garbage cans around him, shoving them out of the way; as he did the cans seemed to disintegrate at his touch.

Tom wasn't paying attention, but the gang was now looking up at him instead of down, fear written all over their faces.

"I'm gettin' outta here!" the first thug turned and began to run.

"Like hell you are." Tom replied in a suddenly booming voice.

Before the thug could move Tom lashed out with a blindingly fast right cross. The man flew from the alley way as if shot from a catapult. He landed in an unconscious heap at the alleyway's end.

Tom turned instantly toward the rest. They all stared at him slack jawed. As one they began to run from him, but with two quick steps he caught up to them. He grabbed two by the neck and smacked their heads together. Both men dropped to the ground unconscious.

"He ain't human!" one of the last two remaining punks said to the other.

"Less talkin' an' more runnin'" the other replied.

"You two aren't going *anywhere*!" Tom shouted.

Tom grabbed both frightened men by the necks and lifted them overhead, one in each hand.

That was when he realized what he was doing. "What the hell?" he said aloud.

Toms' gaze ran down the length of his own arms and stopped at the terrified man in each beefy hand. *"Are those my hands? My arms? What's going on here"*

Tom threw both hoods to the ground roughly stunning them; then he reached up and grabbed the metal slats off of a fire escape, tearing them off as if they were paper. He wrapped the steel bars around each man's chest and tied the gang together like the petals of a five leaf flower.

Then, still looking at his hands in disbelief, Tom ran off, out of the alleyway and, after making sure no one was watching, to his apartment building and in the door.

'I sure hope Jake isn't home.' he thought, *'I'm sure he has a class right now. But with my usual luck...'* Tom trailed off, opened his apartment door and slipped inside.

'Good, no one's around. I need clothes before anything.'

Tom walked by the open bathroom door and glanced at the mirror as he passed. Instantly he stopped and backpedaled to stare incredulously.

"What the hell?" he muttered in a surprisingly unfamiliar voice.

Tom stared for long moments at the face in the mirror, one he did not recognize. It was a square jawed,

122

powerful face with long brown hair, as opposed to Tom's normally short brown hair. It was connected to a body a foot taller than Thomas Jackson typically was used to, and far more muscled than his unexceptionally thin frame.

But the face is what continued to draw Thomas' attention; the strong, powerful face that would shortly become known the world over as the face of Captain Power!

***

"So how'd you get out of the apartment? How'd you learn you could fly? How'd you learn how strong you were?" Dragonfly continued.

"It was all in time Dee. I only absorbed a few garbage cans, so I ended up becoming good ol' Tom Jackson again in a few minutes. That wasn't a problem. After That I started putting costumes together. That was another skill altogether. I had to learn to sew and how to dye things; it was a mess."

"Yeah I guess it would be, Hahaha."

Cap looked at Dragonfly quizzically, "Really kid? You think it was that funny?"

"Yeah I do. I've got this image in my head of you, all six feet eight of you running around with blue dye all over yourself like a giant smurf. It's hysterical."

Cap started to chuckle, "Yeah, yeah you're right kid. It is, or was. Now I just fly over to a tailor I found in the garment district with cash and have him measure me up. He even has a few ready-made spares waiting for me. I buy one he makes another, it works nicely."

"Well it's better than you sewing and dying clothes again, hahaha!"

"Yeah kid you got that right. Listen kid I want to talk to you about something."

"What'd I do now?"

"What? No, you didn't do a thing."

"So what's up then?"

"Dragonfly, until the new guy Stryker proves himself; I want you to give him a wide berth. I don't trust him."

"Why? The dudes cool!"

"And that's the reason right there. You and Silver Shadow seem to be taking a liking to this guy too easily. Almost like he's got you hypnotized. Heck, even Sol was oblivious to it. But there's something not right with this guy. I can't put my finger on it, but I don't trust him."

"Ha! I think you're chasing ghosts or something, Cap. The dudes fine."

Cap shook his head slowly side to side, "I don't trust him kid. Don't fall for his charm. Silver's already school girl giggly about this guy, and that's something I never expected from her."

"What about Creature? What's he got to say about it?"

"Dee, I haven't talked to him about it all yet. But earlier he was playing that video game with you and not paying any attention to her at all, and that's a first. He's usually hovering all over her protectively."

"Maybe he's just learned to relax?"

"Maybe, but I doubt it." Cap stood up, finished his coffee and crushed the cup, "Keep your eyes open Dee, I don't trust this guy at all."

"But what if you're wrong?"

"What if I am? What's the worst that happens? I apologize to our aussie friend? The real question you should be asking yourself Dragonfly, is what if I'm right? Keep it in mind kid."

Cap turned around and flew off into the night leaving his young companion sitting there in deep thought.

Ralph L. Angelo Jr.

Chapter 7

Chaos in Cleveland

Corbo Labs, a high tech, advanced Technology Company based in Cleveland. The morning shift was just getting settled in. Dr. Corbo, the man whose name was on the company's door entered a special lab area sealed off from the rest. He walked purposefully toward other scientists and engineers seated at consoles, all of their eyes were upon him. Two men stood staring at him while he walked toward them.

Corbo was a lean man with greying temples and a receding hairline. His mustache was still dark though.

"Are we ready?"

"Yes Dr. Corbo, everything is readied and prepared as you asked. The gravity multiplier is primed awaiting your hands at its controls."

"Very good Dr. Starkings. Let's get this show on the road, shall we gentlemen? Destiny awaits."

Starkings sat at a control console to the right, the other scientist sat at the console to the left. Corbo sat at the center console.

"Are you ready as well Dr. Peterson?"

The black skinned man nodded in the affirmative.

"Very well gentlemen, we're about to make history here today."

Corbo turned a key on his console, swiveled his head first left and then right to his companions, nodded once and slid a bank of levers upward on the console before him.

Instantly the room about them began to hum loudly as the RPM's of the machinery above them raised to staggering levels.

"All systems are functioning within tolerances sir." Peterson confirmed.

"Very good Peterson. Starkings? How is the power output?"

"Power output is at ninety percent sir."

"Excellent gentlemen, excellent."

Corbo lowered a set of dark goggles over his eyes. The other men in the room watching him did the same.

"Lower the gravity hammer into position Dr. Starkings."

Starkings worked at several controls on his board. A huge device began lowering itself from above. It glowed and hummed with each pulsing revolution. It looked like the gigantic device was a weapon of some kind. But what it was would prove more interesting and dangerous.

The gravity multiplier aimed down into the pit it sat above. Lights all along its large cylindrical body glowed as the three scientists maneuvered it via servo motors into position.

"The gravity multiplier is now primed and working at one hundred percent power. It is ready to be fired Dr. Corbo."

"Very well my fellow scientists; let us begin to study the world within our own!"

Corbo stabbed the fire button. Instantly a beam of blindingly bright energy erupted from the device and streaked into the pit below it.

"I'm getting readings back along the sensor trail," Starkings advised, "There are pockets of granite and igneous rock as well as various metals the further down we go. According to the laser telemetry I am receiving back along the sensor trail we are approximately one hundred miles deep below the surface of the planet now." Starkings looked up at both men seated on either side of him, "It's working. It's working perfectly. The gravity multiplier is crushing earth to dust and drilling a hole deep into the earth itself. We're almost two hundred miles in. This is incredible!"

"Calm down Starkings." Corbo scolded him, "Keep your mind on the task at hand. Dr. Peterson, how are things holding up on the mechanical end of all of this?"

"The gravity multiplier is working within parameters Dr.Cor-" Peterson stopped, and frowned momentarily.

"What is it?" Dr. Corbo asked.

"I-I'm getting some very strange telemetry back along the laser sensor feed."

"What kind of strange telemetry?" Starkings asked.

It appears as if the multiplier is now pushing out more energy than it needs to operate as if something were stealing that power, sucking it out of the machine itself via the gravimetric beam."

Corbo looked at both men, then turned toward Starkings. "What are you seeing there Dr. Starkings?"

"Dr. Corbo, the machine is continuing to drill, but I can now confirm Dr. Petersons analysis. There is a drain on the machine."

Corbo did not hesitate, "Shut it down, immediately."

"Shutting down." Peterson confirmed.

"What the hell?" Starkings muttered.

"What is it Starkings? Speak up man?" Corbo ordered.

"I-I can't control it, it's locked on and running on its own now." Starkings turned and looked at Corbo, and there was fear written all over his face, "Something very bad is happening here."

"Peterson, kill the power."

"I can't." Peterson replied nervously.

"What do you mean you can't?" Corbo demanded.

"The system is locked into a feedback loop of some kind. The power is actually off right now but somehow it's drawing energy up from below on the sensor trail and feeding the gravity multiplier itself."

"What about the redundancies?" Corbo demanded in a shout.

Peterson stood, followed by Starkings, "Nothing is working; we have to run!"

"Like hell! I'm not going to leave this behind I'll shut it down. The pulse emitter plates, yes that's it I'll pull them and everything will shut down."

"We have to leave now, there's no time!" shouted Starkings.

But Corbo was not listening. By now the incessant whine of the machine had built up to an ear splitting crescendo that shook the concrete floor beneath their feet. Starkings and Peterson ran for the doors and punched in codes that opened the vault style, multi-ton door on mechanical hinges.

"Dr. Corbo, you have to come with us!" Starkings shouted.

But Corbo ignored them if he even heard them at all above the incredibly loud sound of the gravity multiplier.

"We have to shut the door." Peterson bellowed above the roar of the machine.

Starkings nodded solemnly. Both men hit their emergency input codes and the door quickly pulled shut on its powerful motors.

"Those walls are five feet thick of solid concrete, if anything can contain what is to come it's that room." Peterson told Starkings.

Both men continued to back away, slowly at first then they ran. The facility, as well as the room they operated in was already cleared out when the first emergency alarm activated. The floor began to rumble as the two men dashed outside towards a car.

Then the implosion occurred.

It was *not* an explosion of great energy flattening everything around it and decimating every building and person in its path.

No, this was a great suction of sorts. It was as if gravity itself had gone mad. First the building itself seemed to collapse, drawn into itself and crushed to fine powder by the strength of the mad occurrence. People were dragged screaming off of their feet and into the vortex now forming where the laboratory building used to be. Cars were next, sucked in whole and crushed to the size of a ball before disappearing altogether.

Then it became worse. For a moment everything seemed to stabilize but an odd pulsating, rumbling sound could still be heard.

What happened next shattered windows and destroyed buildings for ten blocks around. It was as if the earth could only absorb so much, and then it expelled it all at once in a violent explosion that destroyed much of Cleveland.

Survivors were everywhere scattered about the streets. Their clothes torn and ragged, blood on their faces and their limbs. Water shot like geysers out of non-existent hydrants. Sirens screamed from everywhere.

Somehow Starkings and Peterson had survived, they managed to get into Starkings car and drove away as quickly as possible, mere seconds before the implosion hit. They drove madly up I-77 and by the time the resultant explosion itself belched debris from the earth's core upward and across the city, they were already on its outskirts.

Starkings pulled over once the rumbling explosion had stopped. Both men slowly stepped from the car and looked behind them, as did other drivers who stared dumbly behind them at what remained of Cleveland.

"T-that felt like an earthquake." Peterson began.

"It was worse than that. My God man, what have we done?"

"We have foolishly played with the forces of nature I fear, and nature slapped our hands away." Peterson replied.

Both men stared in stunned silence at the rising half-mile wide cloud of dense black smoke that slowly filled the sky over Cleveland.

At the site of the disaster nothing moved. Rescue sirens blared noisily while ambulances and rescue personnel converged in the empty space that used to be Corbo labs.

At the pit that once housed the gravity multiplier a strongly muscled purple gloved hand and arm rose over

132

the rim of the pit and grasped the surface in a powerful grip.

***

Cut to New York City, specifically the grounds of Columbia University. A young man sat in class taking notes when he practically jumped out of his seat as if something had stung him.

"What the hell?" he looked at his arm in surprise, and then he realized the whole class, including the professor were staring at him.

"Sorry," he held his stomach and grimaced, "bad burrito for lunch."

"Lunch?" the female professor asked, "But it's only ten O'clock."

The student brushed past her and out the door of the classroom, "Sorry Professor, I meant yesterday." the door closed behind him and he was out in the hallway, hurrying down a staircase toward the street.

'That was Solaron's emergency alert. He added a chip to my watch, and it just buzzed me. In fact it hasn't stopped buzzing me.' the thin non-descript young man thought.

Heading out to the street, he turned a corner and made his way to a dorm on school grounds. But before entering he took out his cell and called an untraceable number. It rang once and was immediately picked up.

"Captain Power? Is that you?" Solaron's voice inquired.

"Yes Sol, it's me. What's the emergency?"

"You haven't gotten to a TV or used your smartphone to check news recently, have you?"

The thin twenty four year old with the short brown hair shook his head before replying out of habit, "No sorry Sol, I've been in classes all morning. What's up?"

"We have an emergency situation in Cleveland. Most of the city has fallen into a sink hole created by an experiment gone bad, at least that's what it looks like. Reports are saying there are terrible amounts of casualties. From what I see the city is a wreck. We need to be there to offer whatever aid we can."

"You're right of course. Don't wait for me if you're ready to leave. I'll be right behind you."

"Understood Cap, I know how fast you are."

"I'll see you in a few minutes." Tom Jackson broke the connection.

Jackson ran from the campus grounds and headed toward his apartment. On the way he passed a construction site with plenty of debris piled on the side from the last building that had once stood there and had been recently demolished.

'This should do.' he looked around quickly, saw no one around and no camera's aimed at the pile of refuse then the five foot nine inch, one hundred and fifty five pound Tom Jackson placed his hands atop the pile of debris, which instantly glowed, and then disintegrated. Instantly Thomas Jackson began to grow, to fill out, to become much larger, much more muscular than he was. With his left hand he tapped his belt buckle, and in a flash of light Thomas Jackson was no more, in his place stood six foot eight inch Captain Power!

'That costume change tube of Solaron's works great. It makes my life a lot easier instead of having to wear one under my clothes all the time.'

Captain Power took to the air. Energy blazed from his legs as he streaked toward Northern New Jersey.

Cap rocketed overhead, almost faster than the eye could follow.

***

Several minutes earlier...

The team was entering into the Stargrazer as Solaron pressed the button on the automatic hanger bay door opener. The huge hanger door began to slide up. Sol began to head toward the Stargrazer when he realized there were a set of legs standing outside the bay door.

The door opened all the way and a man stood at the front entrance to the cavernous hanger.

The man had on dark sunglasses and a leather trench coat. His jet black hair was slicked back with a lot of product. A cigarette hung from his mouth as he assessed the startled Solaron.

"Who the hell are you and what the hell are you doing here?" Sol asked authoritatively.

The man smirked, and then began to speak, "I'm your new best friend, Solaron. Or should I say Professor Ronald Anderson?"

"Should I be stunned at the revelation that you know my name?" Sol asked coolly, his composure regained instantly.

"Naaah, not at all Solaron. I know all about you an' some of your friends here too."

"You still haven't answered my question."

"The name's Butcher, an' yeah before ya ask, it was the name I was born with. Commander Garret Butcher at yer service."

"You don't look old enough to be a Commander."

"Yer eyes can deceive ya." Butcher dropped the cigarette and stepped on it, grinding it out.

"Pick that up Commander." Sol ordered.

"Really? Yer gonna make me pick up a butt?"

"Damned straight, slick. What do you want and who do you represent? Talk fast and after you pick up the cigarette. I have an emergency to take care of."

"Okay, okay, keep yer pants on, hero."

Butcher bent down picked up the butt and turned back toward Solaron, "There, ya happy now?"

"No. What are you doing here and what do you want?"

"I'm here to ask fer yer help courtesy of the U.S. government."

"Is this about Cleveland?"

Butcher nodded, "It is. We need you and your team to go there ASAP. Something is coming out of that rubble and it's superhuman."

"We don't work for you or the government, Butcher. Let's get that out in the open."

"Look Ronnie, I'm not tryin' ta strong arm ya. But something is happenin' there that's definitely superhuman in nature, an' right now you an' your crew are the only ones the brass thinks has a chance o' stoppin' it."

"So you're not the 'brass' then?"

"Me? Naahh. There are others above me that give me orders. I'm just playin' messenger here. I had a feelin' all a this was unnecessary anyway. I figured you were on your way there to begin with."

Sol nodded, "You figured correctly, Commander Butcher."

By now the Stargrazer had emptied and the rest of the team were standing next to and behind Solaron. To his right was Dragonfly, to his left was Stryker. Next to him was Creature and next to Creature was Silver Shadow. Starbolt stood next to Dragonfly.

Then, Captain Power landed with a roar of spent energy. He walked up past Butcher and then turned and looked him in the eyes, "Solaron, who's this guy? You didn't tell me we had guests."

"He dropped in unexpectedly, but he's just leaving now."

"Yeah I am Captain Power, just leaving that is. We ain't the enemy, we're the government."

Cap chuckled mirthlessly, "That means one and the same to a lot of people these days."

"Maybe so, big man, but I'm tellin' ya we're on the same side. In fact I can help you guys out with a lot of things you might need."

Sol stepped forward, "There's never been so frightening a statement as 'I'm from the government, I'm here to help.' No thanks to whatever it is you're selling Butcher. We're doing just fine without you."

"Listen, I'm not here for trouble, I'm here to let you know we're out here and we're all on the same team. There's a much bigger, much darker world out there that you're just beginning to get involved with. There're places you'll never be allowed to go that we,-I can get you into. Take my card. I'll monitor the situation in

137

Cleveland and if you need back up I'll send my elite agents." he pointed a thumb over his shoulder at the men waiting in the cars on the long driveway behind him, "an' we'll be there in a flash."

"Thanks for the offer, but we won't need you." Cap replied.

Sol took the card from Butcher's outstretched hand.

"I'll talk to you after this mess is over. We can make your teams life a lot easier on a lot of levels."

Sol said nothing. He turned toward the Stargrazer and everyone walked toward it slowly except Cap and Sol who both stood facing Butcher with their arms folded across their chests.

"Time to hit the road Commander. I'm going to be looking into you. If you are who and what you claim to be you'll be hearing from me. If this is some kind of scam you better run and hide in the deepest darkest hole you can find and take your boys with you. You do not want to be on my bad side." Sol advised.

Butcher nodded. He turned and walked away, back into one of the black SUV's that were lined up on the driveway, then they drove away.

Cap watched them disappear.

"I'm not liking that at all."

"Neither am I." Sol replied.

The two men entered the small spaceship. A moment later it hovered within the hanger, turning on its own and then it flew out of the hanger bay, which automatically closed behind it. Solaron waited until the hanger doors had slid shut and then turned to Starbolt, "Okay Prince let's go."

"On our way Solaron." the young superhero replied.

"What's our ETA?"

"Not more than fifteen minutes Solaron. I have to limit our speed this deep within the atmosphere. It's not worth flying up to the edge of space and then back down the angle of ascent and descent would be too steep."

"That's fine Starbolt. Just get us there as fast as possible."

Sol toggled a switch on the console before him, "Marcus, do you copy me?"

"I do Solaron, loud and clear. I stand ready to assist." Mar-Cus replied from deep within the solar observatory.

"Good. Please monitor the situation on all available bands in Cleveland. Also if you have any unwanted visitors, please contact us immediately. Our fastest fliers will be back to you before you could finish your emergency call."

"Are you expecting trouble?" Starbolts' mentor asked, "I saw your confrontation with that Commander Butcher."

"No, I think we're okay as far as he's concerned, but I can't be sure. If a situation does arise, contact us immediately."

"I shall my friend, I shall."

"Good, Hyperforce out." Solaron cut the communication off.

"How are we doing?"

"We are almost there. That black cloud of smoke is our destination." Starbolt pointed at the windshield.

"That doesn't look good." Dragonfly muttered.

"No, not at all." Cap agreed.

"That's a huge area, it looks like half the city may be gone."

"I hope not, from what we were able to discern about all of this it centered on one building, a lab and research facility belonging to a Dr. Paul Corbo."

"Do you know him?" Cap asked.

Sol nodded affirmatively, "Yes I do, but only in passing."

"Okay what were your impressions of the man?" Cap continued.

Sol shrugged, "He was wealthy, driven and brilliant."

"Do you know what he was working on?" Dragonfly asked.

"His field of expertise was gravity manipulation. He was involved in creating a device that could funnel the force of gravity like a weapon. He had always hoped to be able to create a device that could bore to the earths' core if need be in a matter of minutes."

Cap looked at Sol as if uncomprehending, "What drives you guys? I don't get it. Seriously, what practical use can something like that be?"

Sol just shook his head, "It's like climbing the mountain Captain, because it's there."

"Yeah but his mountain just destroyed a city and maybe killed untold amounts of people. Was this worth it?"

Sol sighed, "It wasn't my experiment Cap. I wasn't involved in it at all."

Cap nodded and softened slightly, "You're right Sol, I apologize. I'm just concerned about the people there."

"Understood my friend. We're all under pressure at the moment."

Behind them in the next row of seats Silver Shadow and Creature exchanged worried glances.

"What's wrong you two?" Solaron asked.

"I-I'm getting a lot of worried emotions emanating from that city, or what's left of it. Peoples thoughts- Sol, something climbed out of that pit. Something, no wait a lot of somethings'. One guy who's a big bad, and lots of... I think lots of soldiers or warriors or something. So many jumbled thoughts, but most of it is fear!" Silver Shadow trailed off.

Solaron looked at Silver Shadow grimly for a moment, and then spoke, "Creature, Dragonfly, Cap, you're with me. Stryker, Starbolt, Silver, find a safe spot, park the ship and come join us. Stay together. We have no idea what's down there. Be prepared for anything and everything. Let's go."

The four men flew out of the ship and began to descend to the devastated city below. Cap took point while the others flew in a 'V' formation behind him.

"I'm heading for the pit, where all of this began." Cap informed the rest.

"We're right behind you." Sol replied.

"Wow, look at this. The poor people..." Dragonfly muttered.

"Dragonfly, use your spectroscopic vision as we fly overhead. Look for anything out of the ordinary. People trapped, that sort of thing."

"I am Sol, I am."

An instant later a wave of energy erupted from near the ground, and knocked them all out of the sky, or rather it drew them crushingly toward it.

"Ugggh, what the hell was that?" Cap asked.

"There!" shouted Dragonfly, pointing.

They all followed his direction and saw a big man walking toward them slowly. Behind him were dozens of men, all wearing skin tight suits with goggles covering their eyes.

But the big man in the lead was special. His suit was a dark purple with a full face mask that covered his nose and mouth. His mask went up in the front culminating in several points along the sides. Lenses covered his eyes from view.

A shattered bus lay nearby piled upon the debris. The stranger pointed at it, emanating waves of energy that looked akin to the surface of a calm lake once a stone was tossed into it from his hands. The bus instantly rose into the air, then the stranger pointed in the direction where half of Hyperforce lay helplessly, and the bus crashed down upon them.

The big purple costumed man in the lead stared stoically at the crumpled bus, then turned to face his soldiers and in a booming voice spoke "So die their protectors. If this is the best they have to send against us, the surface will be conquered in mere days and not weeks as I originally foresaw."

"Gravity King!" one of the troops shouted, "L-look!"

The man called 'Gravity King' spun slowly and stared at the bus he had just dropped upon the men he had first pinned to the ground with his gravity powers and stopped to stare. The bus had begun to glow and quickly disintegrated before his eyes. The glow faded quickly, standing before him was Captain Power with his hands outstretched, and behind him under a glowing golden solar bubble stood Solaron, Dragonfly and Creature.

142

"Who are you, where'd you come from and what are you doing here? Why'd you declare war on Cleveland?" Cap yelled.

Gravity King sneered before replying, "Your people attacked my realm, my subjects. You killed thousands."

Solaron walked toward Gravity King slowly, "No one attacked your realm. There may have been something, an experiment that went awry. No one purposely went out of their way to hurt your people."

"Do you think it matters if it was done purposely? My people, they are dead. Thousands of them. There must be retribution."

Captain Power stepped forward, "Look around you. Do you think that this isn't payment enough? We don't even know how many died here, or how many are buried beneath the rubble and still alive. Your attack coupled with the destruction caused by that device has been devastating. No one wanted to hurt your people. Hell, we didn't know they existed. Think this through and stand down."

"No. I will destroy you all for what you have done." Gravity King threw both hands forward at Captain Power, releasing waves of gravimetric force, seeking to crush him into the pavement. Instantly his men raised their futuristic rifles and fired.

Solaron fired blazing blasts of solar heat at Gravity King, staggering the enemy. Creature soared skyward on leathern wings that sprang from his back and attacked the troopers.

"Enough of this, let's rock an' roll." Dragonfly shouted. He flew into the crowd like a missile taking half a dozen of the subterranean warriors down. Creature

landed beside him and together they began tearing
through the troopers. Energy blasts flew from the strange
weapons in all directions. Dragonfly and Creature fought
with fists and claws, while Captain Power walked
toward his enemy. Each step felt like Cap was moving
the earth itself.

"How are you able to walk? You should be trapped
upon the ground, weighed down by your own mass. You
should be cracking the very ground beneath your feet
and sinking into it. What are you?" the stunned Gravity
King asked.

Cap grunted haltingly as he drew near his foe, "I…
am… Power!"

A right cross that would have shattered a mountain
smashed Gravity King from his feet. Solaron stood
nearby blasting their enemy continuously until Gravity
King used some sort of gravity field to deflect Solaron's
blasts. That changed the instant Cap knocked him from
his feet. Solaron fired high density beams at Gravity
King and sent him careening through the rubble like a
ground bound missile.

"Are you okay?" Sol asked Cap.

"Yeah, I'm fine. A little angry, that's all."

"This is a very dangerous situation. This Gravity
King could be a sovereign ruler of another civilization
hidden beneath the earth's crust. We have to be careful
here. There could be ramifications."

"Sol, no offence, but you be careful if you want to.
I'm going to smash this guy into the ground so hard he's
going to end up back where he came from."

The rubble Gravity King was buried in exploded
away from him. He was now floating in mid-air, "I think

144

not Captain Power. You're going into space." Gravity King fired his gravimetric pulses at Cap and suddenly Captain Power was driven away, accelerating upward and out of control.

Solaron didn't hesitate at all; he unleashed solar bolts again and again. But Gravity King blocked them with his gravity shields.

"What did you do to him?" Sol angrily shouted.

"The same thing I am going to do with you, surface dweller. I used anti-gravitons. They will drive you away from the planet and into space, as they did your compatriot." Gravity King fired, hitting Sol squarely. Instantly Solaron rocketed skyward haphazardly and out of control.

"Sol!" Dragonfly screamed.

Instantly a black and gold figure streaked through the sky and tackled Gravity King, driving them both through the war zone-like debris.

"What...was...that?" Creature grunted.

"I think that was Stryker."

Wreckage was hurled about, and revealed in the midst of it all was Stryker trading powerful blows with Gravity King whose fists looked distorted as if the clear gravitic energy encompassed them.

"Another one? Is there no end to you surface dwelling fools?"

"You're wearing a purple costume, an' you're callin' me a fool?" the Australian hero replied.

They stood toe to toe and hammered at each other.

"You are brave, bearded one, but you cannot stand against me for long. I strike at you with the force of earthquakes. You will not last much longer against my power."

"I, ugghh, don't, unngg, have to…mate."

"Fool! I'll crush you under your own weight." Stryker was driven to his knees and Gravity King grasped his fists in his own crushing grip. "I'll force you through the pavement and down to the earth's core where your body will rot for all eternity."

"Not, ungghh, gonna happen mate."

"You are defeated, I have won. Surrender or do not; I do not care." Gravity King stopped and stared at the man on his knees before him, "Why are you so confident yet?"

Stryker looked up at his foe and smiled, "Because I'm part o' a team, mate."

A blast of energy enveloped Gravity Kings' head from above. Instantly he arched painfully backward, an agonized groan dribbling over his lips. He stumbled and finally fell to the ground.

Floating above him was Silver Shadow, her mind numbing stun bolt encompassed him, and filled him with terrible pain.

"I-incredible," Silver began, "he should be unconscious, never mind still fighting to stand."

"Finish 'im! Don't play with 'im!" Stryker shrieked.

The big Aussie struggled to get to his feet. Then he was flying through the air, but not of his own power, and right into Silver Shadow, knocking her from the sky. "No, Silver!" he grunted. Wrapping his arms around her, they were both slammed into the pavement again and again by Gravity King and his gravity controlling power.

"You maniac, get away from them!" Starbolt roared. He threw his hands forward and shouted, "Explosive blasts!"

"Unnggh," Gravity King rumbled while being blasted across the destroyed city streets. He rolled to his feet instantly, throwing waves of gravimetric force at Starbolt, "I'll crush you boy."

"I think not, villain." Starbolt bellowed, "Gravimetric wave."

The gravitational forces between the two men tore the street to shreds in a heartbeat. Pavement became rubble, and then was liquefied.

"Your control is lacking boy."

Starbolt grimaced, "What I lack in control I more than make up for in power."

Redoubling his efforts Starbolt grappled with the gravimetric energies playing about him.

"Incredible," exclaimed Gravity King, "you are actually matching my power. You might actually overwhelm me with my own abilities, were it not for your lack of skill."

Gravity King broke his right hand free and aimed it at a collapsed building behind Starbolt, pulling the rubble over Starbolt instantly.

"Shield!' Starbolt shouted as the rubble fell about him, burying him.

'Very good boy, you saved your life. If you were better at this game you might stand a chance of defeating me."

"He doesn't have to do it alone, jackass. He's part of a team."

Gravity King turned toward the voice and saw both Dragonfly and Creature closing in on him fast.

"Is there no end to you fools?"

"Nope, if that's the way you wanna think about it purple puss, there isn't."

Dragonfly raised both hands and fired explosive fletchettes at the villain, who in a flash raised a gravimetric shield between them. The fletchettes exploded brightly.

Creature took a running start and leapt into the air, his bat-like leathern wings sprouting from his back. Circling around to Gravity Kings blindside Creature attacked, plowing into his foe with a massive roar of anger. He saw his sister lying there unconscious by the equally unconscious Stryker and red rage filled him to overflowing.

Claws grew from outstretched fingertips and slashed the subterranean warriors costume and flesh. Dragonfly meanwhile switched to his electron power bursts or as he called them, 'dragon blasts' with which he immediately peppered the now embattled Gravity King.

But still the big warrior fought back. His gravity fields blunted Dragonfly's attacks, and Creature's own strikes were not causing as much damage as he had hoped.

"You cannot stop me with your puny claws, savage beast. My gravity control already now covers my body with a thick layer of gravimetric pressure, your attacks are now blunted and the boys' energy beams cannot harm me."

"I've had enough of you clown-face." Dragonfly ignited his boot rockets and streaked toward Gravity King, gauntlets still blazing.

"Foolish whelp." Gravity King swept his right hand upward, the ground erupted beneath Dragonfly as a tower of rubble sprang upward and swatted Dragonfly from the air like a bug.

Cartwheeling through the sky Dragonfly swept back and forth trying to avoid the now constant attacks from their enemy. Rubble flew upward repeatedly, each column of stone and debris seeking to end Dragonfly's life.

Creature was now held to the ground by his own weight which was increased a hundred fold. He struggled and growled madly but to no avail.

"You are valiant, all of you are. But you are no match for my skill and power."

"We already took out your troops; you're all that's left." Dragonfly grunted. He streaked through the air, and continued to blast at Gravity King.

"Foolish words from a foolish boy. You can no more stop me than you can stop the raging tides. My power is a force of nature; *I* am a force of nature."

"You talk too much." Dragonfly rocketed overhead and shouted, then he revered his body position and fired his dragon blasts at Gravity King's feet, turning the ground to mush. Instantly the subterranean monarch disappeared beneath it seemingly swallowed whole by the ground itself.

Dragonfly landed, but already the ground had re-solidified where he had driven Gravity King down into the depths below their feet. Looking around Dragonfly muttered, "Good riddance." Quickly he began helping the others up and out of the rubble, "Are you all right Creature?" he asked as he freed the hairy Hyperforcer.

"Where…is…Silver?"

Dragonfly looked around quickly, "I-I'm not sure." he whispered in surprise.

The two men began digging about the wreckage but found nothing. No hide nor hair of Silver Shadow. They were joined almost immediately by first Starbolt and then Stryker.

"Where're Cap and Sol?" Stryker asked, his characteristic Aussie accent wafting through the otherwise silent air of devastated Cleveland.

Dragonfly jerked a thumb skyward, "This guy sent them both packing up into orbit. I guess it was the easiest way to take out our two big guns."

"He didn't take us out, he inconvenienced us." Sol replied. He and Captain Power descended from up above, touching down quietly amidst their teammates.

"Where is he?" Sol asked.

"Back down where he came from." shrugged Dragonfly.

"What's wrong?" Cap demanded.

"Silver's missing." Starbolt replied.

Creature began to growl menacingly.

Sol ordered, "Dragonfly, your spectroscopic vision."

"I've been doing that Sol, but I'm not seeing anything, it's as if she just vanished."

"Not vanished, pulled down with our mysterious enemy below the earth's surface." Solaron replied.

"You…think…he…took…her…with…him?" Creature grunted.

"I think that's the only thing we can assume at this point," Sol answered, "Silver Shadow has disappeared, I think we'd be fooling ourselves if we thought for an instant that this so-called 'Gravity King' didn't have her."

Dragonfly looked around quickly, as if realizing something for the first time, "Sol, Cap, where are they? Where are the soldiers we took out? They're all gone."

Captain Power looked about and returned his gaze to his teammates, "You're right, they're all gone. Somehow this Gravity King not only escaped with one of our own, he also took his foot soldiers back with him. He completely defeated us. We may have driven him off. But he won this hand."

"What do we do now?" Starbolt asked.

"We go after them;" Solaron replied, "and we make them pay.

***

Silver Shadow's eyes fluttered open slowly. She reached up and realized a bandage was wrapped around her head, "W-where am I?"

"You are safe, beauteous one." a deep, powerful voice replied.

Silver looked around and realized she was lying down on a bed or divan of some sort. Spinning her legs off in a fluid motion she stood on her feet in a compact move, and matched her gaze with the man who spoke.

"You. Gravity King. What have you done with me and where am I?" Silver clenched her small fists and her brow furrowed with anger as her eyes locked with his.

"You are safe Silver Shadow, within my realm."

"Within your- How long was I out?"

"Not too long, perhaps two hours at most, but the majority of that time was spent here resting, after my physicians saw to your wounds. How do you feel?"

She snorted, "I feel like someone dropped a building on me." she hesitated a second and then continued, "Stryker. What happened to him? I vaguely remember him putting his body between the falling wall and myself."

"Yes I am sure he perished a warriors' death."

"He's dead?" she asked in wide eyed disbelief.

"I believe so, yes. He was unmoving when I pulled you free of the rubble. In truth I did not check on him, he was an enemy combatant."

Gravity King reached forward to touch Silver's shoulder, "To be honest, I was concerned about you-"

Before he could finish his sentence Silver grabbed his hand and flipped him over her shoulder, slamming him down hard.

Gravity King rolled to his feet instantly and faced Silver Shadow; "You continue to impress me, my lady." he smiled.

"I'm not interested in impressing you. I want out of this place. You and I are not friends, mister. We're not going to share recipes or whatever craziness you have planned. You never answered me, where are we?"

Gravity King walked over to a wall and pulled on curtain cords, opening the curtains and revealing a rocky sandstone colored land stretching as far as the eye could see. A golden orb hung in what appeared to be the sky, but Silver knew that was impossible. Gravity King saw her gaze falling on the glowing orb and smiled.

"Ah our sun stone. The source of our light here. Legend has it that a warrior king in our dim forgotten past climbed up to the sun itself and stole a fragment of that blessed orb to provide light for those who live below.

"Yeah, well I hate to burst your bubble King, but I doubt that ever happened."

He chuckled softly to himself, "Perhaps my lady, perhaps not."

"Why did you take me here? What do you want? You caused enough mayhem and destruction on the surface. No one even knew you existed. No one did anything purposely to harm your people."

"Perhaps not Silver Shadow, but that no longer matters. What does is that I have found you, a warrior princess who is fearless. A woman who could be my perfect mate."

"Your what?" Silver shouted wide eyed in disbelief.

***

"What do you mean you're going after them? You can't do that." Commander Butcher shouted.

"We're going after them, Butcher. You heard me." Solaron replied with equal anger.

"What are you going to do? Fly down that hole after them?"

"Yes we are."

"I-look, this is our job now. Your team did your job, let me and my men go in after them."

"What? These men?" Solaron pointed at the black garbed men gathered all around the hole in the ground.

They wore night vision goggles atop their heads and full
balaclava's. They each carried high powered rifles as
well as a pistol on each hip and a long knife slung across
their chest in a scabbard. They also carried grenades on
their chests in bandoliers.

"I hate to break it to you Butcher, but Gravity King
will crush these men with a thought. This guy is no
pushover, and he has one of ours."

"When…do…we…leave?" Creature walked over to
the two men and growled menacingly.

Butcher looked over the top of his sunglasses at
Creatures furry face, "There's not going to be any
leaving here until we work a few things out. My men are
in charge, you'll be backing them u-"

Creature grabbed Butcher by the collar and lifted him
into the air as if he was a feather. He slammed the man
into the truck they were standing behind and effortlessly
held him there.

"No." Creature growled.

Butchers' eyes went wide in surprise. Creature shook
him once, and then twice, none to gently.

"Put him down Creature." Captain Power ordered.

Creature looked at Cap over his shoulder, grunted
and let Butcher slip to the debris strewn ground.

"Keep your dog on a leash, or next time I might just
put it down." Butcher rested his hand on the holster he
wore under his trench coat.

"No, I don't think you will." Cap walked between
Creature and Commander Butcher, "You said earlier that
we were all on the same side and in so many words you
told us that working together would be advantageous for
us all. Right now I see you coming in here and trying to

step on our toes. Big mistake. We drove this 'Gravity King' off, not you and your shock troopers. You did nothing but show up once the fighting was over with."

"Look ya big jerk, I was trying to save lives and stay outta your way. That 'Gravity King' was throwing around a lot of power, and when you guys started battling him and his cronies you were just adding to the mess. It was such a hot zone in here that a normal soldier probably would have been fried alive."

"Which is why we took this subterranean threat on in the first place."

"Look Cap, I know you guys did the heavy lifting here, but right now we have to invade a hidden nation at the earth's core we never knew existed. There could be armies down there just waiting for us. We can't have civilians mucking things up down there."

Solaron pushed past Creature and Cap now, "Did you *really* just say that to *us*? Think carefully before you answer mister."

"First off, it's 'commander', not mister. Secondly the government wants me in control down there. They want my men running point. I'm under orders. There's nothing I can do."

"Yes there is," Sol replied, "You can just tell them that we refused to comply and that we have the situation under control."

"But that ain't the truth."

"You know otherwise. If not for our intervention things would be much worse than they presently are."

"How much worse than this can things be?" Butcher swept his arms about him, indicating the terrible devastation that used to be Cleveland.

"More loss of life. There Butcher, I said it in words of one syllable for you."

"Solaron, I'm not your enemy."

"So you keep saying."

Butcher pulled out a cigarette, struck a match on some rubble and lit it, then inhaled deeply, finally exhaling after a few seconds.

"Works every time." he indicated the cigarette, "Calms me right down when I need it."

"Yeah, it just kills you in the process. Doesn't seem like such a fair trade off to me." Cap observed.

"Look guys, we're all on the same side here. We could all go down there together. You guys take point and just report everything that you see or happens to me. We share information and everyone is happy, what do you say?"

Cap wagged a finger in Butchers face, "If you're coming down there you better stay behind us and keep your mouths shut. No happy trigger fingers. This is a Hyperforce mission, not a strange black ops team mission."

Before Butcher could interrupt Solaron continued, "I don't want to see your troops shooting everything in sight, only if they are being aimed at or if things go sour. There may still be a way to talk ourselves out of this escalating into a full blown war. But if your men are in danger, well I wouldn't blame them for shooting back."

"All right guys I get it. I agree. We have to work together to trust one another. Chances are this is only the first time of soon to be many missions we'll have to run together."

"Whoa doggy, let's not get ahead of ourselves." Dragonfly interjected.

"Quiet the kid up, Doc. He should be in school anyway."

"An' where should you be gramps?" Dragonfly replied, "The nursing home?"

"I ain't that old pipsqueak. Mind yer mouth."

"Okay all of you shut up." Solaron ordered.

He turned back to Butcher, "How are you proposing to get down there, to wherever 'there' is?"

Butcher grinned, "I thought you'd never ask, Doc."

***

Butcher commented, "We call her 'Bonny'. It doesn't mean a damned thing, we just like the name."

"Butcher, you built a drilling machine?" Solaron spun and looked at the mystery man. Butcher grinned again; his leather trench coat blew about him in the breeze that came off of Lake Erie.

Hyperforce stood staring at the fifteen foot long, ten foot tall, cylindrical machine with the pointed snout.

"The front of that doesn't turn. This is no drill." Cap announced after looking over the vehicle carefully.

Butcher chuckled sarcastically, "It uses lasers. We figured a drill bit that large always has a chance to break or jam up. A laser is just gonna burn baby, burn."

"You're kidding me, right?" Dragonfly shook his head in disbelief, "How much power does it take to run this thing? Are the batteries gonna go dead when it's a few hundred miles down?"

157

"Naah kid, it's powered like a nuclear sub. Same principle."

"So you're tossing a nuke into a hole in the ground and aiming it at your enemies." Cap replied.

"*Our enemies* Captain Power, our enemies."

"Maybe so Butcher, but the idea of handing these guys who just might have more in common with a bunch of backward aliens a working nuclear reactor does not sit well with me."

"You ain't got nothin' ta worry about Captain." Butcher replied.

"I disagree," Sol said, "these guys mean business. Their leader took us all on and almost beat us. If not for Dragonfly's quick thinking we might all be dead. Think about that."

"C'mon golden boy, you know as well as I do that the guy bailed on you all. He musta been getting' tired or somethin'. The guy controls gravity, obviously he flies."

"He flew in front of us." Dragonfly confirmed.

"Yeah, well, it was only common sense that he could have. So what's it gonna be? Are you boys joinin' my crew in goin' down there? Like I said, we'll even let you guys take point, even though we're not supposed to."

"All right we're in," Sol agreed, "but don't get in our way once we find where we're going."

Commander Butcher shook his head in agreement, "You got it Solaron."

"When are you going to tell us what never before heard of agency you represent?"

"You never heard of us, what would be the point?" Butcher grinned.

"I still want to know who, or what I'm saddling up with. You seem to know quite a bit about Hyperforce including where we hang our hats, but you sure have not been exactly forthcoming with any of your information. That ends now. If we're going to work together Commander Butcher, I want full disclosure on your part and I want it now before we step foot into your drilling machine."

Both men stood staring at one another like unmoving blocks of granite. Finally Butcher relented, "Okay chief, you win. We're called 'A.R.M.O.R'."

"And what does that mean?" Cap asked, his brow as furrowed as his patience was becoming.

"It's an acronym. It means Advanced Reserve Military Operations Response unit."

"So you're a special high tech military unit then." Solaron said.

"We can fight if we have to, yeah."

"I gathered as much. What are you? More warriors than super-spies?"

"Yeah that's about right Sol."

"Stop right there. Only my friends can call me 'Sol', Butcher."

Butcher touched his fingertips to his own chest and feigned injury, "Ain't we friends yet Solaron? C'mon, I'm doin' my best here."

"It doesn't much matter what you're doing Butcher. You're not in the trust bucket yet. Let's just say I'm wary of you for now."

"Trust bucket? What the hell is that anyway?"

"Just me saying I'm keeping an eye on you. Prove yourself and your organization to us all and maybe we can work together in the future without looking over our shoulders at one another."

Butcher nodded slowly, "Okay Solaron, all kiddin' aside, I got it. For now let's put our differences aside to work together and get through this disaster to see if we have to save just the country or the whole damned world."

Butcher held out his open hand to Solaron, the golden super-hero took it and shook.

"Agreed Butcher. There's too much at stake to argue about trivialities right now."

A dozen men crammed into the earth drilling machine, including the six Hyperforcers'.

"Tight quarters." one of the ARMOR troopers remarked.

"You could always leave." Dragonfly shrugged with a smirk.

"Sorry kid, somebodies got to be here to change your diaper."

The other black garbed men laughed. Dragonfly smiled. Walked over to the seat of the man who had made the diaper remark and effortlessly snatched the powerful automatic rifle the soldier was carrying from his hands and with a smile and no effort, bent the barrel into a 'U' shape. Then, still smiling he handed the rifle back to the dumbfounded soldier.

"Dragonfly…" Solaron warned.

Dragonfly put his hands up and moved forward to sit in the seat next to Solaron, still grinning.

Cap was seated on the other side of him and said nothing. But Stryker was seated behind him, and thumped him on the shoulder. When Dragonfly turned around Stryker grinned a toothy smile and gave him a thumbs up. Dragonfly turned toward the front of the earth driller and smiled.

"All right enough, all of you." Butcher grunted, "Buckle up, all a ya. We're goin' down."

The engines of the earth mover began to whine louder, building in speed and power. The machine began to slowly creep forward. It pitched down into the cavernous pit formed by the gravity beam weapon of Dr. Corbo and began tunneling down.

Cap spoke first, "This tunnel looks like it's wide open with nothing to block our descent."

Sol nodded, "Yes I see that as well Captain. No one found any sign of Dr. Corbo since all of this began."

After a moment Solaron added, "He's got to be dead. There was too much damage done by his device to the city, especially at the epicenter of the explosion."

The front of the drilling machine had a view screen mounted on the forward section that showed a camera feed from outside the drilling device.

"Nothing so far." Dragonfly commented.

"Hhhmm. This is going to be a long journey." Starbolt remarked.

"How...many...miles?" Creature growled. The soldiers nearest him eyed him suspiciously. Most never realized the hirsute Hyperforcer could speak.

"Almost four thousand." answered Solaron.

"Four thousand? We'll be here all week." Stryker exclaimed.

Sol nodded, "That's about right, if we have to go that deeply into the earth's core, which I doubt."

"So what are you thinking Sol?" Cap asked.

161

Solaron shrugged, "A couple of hundred miles at most. Five hundred on the outset. I know it didn't take these guys any more than a few minutes to climb up this hole from wherever they came from. It's very probable that Gravity King flew the troops to the surface in a gravity bubble up the shaft the device had created, and he simply flew everyone, including Silver Shadow, back down it again at an incredible speed."

"Like most of us could do if we weren't trapped in this tin can you mean." Stryker noted.

"How fast are we traveling, Commander Butcher?" Sol questioned.

"We're approaching a hundred and twenty miles per hour."

"Wow, I'm surprised we're moving that fast. I thought it was a lot less." Dragonfly observed.

"No it ain't. The tunnel that gravity beam cut is wide an' smooth. So far I haven't had to laser anything out of the way except for some loose rubble. Just so you jokers know, the temperature out there is already well over a hundred degrees."

"Yes I had already surmised that." Sol replied.

"Yeah, scientist an' all o' that. I get it." Butcher nodded.

Solaron nodded in reply.

A light began to blink on the control board and a beeping sound filled the small cabin.

"What's that?" Dragonfly asked.

"Somethin's incoming. A lot o' somethin's." Butcher answered.

"Is there an airlock on this thing?" Cap asked.

162

"At the aft section." Butcher replied, "You have to close the inner section which is now recessed into the ceiling. Once it seals you open the outer and can leave the ship. But you can't go out there; we don't even know what it is."

Cap walked swiftly to the rear of the small drilling machine, "Whatever it is it's definitely trouble."

"You're not going alone, Cap." Solaron stood and followed the bigger man to the rear of the ship. Dragonfly shrugged and joined them.

"Stryker," Sol began, "Are you resistant to heat and cold extremes?"

"Uh no mate, sorry. I can fly real fast an' things bounce offa me in flight easily enough wit'out leavin' any damage. But standin' still I got no more protection than any other bloke onna street."

Solaron nodded slowly, "Okay, Creature, Starbolt and Stryker stay aboard 'Bonny' with the soldiers while the rest of us see what's coming our way." Solaron turned to Dragonfly, "Make sure you're in space mode, so your suit seals up."

Dragonfly flashed him a grin and a thumbs up. His face was already hidden behind an indestructible clear plastic shield. "Already done, boss."

"Let's go."

The three heroes exited the inner section of 'Bonny' with the airlock hatch swinging down from above to close them in a short section with another door heading out. Cap began to turn the manual door release, a big wheel upon the center of the door, when Butchers voice boomed over the internal comm system, "Whatever they are they're gettin' closer. By the time you guys exit this thing they'll be here."

"Exiting now Butcher." Solaron replied.

"Good luck gents." Butcher answered and then the comm clicked off.

Cap opened the door and the wave of stifling heat from without hit them all with a physical force.

But none of the three were slowed by it at all. Cap stepped out and flew ahead, immediately followed by Solaron and Dragonfly.

Dragonfly narrowed his eyes, activating his spectroscopic vision and was almost instantly stunned by what he saw.

"Uhh, you guys remember those flying monkeys from 'Wizard of Oz'? Well these ain't them. These guys are bigger and meaner looking and look like they're made out of stone."

Then the howling monstrosities were upon them, swinging axes and pikes made of stone.

"Take them down." shouted Solaron. But he was already too late, as both Captain Power and Dragonfly had dove into the surging mass of winged, flying stone apes.

"Sorry guys, but this is going to hurt." Cap rumbled. His fists tore stone chunks from his enemies, scattering them through the tunnel. Dragonfly wasted no time or energy. He fired his Dragonblasts repeatedly in quick swaths across the tunnel stunning the seemingly endless wave of creatures throwing themselves at them. The stone apes dropped to the ground, insensate.

"Wahoo!" shouted Dragonfly with each blast of his weapons, while Solaron flew ahead of his companions and filled the tunnel with burning solar energy.

"You two stay back, I'm going to unleash a solar blast down here that will fuse this tunnel to glass at the very least."

"Go for it Sol." Cap roared, his fists falling rhythmically like heavy metal pistons, crushing the stone apes with every blow.

Solaron heaved his hands back above his head and then threw them forward, sending a devastating blast of golden solar energy down the depths of the tunnel, incinerating the stone apes and turning them to slag before they could continue their attack.

Dragonfly touched down behind Solaron, followed by Captain Power.

"Wow," an astonished Dragonfly began, "I don't think I ever saw you cut loose like that before."

"That's because I never have, well maybe once, and that was against General Zaring's ship a few weeks back."

"I have to say, I'm impressed Sol." Cap agreed with a lopsided grin.

"You guys realize we just killed a couple of hundred flying apes right?" Dragonfly admonished.

"Really Dragonfly? Did you see any heartbeats with your spectroscopic vision? What about blood flow or anything else that would determine them to be alive?" Solaron asked, a slight smile playing across the corners of his mouth.

"Well, no, not really. They just looked like animated rock. Their chests didn't move to breathe in either. But

165

what if they were some other kind of life form? I mean I'm not arguing that they had it coming and would have done the same thing to us if we gave 'em a chance, but you don't think we killed them?"

"I don't know if they were alive." Sol conjectured. "I do believe they were animated stone sent to kill us by our friend Gravity King."

"How? How could he animate stone?" Cap asked.

"We don't know the extent of his powers. Honestly we have no idea what we're stepping into." Sol considered for a moment and then continued, "We don't even know if he himself is capable of animating those stone men, or if they were actually alive. Also remember their weaponry? They are scientifically years, perhaps decades ahead of what we have on the surface now. The ability to animate stone may be a weapon of some sort for them, or the result of that weapons use."

"Well, I think we have some idea after what happened a few hours ago." Dragonfly allowed.

"Meaning?" Solaron turned toward his young teammate.

"Meaning this guy nearly kicked all our butts. Hey, I know I got lucky. I may be cocky, but I'm not stupid." Dragonfly grinned. "He had no qualms about killing us, that much was for sure, an' now we're going to his home to invade it. We better have a plan before we go down there an' get our heads handed to us. We don't have home field advantage anymore, not that it did anything for us when we did."

"Pretty good kid," Cap began with a smirk, "There might be hope for you yet."

"Thanks big guy, I think." Dragonfly returned the grin. "Now what?" he asked Solaron.

"We continue on. That's what. Again we have no idea how much further we have to go."

Cap looked down the dark tunnel, "How do you think they disappeared so fast? It's like there's nothing to mark their passing through here."

"Think about it; I have no doubt that Gravity King lowered them at tremendous speed using his gravity control powers, probably at thousands of miles per hour. His gravity shields would repel anything that could do them harm, and look at this tunnel the device Corbo was working on created here, its straight as an arrow."

"That brings up another thought," Solaron began, "What did my massive solar blast do where it exited?"

***

"Gravity King!" a guard burst into the room Gravity King stood conversing with Silver Shadow, "Come quickly, sensors we left behind in the tunnel just burned out. There is a massive energy and heat spike heading directly for us. We need you to protect everyone!"

Gravity King was instantly on his feet, Silver followed him.

"Do you see?" he said to her, anger coloring his voice and face hidden beneath his mask, "Your people seek to kill us all for the second time in only a few short hours."

"You don't know that, you don't know what this is."

"Bah," he dismissed her with a wave of his hand and flew away, negating gravity and streaking though the sky toward the tunnels exit point at the far end of the city.

Silver Shadow began to fly after him, out of the open portal and above the small city beneath the earth's crust.

"Hold woman." the guard in the room challenged her, placing his staff across her body, stopping her in place.

Silver Shadow did not hesitate for an instant. She drove a punch toward his nose, but the guard parried it, as he was supposed to. She swept his legs out from under him instantly, and he unceremoniously landed on his butt.

"Now stay there." she commanded and leapt out the stone portal soaring away toward the direction Gravity King had taken.

'Everything looks like it's made out of sandstone or rock. All these houses. But none of this looks dilapidated at all, or antiquated for that matter. I see lights glowing everywhere, all powered by some source of energy. Perhaps that sun stone he had mentioned?' Silver's eyes wandered to the roof of the enclosed city some distance above her head, where the glowing chunk of matter sat embedded in the ceiling illuminating everything.

Then a brilliant burst of light caught her attention, and it was emanating from a hole at the rear of the city some miles in the distance. She aimed toward it and increased her flight speed, skimming over the rooftops.

An instant later she touched down next to the already landed Gravity King, who struggled with the powerful forces that raged all about him. His own power was being used to shield the city from the rampaging solar blast of Solaron's

168

"Do you see Silver Shadow?" Gravity King called to her while looking over his shoulder, "Your teammates-I recognize this power- they try to obliterate my people."

"That's not true Gravity King. You attacked us all first, and then you kidnapped me. Did you really believe they wouldn't come after me? Are you really that naïve?"

"Bah, foolish girl, I am the leader of my people. My only concern is what is best for them all. This city you see before you is called 'Epherezus' and is but one of many spread about the globe. We are an entire civilization and we have been living underground for centuries."

"Arrrggghh!" he suddenly howled, struggling to shield the city from Solaron's blast. With his right hand he maintained his shield, with his left he used his power over gravity to carve a new tunnel back to the surface. Then adjusting the gravitic energy as if it were a thing alive, Gravity King forced the solar blast up the newly formed tunnel he had cut, where it disappeared.

Exhausted he dropped to his knees, breathing heavily.

Silver Shadow walked up to him and placed her hands upon his shoulders from behind, "T-that was really something."

He looked up at her, "The energy required to shunt your friend's solar blast away was devastating. I-I do not believe I can stand as of yet."

"Relax King. What you did was very impressive."
'Why would Sol fire something that powerful down this tunnel? Was he trying to kill everyone here? Including

me? But that's impossible. Why would he do that?'
Silver thought to herself.

"My liege," a guardsman appeared before them both, fear etched upon his face, "There is something coming down the tunnel, something big."

"Prepare weapons, we have invaders incoming."

Silver grabbed his arm, "The same way you and your men were only a few short hours ago?"

He yanked his arm free of her grasp, "This is different."

"How so? How is this different Gravity King? You attacked the surface world, instead of investigating to see what really went on up above. You leaped right in looking for war."

"Bah, you are a foolish girl who knows nothing of men's battles."

She stepped back, her eyes wide in disbelief, "Are you serious? What do you think this is, nineteen fifty-five? Where do you get off talking to me like that, you pompous ass?"

Gravity King raised his hand up as if to back hand Silver, "You dare to speak to me thusly? I am a King. No woman will ever talk to me like that and not suffer for it."

"You're really pushing your luck, Grape Ape." A voice behind them announced, startling them both.

Captain Power stood there arms folded across his broad chest. Behind him and floating in the air were both Solaron and Dragonfly.

"C'mon Silver it's time to go." Dragonfly announced.

"For once I agree with you Dragonfly." Silver looked at Gravity King disgustedly and began to walk toward her teammates.

Gravity King grabbed her arm roughly, yanking her off her feet, "You go nowhere, woman. You will be my wife."

"That's all I had to hear." Dragonfly rocketed through the air, both fists forward, and slammed into Gravity King, smashing him across the ground.

Immediately the underground troops of Epherezus opened fire with their energy beam weapons at Captain Power and Solaron. Both men charged through the barrage. The beams bouncing off of Captain Powers incredibly dense skin and were being deflected off of Solaron by his ever present energy field.

Then the driller dropped through the hole, immediately disgorging Creature, Starbolt and Stryker.

"Sil-ver!" Creature roared. He began running toward her and then after two quick steps jumped into the air. Instantly the great leathern wings grew from his back and he flew through the air toward Gravity King.

Across the street Dragonfly was now being crushed to the ground by Gravity Kings power, "You foolish boy. How quickly the fortunes of battle turn, eh whelp? I will grind your bones to powder, crushed by your own mass."

Dragonfly grit his teeth in pain, but then Creature soared down from above and slashed across the villains unprotected back with his powerful claws.

"Unnghh!" Gravity King howled in agony.

"You...will...pay...for...taking...my sister."

"The beast talks, impressive." Gravity King winced, but waved his hand, and instantly Creature was pinned to the ceiling so far above.

"Gangway, you loser!" Stryker rocketed toward their foe, but instead of hitting him he slammed into a gravimetric field that shunted him off to one side of Gravity King where he careened out of control, and into the heart of the city.

"Hahaha, you are all pathetic. I defeated three of your number in nearly as few seconds. Come the rest of you, come. Your defeat awaits."

"Defeat this!" Cap roared. In a flash he lifted his arms and unleashed his force blasts, while opposite him Solaron fired his high density beams. Gravity King was pinioned between the two, only his powerful gravimetric shields protecting him from being disintegrated by the two powerful forces. The sheer noise and volume of the attack was deafening.

All about the combatants the guardsmen of Epherezus were firing energy rifles at the Hyperforce members.

"All right you bums, let's take these jerks to school!" Butcher yelled, as he led his forces from the drilling machine.

Quickly he and his men engaged the enemy. Now bullets were mixed with ray beams as the area they were fighting in became a true war zone.

"Get down behind the earth digger." Butcher yelled at his men, "Use it for cover."

Gravity King stood pinned between Cap and Sol who continued to hammer at him.

"Give up Gravity King, you've lost this round. Time for you to call it a day and surrender." Solaron ordered.

"No, you surface men have no right to be here, nor do you have a right to give me orders. It is *you* who will bow to *me*!"

Pillars of stone erupted beneath both Solaron and Captain Power, driving them skyward toward the stone ceiling, and into it at terrible speed.

"No!" Silver Shadow shouted. She spun back toward Gravity King, hatred etched on her beautiful features.

"Explosive blast!" was shouted from above her, her eyes raised as Starbolt threw explosive energy at Gravity King, sending him tumbling threw the air.

"Anti-Grav ray, Vertigo effect, acceleration beam." He rapid fired. Gravity King streaked upward and away spinning out of control and immediately sick to his stomach.

"Say good night Gracie." Captain Power barked, as he flew down and punched Gravity King across his unprotected jaw, finally knocking him out.

Cap grabbed his limp body by the back of his suit and flew him to the ground, dumping him at Silver's feet. Solaron and Creature landed beside him, and Starbolt landed next to Silver Shadow.

"Are you all right?" Solaron asked her.

Silver Shadow nodded slowly. Her eyes wandered to the man at her feet.

Solaron looked about and shouted, "All of you stand down, and do it now. This battle is over."

The combatants hesitated, but then Butcher added, "You all heard Solaron. Lower your weapons. There's no more need to fight. This battle is over and done with."

173

Butcher met Sol's gaze, and both men nodded silently to one another.

"Now what?" Starbolt asked.

"Now we take Silver and get out of here." Cap replied.

"Wait, you just wanna leave after all of this?" Butcher asked.

"What else are we going to do, Commander? We have no jurisdiction here. This is as much a foreign land as anything on the surface."

Butcher tugged at his chin a moment then replied, "Yeah but he did attack us first."

"Only after that device of Professor Corbo's went awry." Solaron countered.

Butcher hesitated a moment more then slowly nodded his agreement. "You're right Sol. But what do we do now? Do we just ignore the fact that this guy and his people are living a few hundred miles beneath the surface of Cleveland? How do we justify that? Hell, how do I justify that to the government?"

"What about doing a diplomacy thing?" Dragonfly asked.

"I get yer meaning kid, but I don't know if it's gonna work in this case. I'm willin' ta try, though."

"N-no!" A just awakening Gravity King stammered, "There will be no diplomacy, no peace. You have killed hundreds, no thousands of my people in your attack. That will not go unpunished."

"Thousands of our people perished in the disaster up above. It was not an act of war; it was a mistake, an experiment that got out of control. No one was targeting your subterranean nation."

174

"What of your terrible solar energy attack that I barely contained and blocked? Surely you meant to finish off the job you began."

"What are you talking about?" Solaron asked.

"Do not feign innocence with me, surface man. Your energy attack would have claimed still more lives had I not blocked it."

"Sol," Silver began, "there was a huge blast of your power down here, down the tunnel shaft that he had to block by drilling another tunnel going back upward. Then he used his gravity powers to force your energy up the second tunnel."

"Silver, that blast was in response to a battalion of un-living, animated stone ape men he sent to kill us. I obliterated them and cleared the tunnel of them completely. But he sent them after us. He was still trying to kill us. I assume he had some sort of monitoring system set up in the tunnel, either high tech or a part of his natural power with the earths' gravimetric fields. Either way, once again, Gravity King initiated the attack, and then tried to twist the truth of it to serve his own ends."

She spun on him now, "You lied to me again and again. Did you really think I'd turn on my teammates and friends? Especially for some nut who thinks he's going to charm his way to me? Here's a newsflash, 'King'; that's not going to happen, ever."

By now Stryker had wandered up to the rest of the team, looking dazed and battered.

"Are you okay?" Dragonfly asked.

"I been better mate." Stryker replied hesitantly. He rubbed his head and winced.

175

"Everyone get aboard the driller. Let's close this hole up behind us and make sure Gravity King and his people never return to the surface by this tunnel again." Cap said.

Solaron nodded, "Good Idea, Captain. It's time to go."

"You heard the man, get aboard the earth driller." Butcher ordered his men.

Solaron turned toward Gravity King, "You, never return to the surface again. Not unless you've learned a little bit about humility and diplomacy, because next time we won't be holding back."

Creature was next to his sister, and sneered menacingly at Gravity King as he helped her past him.

Beneath Gravity Kings mask emotions played about his hidden face. But in a half seconds time anger won out.

"No! She will not leave!" He shot gravity beams out of both hands seeking to trap everyone and pin them to the ground, but Silver Shadow spun in mid-air, anger written all over her face as she unleashed a blistering stun bolt from her powerful mind. Gravity King dropped to the ground like a stone, unconscious and unmoving.

She looked at him piteously, "Let's get out of here." she said.

Everyone climbed aboard the earth driller except Captain Power, Solaron and Starbolt.

Sol ordered, "Butcher, get this thing moving. We're collapsing this tunnel and I'm going to fuse it shut behind us."

"What about the second one he created to shunt your blast off?" Silver asked.

"I'll close it from the surface if need be, but I doubt it went all the way through. I have a feeling it fell far short, especially after that blast had gone so far already."

Butcher closed the hatch while Dragonfly, Creature, Silver and Stryker settled into seats aboard the vehicle.

"We're movin'." Butcher announced.

The machine powered up and began to climb back up the hole it had come down. Behind it the three Hyperforce members waited for it to climb a bit up the tunnel and then they began to tear it down behind them. Cap literally tearing the walls down and Sol fusing them solid. Starbolt was flying lookout in case there were any surprises awaiting them all.

After a hundred miles of blocking the tunnel they began to fly behind the drilling machine, and slowly started to compare notes.

"Well that was interesting." Cap began.

"Not how I'd put it, but I see your point." Sol replied.

"What about you Starbolt? Any thoughts on this disaster?" Cap asked.

"It *was* a disaster. Many people were killed by that scientist's device, even though he was trying to create something that would have been of great use."

"Yes, he devastated a great part of Cleveland. It seems that we were lucky the loss of life was not greater than it was." Sol answered.

"Any way you slice it, this was no victory." Cap stated flatly.

Solaron shook his head, "No, it wasn't. This was a mess, and now we have to watch out for reprisals from a new foe set beneath the surface of the planet."

"I considered trying to speak to Gravity King, monarch to monarch. But he was so…angry. So mad. I do not believe it would have done any good at all."

Sol nodded, "I agree Starbolt. The worst part about all of this is that I can almost see his point. People died, on both sides. His people were as innocent as ours were. He was only looking to protect his subjects. It was the way he went about it that became the problem."

"What do you think that was all about with Silver?" Cap asked, "He wanted to make her his wife or something?"

Sol shrugged, "That's what it sounded like. She'll have to fill us in later."

Cap grimaced before adding, "Agreed. For now let's help with the rescue efforts in any way we can and then head home. I'm going to need a bath and a few days' worth of sleep when all of this is over."

"I think that goes for all of us Cap." Solaron agreed. After a moment he continued, "What do you think of our newest recruit now? Are you cutting him any slack after this? He did get as bloody as the rest of us."

Cap shrugged non-committedly, "He had no choice, especially if he's playing a role."

"You really don't trust him, do you?"

"Let me put it this way, his performance today went a long way in changing all of that, but I'm still going to keep an eye on him."

"Fair enough. I know in the short time we've worked together that I've come to trust your judgment."

"Thanks. Let's get out of here. There's got to be a lot of people who are still in need top side."

"Agreed."

Hyperforce

The three heroes sped away flying out of sight of the earth drilling machine with their companions aboard and back to the surface.

Ralph L. Angelo Jr.

Chapter 8

Roar of Thunder...

Deep space, a hundred thousand light years from Earth.

The battered starship of General Zaring held its position and awaited...something.

"Tactical, is there any sign of our...guest?" General Zaring asked.

The tactical officer continued to stare at his display panels, "No General Zaring, there is not."

Zaring walked silently around the bridge of his starship, his hands clasped behind his back, holding a heavy black and purple cape in place.

Minutes passed and then his tactical officer cried out, "General, we have incoming."

"On screen now." Zaring replied testily.

Instantly the image on the viewer at the front of the bridge shimmered and changed. A solitary figure streaked toward Zaring's ship.

"Battle stations." barked the second in command.

"No, belay that. He is here at my request." Zaring ordered.

Heads swiveled about the bridge at that revelation. Station officers looked to one another, but did so in silence.

The only man who questioned Zaring's announcement was his second in command a man named Noc-Turn. Himself a big man with thick black hair and a tightly woven beard, "General, you called this being? The danger he represents…"

Zaring waved him off nonchalantly, "The danger is nothing compared to the benefits he can bring."

The figure flying through space stopped directly before the starship. It was a bizarre looking creature. A man to be sure, but different. His skin was white as the driven snow. His eyes, nose and mouth were all slits. His body was either blue and red or it wore a garment of some type that ended at its ankles, but it was impossible to tell.

"Look at its chest." the communications officer muttered.

"I see it." replied the weapons officer, "A black swirling void that continually changes shape. The black nebula. So the rumors are true."

"The rumors are not your concern Ton-Mar, only your highest efficiency at your position. Is that clear?"

Ton-Mar nodded, "Yes General Zaring."

"Sir," the communications officer interrupted, "It's-he's hailing us."

"Yes," Zaring smiled, "Of course he is. It is only simple radio frequencies after all. Put him through." He waved his hand toward the monitor.

"Why have you called me here?" an eerie voice reverberated through the ship.

"We have discovered a danger on a backwater world, one that will prove disastrous for the entire galaxy. We have failed to contain it, as my damaged ship will attest to."

The being floating there stared at the ship, its eyes flashed as beams shot out of them and played across the hull of the ship.

"Do nothing." Zaring hissed, "He is ascertaining our damage. Let him."

"Where is this world?" the hollow voice asked.

"The denizens of that system call it 'Sol'. They reside on the third world from its star."

"What is the danger called?" the strange being asked.

"It is called 'Hyperforce'. They are under the command of a youth who calls himself 'Starbolt'. He is evil personified, and must be stopped. If not, then soon his thugs will subjugate every world in their path. They are unstoppable. Only you have a sliver of a chance against their evil and foul power. I beseech you, go to that strange third world from its star, the world called Earth and stop this evil plan before its comes to fruition. Stop them Nebula-Man, You're our only hope."

***

Om Earth, at the Solar Energy observatory in northern New Jersey.

Captain Power, Solaron, Starbolt, Creature, Stryker and Silver Shadow disembarked from the just landed Stargrazer.

"I still can't get used to what we're seeing in what's left of Cleveland." Cap said.

"I know," Solaron agreed, "It's horrible. So much death and destruction. So many displaced people. It's a sin."

Silver Shadow shook her head sadly, "It's terrible. I'll never get used to that. It's two weeks since Dr. Corbo's device exploded and we're still finding horrible reminders of it every day, though at least I think we have the last bodies out of there as of today."

Solaron sighed and replied, "I spoke to Commander Butcher earlier. He thinks we've done enough and deserve a rest. I'm agreeing with him. FEMA is in there and taking the brunt of the work cleaning up now. They'll contact us if there's something else they find they need help moving."

"Or if Gravity King returns." Silver added.

"If he does we'll be back there in a heartbeat." Cap commented.

"What's going on?" a new voice called from the entrance to the hanger beneath the observatory.

Everyone turned and smiled as Dragonfly flew in and landed.

"Hey D-fly." Silver greeted him with a smile.

"Dragon…fly." Creature nodded.

"Hey guys, how'd it go today?"

"Better Dragonfly, better." Solaron admitted.

"Aye mate how are ya?" Stryker inquired jovially.

"Good man, doing good." Dragonfly replied with a smile.

Stryker slapped the smaller man on the back and grinned.

"One good thing we have to be thankful for is lack of a new crisis. That's helping us with our efforts to aid that city." Starbolt offered.

They all began to enter the facility when Mar-Cus met them at the door, "My prince, my friends, it is good to see you all."

"Same here Marcus. Thanks for holding down the fort."

"It is the least I can do, Solaron for your allowing young Prince Bol-Ton and I to stay here."

Sol shrugged, "Don't mention it Marcus you're an integral part of this team. Without you keeping us abreast of situations in the field things would be a lot worse."

Solaron turned toward his young nephew, "How was school today Dragonfly?"

"It was cool, Sol. I have to be honest though, I was more concerned with you guys being out there without me"

"Don't be. You have to go to school. We should be able to handle anything we'll come up against and if we can't well, you can always come and save our hides."

"Don't worry, I will." Dragonfly grinned.

"What do we do now?" Silver Shadow asked.

"I don't know about you Silver, but I'm going to go home, kick back, and relax." Captain Power replied, "Even these super strong muscles get tired after a few weeks of acting like a human bulldozer." Captain Power flexed his bicep and grinned.

"Can't say that I blame ya mate. A rest sounds bloody good to me too."

Cap nodded toward Stryker, "Yes it does, 'mate'. I think we all need a rest after this madness."

"Cleveland got lucky if you consider what happened there; relatively few casualties but a lot of scrapes and bruises, along with more than a few broken bones, but very few life threatening injuries. I'd say we got as lucky as anyone could get in a situation like that." Solaron concluded.

Everyone nodded solemnly in agreement.

Cap began to walk toward the hangar bay door, "I'm off heroes. I'll check in tomorrow. If you have anything to update me with call me. Otherwise I'll talk to you then."

"Good bye Cap." Sol waved.

Cap took to the air inside the hanger, energy blasting out of his legs bearing him aloft. He turned, waved to everyone and shot out of the hanger as if from a cannon.

" 'Ey Silver, fancy getting a drink with yer very own Aussie superhero?"

"Not tonight Stryker. I need some sleep, but I'll take a rain check."

"Sounds good luv, next time it is then." he added a nod and a wink to punctuate his words.

Stryker turned to Dragonfly while everyone else walked into the building and offices proper, "What about you mate? Fancy downing a pint or two?"

"A pint or two? I'm sixteen years old, man. Hahaha, I don't think my parents or uncle would like that too much."

Stryker leaned close to Dragonfly and whispered conspirationally, "Do ya always do what they'd like? It ain't nothin' ta be afraid of, Dragon. We're the toast o' the town we can walk inta any pub an' be treated like the flippin' king o' England. C'mon kid, it'll be fun."

Dragonfly shook his head hesitantly, "Ah, I don't know Stryker."

"Mate! It'll be fun. Seriously, yer a flippin' Superhero. When was the last time you had fun just bein' yerself an' enjoyin' yer powers?"

"N-never. Solaron tells me these powers are a gift and shouldn't be about having fun."

"An' is the big golden geek always right?"

"Well, most of the time yeah, he is."

"Okay mate, but when does he ever have fun, ya know, F-U-N fun?"

"Never, but c'mon Stryker I'm sixteen years old. I've never been in a bar before. I don't think I should be."

"Kid you've saved the bloomin' world how many times already? Kick back, relax an' have a few laughs."

Dragonfly hesitated for a moment and then finally said, "Okay Stryker why not? What could happen?"

"Right-o mate. Let's be off then." The big Australian grinned and flew out of the hanger. Dragonfly hesitated a few seconds more, looked hesitantly toward where Solaron and the others had walked into the complex, then turned and flew into the sky after Stryker and joined him.

***

Sometime later…

Solaron, now wearing his white lab coat and regular clothes looked around, then asked "Where's Dragonfly?"

Silver looked up from reading her tablet, scrunched her face up as if in thought and replied, "The last time I saw him he was talking to Stryker, but that was a while ago already."

187

"How long is a while? And what were they talking about?" Sol asked.

"At least an hour, maybe two. I don't know what Stryker was talking about with him, but he asked me if I wanted to go to a bar and have a few drinks."

"You're here and Randy isn't. That can only mean he took my sixteen year old nephew out to carouse around Manhattan. What was he thinking?"

"Who Randy or Stryker?"

"Stryker, Silver. Randy's a kid."

A new voice intruded, "He's also one of the most powerful people on the planet, Sol."

Ronald Anderson and Silver Shadow turned toward the sound of that voice and watched as Captain Power entered the room.

"You're right Cap, he is. So he should know better."

"Did you know better at sixteen? Or did you only think you did?"

"What are you doing Cap? You're taking Randy's side?"

"In a way I am. Stryker's the one you should be mad at, not the kid who can throw trucks around."

Sol fumed a moment then agreed, "You're right. Sometimes I give that sixteen year old kid too much credit and treat him like an adult. I have to remind myself he's five years away from that yet."

Ronald Anderson turned around and exited the room they were in. Captain Power was right behind him.

"Where are you going?" Cap asked.

"To find my nephew. I can use his suits transponder to locate him."

"So you lojacked the kid?"

"You knew that. Every suit that sits in a transporter tube has that tag on it."

Cap nodded, "You're right I did. I still have mixed feelings about it, but I also see where it's a necessity in this line of work."

"Yes, it is."

"So what do you want to do? Go charging in there and embarrass the kid, wherever he is?"

Solaron sighed, "There's no easy way about this is there?"

"Seriously Ron, no there isn't. We might be better off just keeping an eye on him and if he gets stupid drunk we go and pick him up, then kick Stryker's ass as an afterthought."

Ronald Anderson chuckled, "That's the first time you called me by my real name. It's funny hearing it from you."

"Well, it is your name isn't it? And you're not in costume, so..."

Sol held his hands up in a sign of surrender, "I gotcha, I gotcha."

Mar-Cus's voice intruded upon the two men from Captain Powers communicator built into his collar, "Captain are you near a monitor?"

"I am Marcus, what's up?"

"Turn the monitor to channel twelve. There is something there you will want to see."

Solaron did so as Mar-Cus was speaking.

"What the hell?" Cap whispered in wide eyed disbelief.

"He looks...like you?" Sol asked.

On the monitor was a man fighting the police. He wore a costume similar to Cap's except it was a grey in color with a black lightning bolt on the chest. He was taller than Cap was but slightly leaner looking. His long brown hair fell like Cap's did and he wore a grey cape with no markings on it. His face was similar to Caps but he was no twin. His countenance was twisted in horrific rage. He looked on angrily and shouted at the police battling him. Bullets bounced off his chest while he laughed. Then he picked up a garbage truck and hurled it at the police who quickly scattered to safety.

"I've got to get over there, those men need my help." Cap ran from the room, this time Solaron was behind him, "Wait I'll go with you."

"No Sol, You stay here in case Randy and Stryker get into trouble."

Solaron paused, "Do you want to take Silver, Starbolt and Creature with you?"

"No, let them rest. We've all been through enough for the past two weeks. I can handle some doppelganger."

"We'll be monitoring you. If things go bad we'll be right there."

"Relax mother hen, I'll be fine."

Captain Power rocketed away and streaked toward midtown Manhattan.

'I don't know who this guy is, but his costume and look are too much like mine to be coincidence. He may have some answers about the golden lightning bolt that hit me and made me Captain Power.'

Cap flew toward Manhattan from the west, and immediately saw smoke rising from Midtown.

Hyperforce

'I guess I won't need a road map or a GPS to find this guy.'

Cap dove down toward the street, and watched on his approach as the mystery man in question threw a car at a group of riot gear wearing cops. Quickly he accelerated in and caught the car, setting it down gently.

"That's enough mister. Who are you and what are you doing here?"

"Well if it ain't Captain Power. Whoop de frickin' do." the stranger countered.

Cap walked toward the stranger who looked surprisingly so much like him as to be unnerving.

"You didn't answer my question. Why are you here and what are you doing? What do you want?"

"I wanted to get your attention, hero. What'd you think I wanted?"

"Well you succeeded there. Who are you?"

"I wuz gonna call myself 'Cap'n Thunder' but I figured that was gonna be too much like yer name. So I chose 'Thunderfist' instead."

"Really? And that's supposed to be a step up?"

"Oh you're a real smart guy aint'cha?"

"Me? No. what I am is a man who has more questions than answers concerning how I got my powers. Now you show up with identical powers and I have to ask how much you know about how we got them."

"Yer not lookin' at the facts big blue. I got powers an' they're a lot like yours, but they ain't identical."

Thunderfist threw both hands forward and lightning leaped from his fingertips enveloping Cap painfully.

191

Howling in agony Cap fired a force blast from his right hand and knocked Thunderfist through a store front.

Panting painfully Captain Power stood to his full height, "That hurt."

With a growl Thunderfist flew out of the devastated store and rocketed straight toward Cap.

"It's not going to be that easy!" Cap shouted, throwing a devastating right cross, that shot Thunderfist straight up into the sky.

Cap flew after him, streaking skyward.

Above, Thunderfist turned in midair and flew directly down at Captain Power, fists first.

The villain roared, "I'll pound you into dust!"

The two men collided explosively in the sky above New York. Their impact sounded like an explosion.

"What was that?" people down below in the teeming streets asked repeatedly.

Heads turned toward the dark sky and a fear began to grow amongst the people below.

"I-it's like two gods fighting up there." one stunned New Yorker said to another.

"Yeah maybe, but I ain't thinkin' either one gives a damn if they kill us all."

"M-maybe you're right."

The two men looked at one another and ran in opposite directions. The packed New York streets cleared out quickly with people running in packs away from the two battling titans.

"What do you know about how we got our powers?" Cap shouted, emphasizing his question with a left cross.

"Idiot! I ain't tellin' you nothin'!" Thunderfist kicked Cap in midair, catching him in the stomach. Cap doubled over from the impact. Thunderfist grabbed Cap's head and smashed it against his knee. He shoved Cap away from himself and shot lightning bolts from his hands at him.

Cap tumbled through the sky like a rock to careen into an outdoor car lot, smashing a dozen cars to scrap.

"Oh my God!" a car lot attendant ran from the lot.

First one then another and another car exploded from Captain Power's impact with them. Flames jumped thirty feet into the air and a wave of heat rolled over everything nearby.

Thunderfist landed smiling. "I thought you were gonna be tougher than that, big guy. You were a little wimpy."

Before Thunderfist' surprised eyes the flames began to die out quickly and the mass of wrecked vehicles disappeared.

A man stood up, silhouetted by the raging flames all about him.

"Did you really think it was going to be that easy, Thunderfist?"

Cap streaked from out of the flames like the fiery phoenix of legend and struck Thunderfist with incredible force!

Buildings shook for blocks around from their impact.

"What the hell?" Thunderfist began, "I was sure you were down for the count. Did you get stronger or somethin'?"

"Yes, or something." Cap replied. They rained punches down on one another now, one after another.

193

High impact blows that shook the ground like earthquakes and sounded like thunder. The ground gave way beneath their feet and both men disappeared into the subway tunnels below.

"Why don't you die?" Thunderfist shouted.

"Yeah, I'm just going to lie down and do that for you, to make you happy." Cap connected with a punch thrown from his hip that shot Thunderfist back through the subway tunnel. Cap flew after him immediately, tackling him and pinning him to the ground.

"Tell me what you know about our powers!" Cap roared. He continued to bludgeon Thunderfist now with fists fueled by a long guarded rage.

A train whistle suddenly sounded in front of them. Cap looked up at the train's oncoming light and without hesitation Thunderfist kicked him off.

"Ha! Chump! Din'cha yer momma ever tell ya not ta take yer eyes offa the prize?"

Thunderfist rocketed off down the tunnels.

"Ohhh." Cap stood and rubbed his head, "Oh no, the train!" Cap leaped into the air, and flew off after Thunderfist narrowly avoiding getting run over by the speeding subway train.

Cap streaked through the subway tunnel after his mysterious double. Past a station and a landing where people stood in awe as he flew by.

'I see him up ahead, I've almost got him.'

As if sensing Caps thoughts, Thunderfist changed his trajectory and punched a hole back to the surface. Cap emerged from the newly made hole a heartbeat later, and flew right into a double fisted punch.

"Arrggh!" he shouted in more surprise than pain. He arced away over the city haphazardly to land in the river with a powerful splash.

Instantly Thunderfist was overhead and diving toward the water.

Cap exploded from the river, flying straight into his enemy, smashing him from the sky with a powerful right, and down on to the deck of the decommissioned Intrepid air craft carrier, which was now an air and space museum.

Cap landed near Thunderfist and immediately shouted "Are you insane? Stop this madness, we're tearing the city apart."

"D'ya think I care?" Lightning exploded from Thunderfist's fingertips, but this time Cap matched them with his powerful force blasts. Incredible energies played about between the two men on the deck of the ship, lighting up the night time air between them like a small sun.

"You can't win this Thunderfist. I don't know what you want but enough's enough."

"I don't want nothin' but to let you know that I'm out here an' I'm better'n you. You gettin' tired again Cappy? Ya notice I never do? I know you gotta absorb stuff ta keep yer strength up. Me? That's a handicap I ain't got ta worry about. I stay strong an' powerful. I'm your better."

"No, you've just got a bigger mouth."

Changing tactics Captain Power flew into Thunderfist again, below his foes blast of lightning.

Grabbing Thunderfist by the cape, Cap flew upward and then heaved his enemy to the ground from a

195

thousand feet up. The impact shattered windows for two blocks in every direction.

***

"What the heck was that?" Dragonfly asked. He slurred his words slightly. Stryker stood next to him in a private box within a club with pounding music and lights.

"I don't know kid, but I bet it wasn't anything good. It felt like a bloomin' earthquake."

"Mah uncle says we can't get earthquakes here. Somethin' about the city bein' built on bedrock or somethin'?" Dragonfly continued.

"All right my friend let's get outta here an' go see what that trouble is."

"O-kay." Dragonfly replied with a grin.

"How many didja drink tonight boy?"

"Only a few, I think six maybe?" Dragonfly answered with a drunken grin.

"Ohhh boy, yer uncles gonna have me head I think."

The two men exited the loud night club, leaving the thumping beat behind. The cool night air washed over them and was like a slap in the face of Dragonfly.

"Whoa…" he stumbled slightly.

"You okay kid? Yer not gonna lose yer lunch on me now are ya?"

"N-no Stryker, I-I'm-blorch!" Stryker looked away grinning. Dragonfly heaved his guts out all over the sidewalk in front of the nightclub, stumbling badly as he did.

"Ohhh yeah yer uncle's definitely gonna have me head." Stryker grinned. He grasped Dragonfly by the back of his costume, "C'mon kid, I'll fly."

Stryker rocketed away over the city, dragging the sick to his stomach Dragonfly with him.

"Snap out o' it kid. Yer uncle will kill us both if you show up lookin' like this. Besides, he ain't exactly the most fun individual on his best o' days."

"Uncle Ron's okay." Dragonfly slurred. "He jus worries 'bout me."

"I got it kid I got it. He's an ace all right, he just always seems ta be holdin' ya back is all. Just don't tell him I told ya so." Stryker grinned slyly.

"I-I won't Stryker, you an' me, we're buds."

"That we are kid. Look below."

Dragonfly fought another wave of nausea as he shook his head. "Wh-what is that? Two Captain Powers? Am I just seein' double?"

Under his mask Stryker furrowed his own brow, "That's what it appears ta be kid. You try an' sit this one out hotshot I don't wanna see ya gettin' hurt."

He landed on a nearby rooftop overlooking the battle and released Dragonfly, letting him slump against a chimney.

Stryker stared for a split second then turned toward Dragonfly, "Cap's takin' a lot o' hits from that guy and he might be in trouble."

Stryker disappeared, hyper accelerating away and directly at Thunderfist in less than an eye blink.

He slammed into Thunderfist with an earthshaking fury that sent both men careening across the debris strewn ground.

197

"Who the hell're you?" Thunderfist roared.

Stryker unleashed a left cross to Thunderfist's jaw, "Name's Stryker, mate. I'm a friend o' the big guy over there." Stryker punctuated his words with a right-left combination to the face.

Thunderfist back fisted Stryker away, sending him careening like a rag doll into a demolished and dilapidated store, that immediately collapsed upon him.

"Are you kiddin' me Crocodile Dundee? You might be stronger than most, but you ain't in *my* league."

"No," an angry voice growled behind Thunderfist. The villain's eyes widened as he turned in surprise. Behind him was Captain Power, his hands glowing with energy. Behind Captain Power was what was left of a cement mixer. A minute ago it had been whole. "but I am, and then some." Cap finished.

Captain Power ran toward the grey suited Thunderfist, and sent his right fist exploding into his evil double's jaw before Thunderfist could even move.

The force of the blow was incredible! It cracked the ground beneath their feet and threw Thunderfist a block.

Before he could really get to his feet Captain Power was back on him, streaking through the air and tackling his enemy.

"Tell me what you know!" Cap roared. "With his left hand he heaved Thunderfist skyward akin to a meteor in reverse, then he rocketed after him.

On the rooftop, Dragonfly watched in disbelief as Cap disappeared into the clouds after his grey costumed foe.

"Wow. All this damage. Yet this is nothing compared to Cleveland." Dragonfly stood, his stomach ached and his head hurt, but he felt better than he had fifteen minutes earlier.

He ran three steps and flew into the air, then down to where Stryker had disappeared into the rubble.

Dragonfly landed shakily, but forced his way toward the rubble he knew Stryker lie under.

'I can't use my Dragonblasts cause I might disintegrate Stryker.'

He began to heave the rubble away, digging through it like a human sized bulldozer. His hands ripped thousand pound chunks of rubble apart and heaved them like Styrofoam. He dug like a man possessed until he saw a black and yellow gloved hand sticking out from beneath the rubble. It was not moving.

"No!" he shouted, digging with renewed vigor. An instant later he pulled Stryker's unmoving form from the debris. "Stryker! Don't be dead, please don't be dead, man."

"I ain't." Stryker groaned, "But I almost wish I was."

Stryker stumbled to his feet and rubbed the back of his neck.

"You okay?" Dragonfly asked.

"Yeah kid, I just need a minute. Where's the big guy?"

Dragonfly pointed upward with his thumb.

"Okay, are you straightened out enough to fly?"

"Yeah, yeah I am Stryker."

"All right then mate; let's go find the two bruisers."

Stryker disappeared in a black and yellow streak.

"Wow, he's really fast. I think he's the fastest one of us all." Dragonfly commented in awe.

Dragonfly ignited his boot rockets and raced after Stryker into the sky.

'My stomach is still a mess and my head is throbbing. But at least I can fly straight now. I think my super metabolism must be burning off the alcohol. But I guess this is the hangover I'm left with. This ain't any fun.'

Dragonfly had his arms straight ahead of him; his red underarm wings glistened in the sunlight as he pierced the clouds.

Pausing above the cloud cover Dragonfly activated his spectroscopic vision.

'Where are they?'

He scanned the sky for miles in each direction, then his vision picked up three heat signatures miles off.

"There!"

His boot rockets flared and Dragonfly soared toward the battle.

Captain Power had Thunderfist by the throat with his right hand and unloaded his left again and again into his enemy's face.

"Get away from me!" Thunderfist shouted, unleashing a blast of his lightning.

Cap flew backward, but stopped and righted himself.

"How'd we get our powers? Who gave them to us? Tell me what you know."

"I don't know anything and if I did I wouldn't tell you anyway, you crazy bastard!"

He released another blast of lightning enveloping the raging Captain Power. But he himself was then hit by beams of explosive force. Stryker floated behind Thunderfist and fired his explosive energy blasts.

200

Thunderfist flew off to one side, putting his arm up to ward off the explosive blasts.

"You got some cojones Dundee, I'll give you that, but like I said, you ain't in my league."

Thunderfist fired his lightning blasts at Stryker, but then a red and blue blur was between the two, blocking the blasts on his underarm wings, using them like shields.

"Heads up dirtbag." Dragonfly shouted.

He arced through the sky until he was above Thunderfist, and then he fired his Dragonblasts. The big villain screamed in agony.

"End of the line grey and black." Captain Power roared. He slammed into Thunderfist at waist height, tackling him while he was stunned. Cap grabbed Thunderfist by the collar with his left hand and drew back his right. Then with a growl of rage he put all his strength into a punch to his foes jaw that shot the big man away from him as if out of the barrel of a cannon.

The sound was akin to an explosion in the upper atmosphere. Thunderfist shot down toward the Earth miles below at astonishing speed.

"Are you two okay?" Cap asked Dragonfly and Stryker.

"Been better mate that's fer dang certain."

Dragonfly nodded, "I'm fine. Let's get after him."

Cap returned the nod and dove beneath the cloud cover, followed by his teammates.

But...

"He's gone!" Dragonfly exclaimed, "I'm scanning everything with my spectroscopic vision and I can't find

a trace of him. He must have sped off after you knocked
him flying."

Cap looked around stoically in every direction, but
found nothing below the wispy cloud cover.

"He got away." Cap said aloud.

"Let's head back to the observatory. I think I've had
enough excitement for one afternoon."

Cap nodded, "All right Dragonfly, let's go." He stole
a glance at Stryker who was floating there grinning like
an idiot. Then the three men sped off.

***

"What were you thinking? Both of you?" Solaron
bellowed at Dragonfly and Stryker.

"Haven't I preached to you enough about acting like
an adult? You're strong enough to lift a fifteen ton truck.
Don't you realize the damage you could do? My God
Randy, you could tear a man apart if you lost control.
Drinking? How am I supposed to explain this to your
parents? And you Stryker, what was going on in your
head? Was anything going on in there? You take a
sixteen year old out binge drinking? Do you know what
the term 'responsible adult' even means?"

"Yer getting' all worked up over nothin' mate; in Oz
we're drinkin' in the outback a year or two younger than
he is."

"But you're not in Oz anymore, Stryker. Here we're
a little more staid than you are back home. You can't
take a kid out and get him drunk. Especially a kid who
can bench press cement trucks. What if he had hurt or
killed someone?"

"Stop it!" Dragonfly shouted, "What's wrong with you? We were out having a little fun; blowing off a little steam. You're always trying to hold me back, you never let me laugh and just act like a kid."

Stryker looked away and grinned for an instant, then looked on stoically.

"A kid doesn't go out drinking until he can't stand on his own two feet. A kid doesn't go out drinking at all, especially not a responsible one."

"C'mon Uncle Ron, I see all those movies where kids are having fun at drinking parties and sneaking into bars getting wasted."

"Those are movies, Randy. They never show the downside, the kids so sick from alcohol poisoning they end up in the hospital for days. Some die there. Do they show that in the movies? Do they show the kids who drive off drunk and kill someone and themselves on the way home? Or the ones who just get caught and arrested? Do your party movies show any of that?" Solaron walked around his nephew in a circle, his anger spilling out all about him in his wake, as an almost palpable thing.

Behind him and leaning against a counter Captain Power stood with his arms crossed. Dragonfly stood in the center of the room with his head downcast. Stryker next to him, his own face grim.

"Stryker, I understand this is normal where you come from. I get that. But it's not normal here. You have to wake up and realize you're not in the outback anymore or wherever it is you come from. We do things differently here."

"Noted mate, I'm sorry, I apologize."

Solaron nodded and turned toward Dragonfly, "What am I going to do with you? Do I ground you? Do I take your battle suit away from you? All that would do is leave you without flight, some offensive weapons and your wing shields. You'd still be able to throw trucks."

"I-I'm sorry Uncle Ron. I really am."

"Randy I want the best for you. I want you to be the best you can be. You're my sisters' son. I'm only fourteen years older than you. You don't realize that now, but that's nothing. It's the blink of an eye. Wake up son. You have to be smarter than this. You have to do better."

"I-I will Uncle Ron, I promise."

"Go on, get out of here. Call your mother and tell her you're staying here tonight, that we were working late on an experiment and that I'll drop you off in the morning. I can't have you going home smelling like throw up and liquor. Go take a shower, then clean your costume up."

Dragonfly silently left the control center.

Solaron turned toward Stryker once again, "You have to think more as well. You're powerful and good in a fight. You're a good addition to the team. But you can't screw up like this again, got it?"

"I got it Solaron. Thanks. I appreciate the second chance mate."

Solaron waved him off. Stryker left the control room, leaving Cap and Sol alone.

"You've got nothing to say?"

Cap shrugged, "What do you expect me to say? You were right on every count."

"I think you were too, about Stryker."

"Yeah, I get that. The other side of the coin is that he could just not understand how we do things here, like he said."

"Do you believe that?"

Cap shrugged, "Maybe, maybe not. Right now he's an asset that bears watching until he's no longer an asset. He *is* good in a fight. He helped me out against this Thunderfist lunatic."

"Do you think it was just to serve his purpose whatever that may be?"

"It could be. Remember 'keep your friends close and your enemies' closer.' Those are words we should be heeding where he's concerned."

"But 'Which is he?' is the question."

***

Outside the observatory, floating in the sky a mile above the building Stryker spoke into his costumes wrist, with a decidedly un-Australian accent, "Hey boss, do you hear me? I've only got a minute or two before they realize I'm gone."

A voice rumbled in reply within his form fitting masks ear pieces, "I am receiving your transmission Stryker. Does the plan proceed apace?"

"It does. The seeds of discontent have been sown. Now they've got to be nurtured." he closed the communication with a grin, and flew back toward the observatory.

Ralph L. Angelo Jr.

Chapter 9

It came from beyond the stars

At a small tavern a few miles from the Solar Observatory…

At a table in regular clothes sat Silver Shadow and Stryker. She sipped on a beer, while he guzzled one after another.

"Aren't you worried about drinking so much after what just happened with Randy last week?"

He guffawed, "Why should I be Silver? I'm a blinkin' adult an' so are you. What? Is big daddy Solaron gonna paddle us both an' ground us if we come home drunk? Believe me gorgeous, this is one Aussie who can handle his liquor." he tapped himself in the chest with his thumb for emphasis.

"It has nothing to do with Solaron. Well, not really at least. I mean don't you feel like he's been good to us? He lets us stay there, gave us rooms of our own; feeds us. Heck he even gives us some spending cash. I mean I know the guy is loaded and all, but he really goes out of his way to be good to us. Don't you think you could be a little more, I guess the word I'm looking for is considerate?"

"Considerate? I'm puttin' me life on the line every time I put the uniform on. I think we're even Steven at least. Heck, ol' glow bug may owe us the ways I'm lookin' at it, babe."

She shook her head negatively, "That's really not how I'm seeing it."

"Well then I think you should be thinking about it all a bit more carefully then. It's just a thought, luv. Somethin' ta mull over. We're all important cogs in this wheel called Hyperforce. No one is more important 'an another."

"I-I get that," Silver answered hesitantly while she swirled her beer around in her mug, "I don't know. I just feel like we're talking treason almost. I mean the guy has been nothing but great to us," she looked up, "why would I want to leave the team in the first place? I like it here. This is the first place Creature and I can be that we both feel like, well, normal people."

"Darling, no offense, I mean I love yer brother like a, well brother, but you're the normal one. Dontcha realize babe this is the first time in probably years that you've gone out on a date without havin' ta worry about him? All I'm sayin' is that it may be time ta let little Billy fly the coup an' be a man. If you an' me leave the team an' he stays you can have some freedom without worryin' about him all a the time."

Silver looked at him and her eyes seemed to smolder with anger, "You don't understand, Stryker, he's my brother. It's not a burden to me. I love taking care of him. Let's change the subject. You asked me out, and I'm sure it wasn't to tear apart our friends and talk treason."

"You are right, beautiful." Stryker stared into her eyes as he took her slim hand in his own powerful one, "I gotta say you are one gorgeous girl. I'm amazed at how flippin' pretty you are. How come you ain't a model?"

"Oh, well you know because of my brothe-" she stopped herself, "Uh just for reasons. I'm too short, didn't have the time or the heart to put into it. Plus my powers, I can always hear everyone's thoughts. It took me years to learn to turn that off." She giggled as he stroked her hand gently.

"Well it's a good thing you did, cause I'd hate for you to see what I'm thinkin' now." he grinned, looking in her eyes.

But before either of them could move both their phones received text messages. They each looked simultaneously, then looked at each other.

"Papa bear calls." Stryker said.

"Perfect timing too." Silver lamented.

Both stood quickly while Stryker dropped a twenty on the table and pointed to it so the waitress would see. She nodded at them.

"Let's go." Silver hastened him.

They went outside and opened the doors of a black Camaro convertible, with Stryker sliding behind the wheel.

"We're off m'lady."

The car started with a roar and powerfully headed off toward the observatory a few miles away.

Minutes later they entered the underground facility beneath the observatory itself, heading straight for the main meeting room.

Dragonfly, Solaron, Creature, Starbolt, Captain Power and Mar-Cus were seated at the table already. On the main monitor was a still image of space and something glowing at its center.

"I'm glad you two made it back so fast, thank you." Solaron began, "We have a situation and it may be a bad one."

"What's going on?" Silver inquired.

"Something is on its way here, and we don't know what it is." Solaron replied, "I was using the telescope tonight to take solar flare readings when I happened to turn toward the darkest part of space to recalibrate its lenses, and then I saw it."

"Saw what mate?" Stryker asked.

"This." Sol aimed the remote at the monitor and clicked. Instantly the image came to life.

"What the heck is that?" Dragonfly asked.

Mar-Cus and Prince Bol-ton exchanged nervous glances.

"I believe we know what or rather who that is." Bolton replied.

"It..is…a…who?" Creature asked in disbelief.

"It is. But in truth it could mean much more if it is who we believe it to be." Mar-Cus advised.

"Don't mince words Marcus, tell us what you know. This person is flying toward earth faster than anything on record. It is well beyond light speed. How we are even seeing it is only because of the observatory's visual computer system slowing down the feed to something our brains can comprehend."

Mar-Cus stared at the image a moment longer then added, "Solaron, perhaps you had better contact Commander Butcher as well. His ARMOR will want to know about this."

210

Solaron nodded and began stabbing buttons on a console before him. An instant later a black suited blonde haired young woman appeared on half of the monitor, moving the once again frozen image to the right hand side of it.

"Who is this? How'd you get this frequency?"

"My name is Solaron. Tell Commander Butcher I need to speak to him immediately. It's a matter of world security."

She nodded and gulped hard at his name. Ten seconds later Butchers countenance, dark sunglasses and all, filled the monitor, "I guess you're seein' this too?" he asked without any fanfare.

Solaron nodded, "We are, and our two alien visitors tell me they know what it is; except it's not a what, it's a who."

"Yeah, too small to be a ship. We kinda figured it was some kinda super-freak. No offense." Butcher quickly corrected himself.

"None taken." Sol replied.

"So what've we got?" Butcher asked while lighting a cigarette.

Mar-Cus cleared his throat and began to speak, "That is a being called 'Nebula-Man'. It is said to be astronomically powerful, and absolutely unstoppable. The creature is believed to have been a normal mortal at one time, but a trip inside the legendary 'Black Nebula' changed all of that."

Butcher shook his head on the other side of the monitor, "What does any of that even mean? What is this…thing?"

211

"Commander, it is power personified. It is said he is able to tear a star asunder. He is a law unto himself, a force of nature on a cosmic scale. When he perceives a threat to galactic peace on a scale beyond imagining he takes matters into his own hands."

"So why's he comin' here?" Butcher asked.

"I can only assume General Zaring has coaxed him into coming here to kill Prince Bol-Ton."

"What is going on over there Anderson? You've got aliens on your squad and now you've got some psycho spaceman coming down from the depths o' space after them to kill a kid or something?"

"Those 'aliens' as you put it are trusted teammates who have proven themselves over and over again these past months. They are also friends and colleagues I would vouch for in an instant, Commander."

Butcher held his hands up, "Okay, okay I get it Solaron. What do you want ARMOR to do?"

"Nothing; just stand pat, monitor the situation from wherever the heck you are. If we fail, well I don't see you or anyone else having much luck against this guy from what Marcus just said. Whatever you've got in your bag of tricks, Commander, I'd bring out the best of it. If we fail you may be all that stands between this alien and earth's survival."

Butcher pulled heavily on his cigarette, then dropped it to the floor out of the camera's range and stepped on it. "We'll be ready for this Nebula-Man if you guys fail. Solaron, don't fail. This doesn't look like anything small time. I've got a feelin' this guy is gonna make Gravity King look like a first grader."

"I know Butcher. That's what I'm afraid of too. We'll be in touch."

Butcher nodded, "I'll be watchin'."

The monitor went black save for the image of the man sized shape hurtling toward them.

"How far is he now?" Captain Power asked.

"He's passing Neptune now, but for some reason he slowed down, but he's still moving well beyond light speed."

"He slowed down because of the planetary gravity wells of the giant worlds in your system. Even he must obey basic laws of cosmic nature, though he will still be here in mere minutes." Starbolt offered.

"I'm going to go charge up." Cap advised.

"Where are you going?" Sol asked.

"There's a junk yard a few miles from here. It's going to be missing a few scrap metal cars. Where do you want to meet this guy? In space?"

"I don't think we can. He's coming directly toward us I believe. Somehow he must have tuned in to Starbolt's power."

"That is a likely assumption, Solaron. Make no mistake. This being is unstoppable. He is unto a god gone mad. No power has ever been able to slow him."

"He hasn't met me yet." Cap replied with a slight grin.

"Captain, Nebula-Man has never been bested, by anyone. It is best you charge your powers up to their maximum, for we will need you. We will need all of you." Mar-Cus informed them all grimly.

Cap nodded and flew off, out of the hanger bay and toward the junkyard.

"How long until he gets here?" Dragonfly asked.

"It could be minutes for all I know." Sol replied earnestly.

"I'm going to top off my fletchettes and put in a freshly charged power cell, just in case." Dragonfly exited the room without a backward glance.

"The field where we first met." Starbolt said, "We could draw him there."

"It *is* large enough to avoid innocents and we might be able to contain the damage there." Sol admitted thoughtfully. "I'm going to contact Butcher again and have him announce a five mile evacuation area surrounding that field to begin with."

He turned back to Mar-Cus, "I need to know everything you know about this Nebula-Man. What powers him? You mentioned a Black Nebula?"

"Yes it is surmised that he receives his power from the Black Nebula, a mysterious area of space which nothing ever returns from. Every star spanning civilization gives it a wide berth. On his chest is a swirling, ever changing image of stars and galaxies thought to be within the Black Nebula itself."

"So it would stand to reason he receives his power through his chest then. All right this is something I can work with."

Dragonfly returned, "All set. Are we ready to go?"

"Yes. Stryker you're the big gun until Cap returns. I'll be right behind you all. I have something down in the labs that might help us. I'll meet you there. Now hurry all of you, get to that field and don't do anything stupid."

Silver touched her belt buckle and immediately switched into her costume. Stryker did likewise.

214

Creature thundered toward the door, his heavy footfalls reverberating through the room, mixing with his growls.

"Be careful Prince Bol-Ton." Mar-Cus placed his hands on Starbolt's shoulders, "I have never told you this, but you are as much a son to me as if you were my own flesh. Do nothing foolish where Nebula-Man is concerned. Our only hope is to handle him as a team."

Starbolt grinned and hugged the older black man.

"You are a second father to me as well, Mar-Cus."

Silver Shadow was already out with her brother. Stryker waited with his arms crossed just within the hanger. Dragonfly hovered in the air awaiting the rest of the team to get airborne.

"All together?" Dragonfly asked.

"Yes." Silver replied for the rest who now were taking to the air.

"Then let's go and show this guy that Earth isn't like any world he's ever stuck his nose into before." Dragonfly completed.

They all rocketed away toward the huge field several miles distant.

Starbolt led them toward the rolling hillside which still showed scars from the battle first seen there, only several weeks prior.

Starbolt touched down lightly, holding the ends of his cape.

Creature, Dragonfly, Silver Shadow and Stryker landed beside him.

"I wish our two big guns would get here already." Silver muttered.

"They will, in the nick o' time too, I'm willin' ta bet." Stryker replied.

"Be…ready." Creature grunted.

Dragonfly scanned the sky, his eyes mere slits.

Long minutes, laden with anxiety passed until Starbolt asked, "Do you see anything Randy?"

"Yeah just now. It's a long ways up, but coming in hot. He's glowing like a fire ball to my spectroscopic vision. Like Sol said, he must have attuned himself to your power somehow."

Starbolt nodded, "Yes I agree. That is the only way he could have tracked me here."

"Everyone get ready, he's almost here I-"

A startling figure slammed to the ground between them all. Tall, athletically built, with pale white skin and slits for eyes. He wore a blue and red uniform from his neck down to his ankles with a swirling back mass upon his chest.

The strange creature exuded power. It was an aura about him. Slowly the strange being who would be called Nebula-Man surveyed those he stood in the midst of, scanning every face unemotionally while his grim visage was met with defiance and determination. Minutes passed before he finally spoke.

He stared directly at Starbolt, "You will come with me. You have much to answer for."

"No. He will not." Dragonfly replied, imposing himself between Nebula-Man and Starbolt, "You've been duped by someone, probably that nut bag Zaring. Starbolt's done nothing wrong. In fact he's the guy who was wronged."

"Stand aside youth. This is not your battle." I will take Starbolt to face justice for his crimes."

"He has no crimes. He is the rightful heir to that world's throne. His father is the king, who's being held hostage by Zaring."

"Your words have no meaning to me, youth. If there is a question to all of this, Starbolt will meet his fate when that question is answered upon his home world. He has done much harm and you all represent a grave threat that must be dealt with. I have been told how you damaged General Zaring's ship. An imperial dreadnaught that was thought to be indestructible."

"We damaged his ship because he came here looking to kill Starbolt. That's something we weren't going to allow." Silver Shadow answered.

"You all stand no chance of victory against me. Even with all your combined might. I have scanned you all and I know my power is the greater."

"This isn't all o' us mate." Stryker replied with a grin.

Nebula-Man spun to face him, "It matters not if there be three of you or three thousand. I will win the day. I am justice on an interstellar scale. I have been sent here to stop a wrong on a cosmic scale from occurring."

"You...will...not...harm...him." Creature rumbled.

"You are all protective of this Starbolt. You have grown close and have bonded. I have seen the damage you all have done against a valiant defender of his world. I was informed of how you drove his ship away from this backwater planet. Zaring came here seeking the traitor to his people and you earthlings denied him access to this villain."

"Zaring is the villain. Are you mad?" Starbolt exploded, "Everything you have heard this night is the truth. Zaring holds my parents hostage by right of combat. As I am the next heir in line for the throne I must battle him to meet his challenge. My father is too old, but I am not ready yet. He used a long forgotten clause to attack me, to challenge me. If I die he becomes ruler of my world. He initiated the challenge now, while I am still young and barely trained in my powers."

"That is not what General Zaring conveyed to me." Nebula-Man pointed at Starbolt, "The time for talk is over. You will come with me now. You have no choice in the matter."

Nebula-Man grabbed Starbolt's arm, but before Starbolt could even begin to try to free himself a figure streaked out of the sky and slammed into the powerful alien, impacting him like a runaway meteor.

Both figures hurtled across the field for a hundred yards. Then Captain Power was on his feet, pulling Nebula-Man to meet him eye to eye.

"The kid's not going anywhere, Nebula-Man. You had better consider standing down. I don't want to hurt you."

Nebula-Man looked at Captain Power through his slit eyes, then moving faster than the eye could follow, he backhanded Cap into the sky, sending him possibly miles away with one slap!

"Oh my God!" Dragonfly exclaimed, "Don't hesitate, let's take this guy down."

Dragonfly sprang skyward and began firing his explosive fletchettes at Nebula-Man. Starbolt stayed on the ground and shouted "Force beam", instantly crimson energy blasted from his hands, hammering at his enemy.

Stryker unleashed his own explosive energy blasts, pinioning Nebula-Man between both energies. "Pour it on, mate!"

Nebula-Man seemed almost oblivious to the attacks as he scanned around him calmly.

"I'm going to try something." Starbolt shouted. Creature and Silver shadow stood back, for either of them to get in closer to the battle would only get them both hit by their own teammates attacks.

"Anti-Grav ray, acceleration ray, vertigo effect!" Starbolt shouted quickly.

Nebula-Man disappeared instantly, shooting skyward spinning around uncontrollably.

"What'd you do to him?" Dragonfly asked while landing next to his friends.

"The same thing I did to Gravity King. But I do not know how much time this will afford us."

"Not much he's already heading back. Where the heck is Sol?" Dragonfly asked.

"Let's see if I can buy us some more time mates."

Stryker disappeared, his instant acceleration power taking him from zero to fifteen hundred miles per hour. He barreled into Nebula-Man high above the earth, knocking him off course immediately.

"Crazy nut! He's going to get himself killed." Dragonfly bellowed.

"Don't go after him." Silver shouted.

"What? Why?"

"We can't afford to get separated. We're stronger together."

"A fat lot of good that's done us so far." Dragonfly replied.

"We...still...live." Creature commented.

"You're right we- Get out of the way!" Dragonfly shoved both Creature and Silver clear as the unmoving form of Stryker plowed into the ground.

Immediately Nebula-Man landed again, facing them all. "Enough of this foolishness. This game is finished. I will take the boy and go, or I will destroy you all."

"Oh no you won't." A voice from above shouted. Captain Power returned, swooping in and unleashing a powerful right haymaker that lifted Nebula-Man into the sky once again.

Then a blast of golden energy erupted from elsewhere in the black night sky, hammering their foe.

"Solaron!" shouted Dragonfly.

Solaron rocketed across the sky, blasting their enemy again and again unrelentingly.

Cap turned to Starbolt, "Can you get him back down here? Maybe increase gravity around him a thousand times?"

Starbolt nodded, and then shouted, "Heavy gravity beam!"

Energy leapt from his fingertips enveloping Nebula-Man who immediately fell from the heavens to slam into the ground like Icarus with his wings cut.

"Hold him there." Solaron ordered while landing.

"I will do my best." answered Starbolt.

Nebula-Man laid on his back struggling to stand. The ground around him began to indent from his incredibly increased mass.

Solaron unhesitatingly walked up to him and placed a metallic disc on his chest that covered up the chaotic swirling mass of stars and black space there. The disc glowed momentarily, Nebula-Man stiffened in pain and then collapsed after an instant.

"What is that?" Cap asked.

"It's something I whipped up to block him from drawing power from the Black Nebula."

"You cannot stop me man of Earth." Nebula-Man bellowed. He fought his way to his feet, even while Starbolt continued to increase local gravity upon him.

"I will have this boy. You will not deter me."

"Starbolt, now." Solaron ordered.

Starbolt nodded and barked, "Anti-Grav ray!"

Instantly Nebula-man disappeared again, streaking skyward completely out of control.

"He's turning already and heading back to us." Dragonfly advised.

"I figured as much. Silver, how's Stryker?"

"I'm okay mate, a bit light headed but otherwise I'm ready for another tussle."

"Okay different tactic. When he lands Silver, use your stun bolt on him. Maybe that can buy us some time."

"Time for what?" Cap asked.

"For him to run out of energy, or at least use up enough to become more manageable."

"I don't think that's going to happen." Cap replied.

"Here he comes." Dragonfly warned.

This time he landed and released energy blasts from both hands, firing in a circle about himself.

"Force field!" yelled Starbolt.

An energy barrier sprang up between the team and Nebula-Man.

But almost instantly it shattered under his power.

"Not so fast pasty face." Cap grunted. He hurled himself into his foe, forcing him backward.

"You're not going any further, space-man." Cap roared. He punctuated his sentence with a powerful left cross, followed by a thunderous right. Nebula-Man said nothing, merely replied in kind. Punch after earth shaking punch was thrown by both combatants. Silver was actually knocked off her feet from the earthquake-like reverberations. Creature flew to her side and scooped her up, taking her into the air.

"This is crazy!" Dragonfly told Solaron, "They're hitting each other so hard the ground is starting to crack."

"What's worse," Sol replied, "is that neither one is gaining ground over the other. How long can Cap maintain this level of strength before he runs out of power?"

Now the two combatants began to grapple, locking hands and forcing one another back and forth.

Nebula-Man broke the silent tableau, "You are strong earthman. Perhaps the strongest being I have ever met. But my powers go beyond mere physical might."

Energy beams lanced out of his eyes, striking Captain Power full in the face. Cap stumbled backward holding his face.

"Cap!" Silver Shadow shouted. She turned angrily and unleashed her mental stun bolt from her forehead.

Her blast smashed into Nebula-Man's own forehead, snapping his head back unexpectedly.

For a moment nothing happened. Silver maintained her psionic attack, clenching her fists at her sides tightly and gritting her teeth.

Then Nebula-Man slowly righted himself and turned to face her onslaught, "You humans of earth continue to surprise me. But you are not the only one with powers of the mind, woman."

The beam from Silver's mind to Nebula-Man's seemed to change color to a much darker hue than its normally silver color and reversed flow back at her.

"Aaaaa!" Silver screamed.

But her scream was cut short as Dragonfly and Creature attacked simultaneously. The shape shifting Hyperforcer tackled the alien powerhouse, mauling him while bellowing bestial roars with each powerful blow and slash. Dragonfly streaked through the air fists first and plowed into Nebula-Man, knocking him down under their combined assault.

"You are both as nothing compared to my might." Nebula-Man threw both his arms wide, and smashed both heroes from him.

He turned, only to receive a face full of high density solar energy beams, courtesy of Solaron.

"What? Y-you attack me with the power of a star? I-I have ripped stars asunder, I have w-waded through them!"

"You don't sound so confident about that right now." Solaron replied.

"No he doesn't, does he?" Dragonfly affirmed.

The teenaged Hyperforcer began firing his Dragonblasts, holding them steadily on his enemy. Now Nebula-Man put his hands up in front of his face, trying to ward off the attacks, or trying to deflect them.

"What's happening to him?" Dragonfly yelled over the thunderous din.

"He's finally starting to lose strength. I was right. He draws power from that Black Nebula; probably in some sort of subspace conduit. My power dampener is acting like a cork, blocking power from getting to him, cutting him off."

"We have to keep up the attacks on him until he runs out." Dragonfly noted.

"Less talk, more action." Sol replied.

"You want action mate? I'll give ya action." Stryker flew into Nebula-Man shoulder first, knocking him to the ground.

But almost instantly a blast of energy from Nebula-Man sent Stryker heavenward where he disappeared instantly into the star speckled night sky.

"He's still got juice left in him." Solaron roared while flying upward.

Arcing around Solaron began hammering at their foe from above with a steady stream of powerful high density solar blasts.

Dragonfly grasped his underarm wing with his right hand and in one smooth motion, unhooked it from his costume and hurled it. The crescent shaped wing spun on edge and slammed into Nebula-Man.

Nebula-Man was staggered, falling several steps backward from the impact.

"Why can't he remove that thing?" Dragonfly asked.

"It uses a molecular bonding component I came up with. It's basically becoming a part of him." Solaron replied.

"What's he doing now?" Starbolt asked.

"I don't know he's begun glowing brighter and brighter I-he's trying to burn the power dampener off of his chest. Get him!"

The team sprang into action as one. Dragonfly ran in deftly avoiding the chaotic energy blasts, leaping over them, ducking beneath until he was finally within striking distance. Shouting "Cowabunga dude!" he threw a side thrust kick into Nebula-Man's stomach with all his prodigious strength.

"Ugggh," moaned Nebula-Man while stumbling back several steps. Dragonfly executed a perfect spinning wheel kick at his enemies head. Nebula-Man again staggered back, anger beginning to show on his otherwise impassive face.

He raised his hands quickly, about to unleash his Black Nebula energy at Dragonfly when Solaron threw a gleaming blast of solar power and knocked him from his feet.

Silver Shadow appeared, hovering above him, firing her stun bolt again and again.

"That's it, keep him off balance." Sol ordered.

"Oh I'll keep him more than off balance." Captain Power replied, as he flew down from above and hammered the strange alien being straight down into the ground, literally burying him to his neck in the densely packed earth. His impact shook the ground for miles around.

"Cap! Are you all right?" Silver asked.

"I've been better. It took me a few minutes until my vision came back, that's why I was holding back. Even now things are kind of blurry, but getting better every minute. Where's our resident Aussie?"

"Stasis field!" Starbolt shouted. Energy ripped from his fingers and spread over Nebula-Man. Instantly he froze in place.

Everyone turned toward Starbolt.

"Why didn't you do that from the get go? It would have saved us all a lot of trouble." Solaron asked.

"I just thought of it now." Starbolt shrugged sheepishly, "When he shattered my force field I was barely conscious. The feedback almost took me out of the fight. He's just too powerful. When I saw you all expending so much energy to just hold our own it came to me to just hold him in place."

"But how long will that last?" Cap asked.

"And what do we do with him when he breaks free of it?" Dragonfly added.

"I'm going to check on Creature and see if I can find Stryker." Solaron announced, Silver, see if you can use your psionic abilities to maybe find out what this guy's deal is."

"I-I don't really have anything more than a stun bolt and some low level telepathy."

"I know but use that, the telepathy. Try to read his mind. Maybe there's something there we can work with. I can't think of anything else at the moment. If he burns through that power dampener I affixed to him we're all in trouble, and I don't think Prince Bolton can hold him like this for too long."

"Okay Solaron. Check on my brother, he took a hard shot from this guy."

"I'm checking him now." Sol walked away toward the insensate Creature.

Silver watched him kneel beside the hairy behemoth for a moment until she saw Creature begin to move, then she focused her attention on the powerful alien.

Her mind opened up and began to probe Nebula-Man's, folding back the layers hidden within, extracting what she believed was useful and then with a start she uttered, "Oh!" She stood up and stumbled backward, then called out, "Sol, I have to talk to you."

"What is it Silver?" He was at her side immediately, Creature was right behind him, rubbing the back of his head. The rest of the team gathered close.

"You're not going to believe this, but he doesn't remember who he really is."

"What do you mean? Is he someone else besides Nebula-Man?" Cap asked.

"He was. But he lost that memory. It was buried deep within him and inaccessible, until now."

"Silver what are you getting at?" Sol prodded.

"Sol, he's an earthman. He's from here. His name was Jim Carroll. He was abducted from Earth years ago by aliens. Sometime later they were trying to escape a patrol ship of some kind that was after them and they flew too close to the Black Nebula. They ended up getting sucked in. He was changed within it into who and what he is now."

"Does he realize this at all?"

"He didn't. Or he didn't at least until now." she corrected herself.

"Starbolt drop your stasis field let's see what happens." Solaron commanded.

Starbolt nodded cautiously and stopped bathing Nebula-Man in the stasis beams.

Instantly the ground around Nebula-Man exploded furiously. He rocketed upward from the devastated earth. The device Solaron had adhered to his chest melted away to slag from within, once again exposing the swirling Black Nebula upon his chest and stomach.

Without hesitation Captain Power and Dragonfly flew into the sky after the now hovering Nebula-Man, ready to immediately resume the battle.

"Hold!" Nebula-Man calmly ordered, "I will battle you no more this day. What Silver Shadow showed me, it was something I dared not guess before; something that was hidden from me by the Black Nebula itself when it remade me into the cosmic avenger that I have become. You have all fought valiantly this day. That is something I did not expect. Further, Silver Shadow's link was two way. I was able to see the truth of your words. General Zaring is an evil man. He sought to use me in his own nefarious schemes to destroy you all, and to drag Starbolt back to his home world where Zaring may execute him. You have my that on this matter that we will not come to blows again. You are all powerful and worthy opponents. Never in my second life have I fought such a group of individuals. You have done what no one else in all of existence has ever done. You had me defeated. I salute you all."

"What will you do now?" Solaron floated upward until he was face to face with Nebula-Man.

"I will begin to explore my former home once again. I must see if those who were-are my family still exist. All of these memories…They flood back into my mind now. I must come to terms with them."

He turned and began to float toward the stars.

Dragonfly looked at Cap and Sol, and beside them now hovered Silver and Starbolt, "Are we just going to let him go?"

"I don't think we could stop him if we wanted to." Cap replied, "I know I've had enough, and if there's no longer a point to it all, I'm not going to spend the next week here hitting this guy."

"My power dampener is gone; his power finally melted it from within. I don't know what else we could do to stop him, and considering the way he fought us all to a standstill, I'm not sure I want to." Solaron stated.

"Good point, I guess." Dragonfly agreed.

Silver looked around now as if something had just come back to her, "Has anyone seen Stryker? Nebula-Man hit him at one point and sent him into the clouds. He never returned."

"Don't worry Silver, we'll find him." Cap answered her.

"I'm heading back to the base. I have a device there that can track any of us through our communicator."

Dragonfly mentioned, "I'm going to stay and see if I can find him with my spectroscopic vision. Maybe Cap and I can track him down."

"Ey!" a familiar voice interrupted over the comm units built into their costumes, "Anyone hear me? That bloody bastard knocked me clear into Pennsylvania. I don't know how long I was out cold for, but I woke up in a bloody field next to a cow that was lickin' me face."

"Bad penny's." Cap added sarcastically.

Solaron looked at Cap with annoyance, "We read you Stryker, where are you now?"

"Headin' back to yer position."

"Don't bother. Go back to the observatory. We're done here and Nebula-Man is gone."

"Bloody hell! How'd you beat him?"

"I'm not so certain we did, but I'll consider this a win anyway. Meet you back at the base, Solaron out." He tapped his cheek, shutting off the comm unit hidden in his cowl.

Creature flapped his wings and rose up to float beside them all, his wings slowly pinioning the air to keep him aloft.

"Is everyone okay?" Solaron asked.

They all nodded in the affirmative.

"Let's head back. This this has been one hell of a night."

The team flew upward and disappeared into the sky.

Hidden within the clouds a small device no larger than a microwave oven, but shaped like a saucer hovered and slowly transmitted their every move.

Fifteen hundred miles away, on an island in the Caribbean, an island not on any map, a massive figure sat in what could only be termed as a throne room. Black smoke hung about his massive form and shadowed brow. He wore shiny black leather from the top of head to his massive boots. If he were standing his height would have tipped eight feet. A belt of blackened skulls hung about his waist. They were not simply ornamental. He leaned back in his throne of sorts, slouching actually, and took a long pull on a goblet of wine he had next to him on a finely crafted stand. Then he clicked a button on a remote he held and the monitor with Hyperforce' fading images clicked off.

He drank again of his wine. The grey skin that showed on his face beneath his head covering marked a stark contrast against the red of the wine itself.

"Interesting." was the only word he uttered in a voice like unto gravel and thunder. Then the grey skinned, black garbed behemoth stood and left the room, shutting the light behind him and plunging the room into abject darkness.

Ralph L. Angelo Jr.

Chapter 10

So now what?

Ronald Anderson peered through the high resolution solar observatory telescope. After several moments he tapped into a tablet he had at his side and entered his findings which were automatically slaved to the mainframe in the observatory's control center.

"Hey Uncle Ron."

Ronald raised his head and looked at his nephew Randy, who had just entered the lab and the professor smiled.

"Hello Randy. What are you doing here?"

"Not much Unc. I haven't seen you in a few days and figured I'd stop by and say 'hi'."

Anderson chuckled and walked past his nephew, tousling his hair as he did, "you mean there's been no Hyperforce action for the past week since Nebula-Man took off for parts unknown, and you're starting to get bored, isn't that right?"

Randy Anderson smiled and looked down at his feet, not trying to show how correct his uncle was. Finally he gave up and met Ronald Anderson's gaze, "Uncle Ron, you have to realize, it's not that I don't have other things I could do, but compared to this they're all boring, and not exactly much of a challenge. I mean, yes, I could be on the school's baseball, football, track or basketball teams. The only problem is I would be the MVP of every league and game. Nothing is really a challenge anymore. Except this. It just wouldn't be fair to anyone else."

Ronald Anderson looked at his nephew and slowly nodded; a slight grin began to crack around the corners of his mouth, "All right sport, hang out with me here today, maybe we'll get lucky and have to save the world again."

Randy smiled and relaxed, "Where's Starbolt and Marcus? Or even Silver and Creature for that matter? And when are we going to learn their real names?"

"When they choose to tell us, Randy. I'm not going to push them on that. When they're comfortable we'll learn them."

"Uncle Ron, have you found Nebula-Man yet?"

"No, Randy. Not at all. Not hide nor hair. He's disappeared, or went back off into space."

"Or maybe he's hiding himself from detection?"

"That could be Randy. In fact that is probably the case. I have to think if he doesn't want to be found, he's one guy who can hide himself from any type of detection we might come up with."

"What about Commander Butcher?"

"What about him?"

"Well, has he been looking for Nebula-Man?"

"Of course, and he seems pretty much on the level about sharing information with us, but I don't know how much I trust this man Butcher. So far he seems on the up and up. In fact he invited us to their headquarters to sort of meet and greet and check out the facility."

Randy grimaced, "Wow, do you think he could be trying to trap us there?"

Ronald stared at his nephew with a perplexed look on his face, "Why would you think that?"

"Well, I don't trust him either."

234

"It's not that I don't trust him, to be honest he's done nothing so far that would make me think he's out to get us in any way. If anything I think he's been pretty straight forward. But that being said, I'm not going into anything with these government types and acting blind to what could happen."

Randy nodded, "I gotcha Unc. So like I asked already, where is everyone?"

"Oh they're around somewhere. Creature is probably down in the game room playing X-Box again. Silver may be out with Stryker, yet again. I haven't seen either of them for a few hours."

"Gotcha Unc. I'm gonna go see if I can find Creature, maybe I can get a game going with him."

"You know, it wouldn't hurt you guys to get outside once in a while."

"He doesn't like to go out. He doesn't want anyone to see him, unless he's in action."

"We have to break him of that Randy. He needs to see the world from more than just inside these walls."

"I know Uncle Ron, but he's really self-conscious about his hairy hide when we're not on a mission."

Ronald Anderson stood, contemplating for a moment and staring into space. "Randy, here's twenty dollars. Go change into your costume and take Creature with you to that ice cream shop in town that the kids hang out at."

"Uncle Ron, are you sure? I mean he's not really sociable as it is. Do you think this is a good idea?"

"Yes, I think it's something that has to be done. This young man has to deal with who and what he is. He's a hero and he has to see himself as such and not a monster. He also needs friends. Can you be his friend Randy?"

"I already am, Uncle Ron. When he loosens up he's a lot of fun."

"Then take him out and make sure he gets loose. He has to socialize."

"Uncle Ron, you do know he's about six years older than me right?"

"I realize that Randy. But he's not too old to hang around an ice cream parlor and look at girls with you. Plus you two are now world famous superheroes. Go out and enjoy some notoriety."

Randy sighed, "Okay Unc. I'll go talk to Creature." Randy touched his belt buckle and instantly his costume appeared, exchanging places with his clothes in the transport tube.

Dragonfly walked down to the rec room where Creature was indeed playing with a video game. "Hey buddy. C'mon let's go into town and have some ice cream."

Creature looked at him quizzically, not believing what he heard, "Are...you......kidding? I can't...go out...like...this." He held his hands out in front of himself, palms up.

"Why not? It's who you are, and we're both celebrities now, kinda anyway."

"No. I...cannot do this...to...myself."

"Yes you can, now c'mon, it's time you came out and had some fun instead of hidin' in here all the time."

"B-but look at...me."

"I am. I see a super-hero. A world famous super-hero who has saved the world a few times already."

"But...I am ...ugly."

"No you're not Creature. You're just different, that's all, and who isn't?"

"N-no one…is this…different."

"C'mon man it doesn't matter. Come with me. Let's go hang out and be celebrities. They'll be chicks…" Dragonfly smiled.

Creature shook his head and then looked at his friend before throwing his hairy paws into the air as if resigned to his fate.

"C'mon buddy, it'll be fun." Dragonfly said with a grin.

"This…can't be a…good idea."

***

Fifteen minutes later…

Dragonfly grinned, "See? I told you it would be fun."

"You are…crazy." Creature groaned. Around both men were high school girls wanting autographs. Creature had two girls sitting on his lap giggling and smiling while their friends took pictures with their cell phones. Dragonfly had a girl under each arm while he gave the thumbs up sign with each hand and a wide grin plastered across his face. Creature, for all his complaining, was smiling and actually enjoying himself.

"You boys can come in here any time you want and whatever you want is on the house." The owner of the ice cream shop said. There was a line out to the street, all high school girls and boys wanting to see the super-heroes.

"See Creature? I told you this would be cool."

Creature tried to grunt disapprovingly but a high school girl in a cheerleader uniform sitting on his lap

turned around and tickled him under the chin. Try as he
might not to, he laughed.

***

Across the street in a beat up black van…
"Do you see this? Are you kidding me?" The man
talking looked in disbelief out the van's window. He was
a powerfully built black man with long dreadlocks. He
wore a domino mask and his red costume shirt was open
to his waist. Black leather pants and laced up combat
boots completed his look.
"War Roar, what do you want me to do? I had no
idea these clowns would be here. This is not my fault."
"Well it ain't mine, Benny-"
"Code names!" Benny interrupted.
War Roar waved his hands in disgust, "Okay, okay
Brass Tiger. But this still blows this right out of the
water. We can't rob this bank now with these two idiots
next door eating ice cream."
"Why not War? Look at them, they're two kids.
They ain't got a clue what's about to happen. Hell, you
could blow the wall down and I could stop these two
morons before they get into the street. They'll never
expect a fight here."
"Are you kiddin me Tiger? They are super-heroes,
the first the worlds ever seen. They live for fighting guys
like us, we're villains, super-villains. We were made to
clash with these two fools. It's all in the cards."
"I'm tellin' you we can take them, War Roar."
"An' what if we can't? How many fights do you
think these two clowns have been in already? Hell, a

week ago they fought some alien, from space even! An' they drove him off."

"Yeah they did. Them and a half dozen other so-called he-roes. Well them other he-roes ain't here with them War. Look at the one in the red an' blue; he's a kid. How smart could he be? You don't think the two of us could out fight an' out think these two punks? Do what I said. Drive around the building. You take down the wall going into the vault with your sonic scream-"

"It ain't no scream Tiger, it's a roar."

"Okay, take it down with your roar. Just make sure it's a deafening, ear splitting one. We want them to hear that wall going down. They run out the door, I'll be waiting. You clean out the vault, load as much as you can carry-"

"Ah can carry everything in there, I'm really strong, remember?"

"I know War Roar. But you remember, I'm stronger an' faster than you."

Brass tiger looked at his partner. He wore what appeared to be a Tiger skin, with his face hidden within the mouth and jaw. His wrists had what appeared to be brass armbands wrapped around them.

War Roar shook his head in annoyance, "This is the dumbest thing I ever let myself be talked into."

"This dumb thing is gonna make you a rich man."

"It better Benny, it really better. Otherwise you an' me, we are gonna have us some words."

Brass Tiger smiled, "Relax War Roar. This is all gonna work out beautifully, I promise you."

***

239

Back inside the ice cream parlor, Dragonfly and Creature were drinking ice cream sodas and enjoying all the attention being foisted upon them.

Creature sucked on the straw in his soda and smiled as the soda emptied.

"See?" Dragonfly said with a smile, "I told you this was going to be fun."

"Yes…you did." Creature smiled.

"Man, you are relaxed for the first time since I met you. That's gotta feel better than being cooped up back at the uh, base. Yeah base. That's what we'll call it."

Creature smiled, his hairy face twisting comically, "Yes…base sounds…good."

Suddenly a blaring howl cut through the air. Instinctively everyone within the ice cream shop covered their ears and grimaced in pain.

"What the heck was that?" Dragonfly barked. He ran for the door of the Ice Cream shop with Creature quick on his heels.

They both exited the door and were immediately run over by a slashing, growling lunatic.

"Raaarroar!" howled Creature. He leaped onto his mysterious foe, while Dragonfly cartwheeled away.

Both feral opponents were now on their feet and circling each other, deep animalistic sounds emanated from both their throats.

"Have you got this?" Dragonfly shouted.

Creature nodded slowly, his eyes never leaving his opponent, "Go." he rumbled.

Dragonfly didn't hesitate and flew off, over the ice cream shop to the back of the small row of stores.

'The back wall of this place is blown out.' he flew into the gaping hole, and an instant later was hurled bodily back out of the hole on a wave of sound.

"What the heck?" Dragonfly shouted.

Following him out of the shattered bank wall came the second thief, howling madly, shooting off waves of sonic power, turning brick, concrete and tar to rubble. Dragonfly deftly flew over and around each blast, then returned fire with his own dragonblasts, catching the big dreadlocked villain in the chest and eliciting a cry of pain and surprise, "What the hell was that kid? That hurt."

"They're called my dragonblasts, doofus. Now who are you? Just so I can tell the cops when they arrest your unconscious butt."

The villain chuckled, "M' name's 'War Roar' kid, remember it when you wake up in the hospital."

War Roar reared back again and then forward howling madly. Dragonfly instinctively raised his right underarm wing up in front of himself, fending off the blast. But then War Roar turned his aim at the ground beneath Dragonfly's feet tearing it up and tossing Dragonfly into the air.

Back in front of the ice cream shop Creature and Brass Tiger slashed savagely at each other. Both giving no ground. Like two wild beasts they tore at one another.

"What are you? Some kind of monster?" Brass Tiger asked.

"I could…ask you…the…same." Creature replied. He rubbed blood from his mouth and snarled.

With a leap he hurled himself at Brass Tiger, who ducked below and surged upward, throwing Creature from him.

Like a cat, Creature landed on all fours. He stared at Brass Tiger and grunted with exertion. Immediately his fur began to change shape becoming thicker and larger.

"What are you-" Brass Tiger began, and then stopped himself as his eyes went wide in disbelief at what he saw. Creature smiled as his fur turned to quills, and every one of them exploded out of his body and at Brass Tiger.

Behind the bank, Dragonfly leaped into the air and landed on a wall, hanging there sideways. Without hesitation he fired explosive fletchettes, blowing War Roar off of his feet and onto his back.

"You can walk on walls? You're jus' like that other guy."

"Sorry rocket scientist, I'm not like anyone you ever heard of."

Dragonfly leaped at him, covering the fifteen feet between them easily, and finishing his leap with a solid left cross to War-Roar's jaw.

"Ugghh." the villain grunted. He slid across the ground and slammed back first into the banks wall.

"Give it up big guy. I can dance around with you all day."

War Roar sneered, "Kid, you got a big mouth." He roared again, sonic energy slammed Dragonfly backward and into the back wall of the adjoining store.

The young hero ducked below a second blast of sound, then rolled across the alley while War Roar followed him with a long drawn out blast of sonic energy.

Leaping upward, Dragonfly ignited his boot rockets and streaked skyward, "Eat hot dragonblast, chunky!" Dragonfly unleashed his atom disrupting energy blasts again, and caught his opponent with both beams square in the chest.

War Roar arched his back and howled in agony, by pure chance releasing another sonic blast across the sky, smashing Dragonfly in the chest and knocking him to the ground.

With a thud the young super-hero slammed into the pavement, and lie still.

"Sorry kid, I'll make this short an' sweet an' as painless as I can. What you shot me with, those dragon things? They hurt like hell, so you got this coming."

***

Back out in the street, Creature punched Brass Tiger with all his might, sending his furry antagonist sailing through the air, to land very uncat-like on the hood of a car. Immediately the two front tires blew out from the impact.

Brass Tiger shook his head to clear it, but Creature was on top of him in half a heartbeat. He brought both of his powerful arms upward and slammed them down together like hammers upon his enemies shoulders, smashing him through the hood of the car.

"Freeze!" a newcomers voice shouted.

Creature looked toward the sound of the voice and saw a dozen police officers lined up and pointing guns at him!

***

Back in the alley behind the bank, Dragonfly lay unmoving. War Roar walked up close to him and reared back, prepared to unleash a sonic blast at point blank range.

In a blur, Dragonfly ignited his boot rockets and slammed War Roar in the gut, knocking the wind out of him and rocketing him skyward.

"Surprise!" he laughed. Dragonfly flew upward after his opponent. Faster than the eye could follow Dragonfly gasped War Roar by the throat, preventing him from roaring once again.

Arcing over the building, Dragonfly immediately saw the cops surrounding Creature and Creature's own unconscious opponent.

War Roar gasped for air, but Dragonfly smiled at him and said, "This is your stop dreads, time to get off."

With a heave of his arm he hurled War Roar down onto the unconscious Brass Tiger. The police immediately looked upward at the hovering super-hero who smiled and said, "These are the droids you're looking for."

"What? What was that supposed to mean?" one of the cops asked.

"It means these two are the bad guys and we're the heroes." Dragonfly landed next to Creature with his hands on his hips.

"Yeah everyone knows who you are by now Dragonfly. But don't kid yourself, not all of us are happy you vigilantes are operating out of our town. You end up bringing scum like this with you."

"Okay officer, first off, think about this; if we were such bad news, why would the bad guys come to any town we hung out in? I mean I think that would be counterproductive or somethin'. I mean, if I was a super-villain the last thing I'd do is go to a town where Super-heroes hung out in. In fact I'd move to the other side of the country."

The officer shook his head disgustedly, "Go on, get outta here before I run you in just for the hell of it." Creature began to growl but Dragonfly silenced him quickly, "Let's go Creature."

Creature turned his head one last time and looked at the officer and then at the front of the ice cream shop which was filled with the high school students. A girl in her cheerleader's uniform waved at him forlornly. Again he returned his eyes to the officer and a deep seated growl emanated from within his soul.

"Yes... leave this...place." Creature snarled at the police again and then his leathery wings grew out of his back.

Both men flew skyward; Dragonfly turned toward Creature and asked, "Are you all right?"

"No." after a moment's hesitation he continued, "For the...first time...in years...I was...having...fun."

An instant later Dragonfly and Creature disappeared into the sky.

Ralph L. Angelo Jr.

Chapter 11

Fire from the sky

"What happened?" Ron Anderson asked his nephew, who was still wearing his Dragonfly uniform.

Dragonfly sighed; it was almost as if he had deflated. He looked up at his uncle and began, "Like you asked, we, Creature and I, had gone to town. I wanted to see if I could get him to just relax around regular people. You know, to put his guard down a little and just hang out, and it worked. We were having a good time. A bunch of girls from the high school came in and started talking to the two cool super-heroes. We were both having a great time. The girls were taking pictures with us both. Some guys came in and wanted to shake our hands. It was cool. All of it was. Creature freakin' smiled Uncle Ron!"

Ronald Anderson nodded, touching his chin pensively, "That's a first, without a doubt."

"But then some idiots decided to rob the bank next door; and they were super-powered idiots to boot."

"Go on."

"We beat them; we tied the whole thing up nicely. That's when one of the cops started acting like a jerk. He told us outright he didn't like super-heroes and called us vigilantes. I thought Creature was going to attack him he was so angry. But he didn't, he just looked back at the ice cream shop, where even the owner had been really cool with us and told us to come back any time we wanted...on the house."

247

Ronald Anderson walked around his lab quietly a moment, his white lab coat fluttering behind him as he thought.

"I see two ways around this. One, we go back as a whole team and buy everyone who comes in ice cream and do a meet and greet, maybe even announce it with the mayor and make a day of it."

"What's the second way?"

"Something I'm dreading to even suggest. I'm considering contacting Butcher and seeing if he can give us some kind of official government agent status. But what I fear there is that we would be at the government's beck and call, which I'd rather not be. I don't mind us helping out if called upon, but I don't want us to become their secret weapons and being ordered to do their bidding whenever they need us. The other side of the coin is, I may be wealthy, but I'm not made of money. Since we became Hyperforce a few months back I've had less time for research, and less time to rent out the solar observatory, which equates to a slowing of income. I'm far from in trouble, but I have to think ahead about all of this. If we hire out to the government on occasion we can ask a high enough price to make all of this financially worthwhile too."

"Yeah but that makes us guns for hire."

"Only against threats we would normally face anyway. The way I'm seeing it is that we'd get paid for what we'd normally do. But it is a thin line we'd have to be careful about crossing as far as I'm concerned. I don't want them to think we're government employees maybe 'instead of just free lancers. That's where we'd have to put our feet down." He turned back toward his nephew, "How's Creature now?"

"He's back down in the rec room playing his video games. He looks kinda, I dunno, sad."

"Why? What happened to him?" a female's voice interrupted from the doorway.

Both men turned and saw Silver Shadow standing there with her hands on her hips.

"Ahh we had a little problem in town." Dragonfly replied.

"What kind of problem?" Silver Shadow demanded.

"Some cop gave us a hard time after the two of us took down some super powered thugs, that's all. He didn't like vigilantes he said."

"Why was my brother out in the open?"

Ronald Anderson stepped between Silver and Dragonfly, "He needs to have some fun and hang out with people once in a while, Silver. He can't hide in here or anywhere for the rest of his life."

She met his gaze and softened after a few seconds, "Y-your right Ron. You are. He does need to be out, no matter what he looks like. He has to learn to accept himself before others can accept him."

"Others were accepting him." Dragonfly pointed out, "We were hangin' out with some high schoolers and everything was going good."

"This probably hurt him." Silver thought aloud.

"I would think it did." Ronald Anderson agreed.

"I know it did. I was there. I thought he was going to tear the cop apart." Dragonfly said.

"What do we do now? For him I mean?" Silver asked.

"Let it all settle down a day or two. I'll go to see the mayor of this town. After that the rest of us will all go out for dinner together somewhere very public and very loud. I'll make sure every paper in three states knows we'll be there too." Ron Anderson concluded.

A loud alarm sounded and the many monitors around the headquarters section of the observatory flashed red with a banner that said 'incoming message from A.R.M.O.R.'

Ron Anderson ran his fingers across his belt buckle and his costume instantly appeared. Professor Ronald Anderson had reached the switch to answer the incoming communication, but it was Solaron who actually answered it.

Commander Butcher's face appeared on the monitor "What is it Commander?"

"Solaron, we have a situation."

"First, we're going to have a talk about our availability to your beck and call when whatever this new emergency is over. We don't mind helping our country out against enemies, especially super-powered ones. But that being said, there's going to have to be some concessions on the governments' part for these occasional missions we undertake for you."

"Look Solaron, we can dance around that pole another night, right now we got a situation, an' it's a doozy."

"What have you got, Butcher?"

Something just went off in both Antarctica, and the arctic circle. Something big, an' bad."

"Define 'big and bad'."

"It looks nuclear. That's all we know. I have ships on the way. But my planes can't get anywhere near either site because of the radiation. I'm hoping maybe some of your guys would be immune to radiation so we can find out what this really is."

"Myself, Captain Power and probably Starbolt would be able to shield or be immune to radiation on all levels. Also the shields on the Stargrazer can protect the rest of the team."

"How fast can you be on site?"

Sol shrugged, "Cap and I can fly there in minutes. We're faster out of atmosphere, and Starbolt is probably faster than any of us."

"All right I'll leave this all to you. I'll keep comm lines open just in case you need back up."

Solaron nodded, very good Butcher, Solaron out."

Sol cut the communication and turned to his team who had gathered behind him during the conversation with Butcher. Everyone was there including Stryker and Creature.

"We have a situation, and it's a bad one. It looks like nukes, or something approximating them went off at both poles simultaneously. We have to find out why, or who caused this."

"We're going to have to split up." Cap commented.

Sol nodded in agreement, "I was thinking the same thing."

"You and I down to the South Pole and the rest of the team to the North?"

"Yes Cap, that sounds right."

Sol turned to Starbolt, "Prince Bolton, can your render yourself immune to radiation?"

251

"I can Solaron, yes."

"What about your ship?"

"Its shields will easily protect those aboard from the radiation from one of your nuclear weapons."

"Very good. Captain Power and I will proceed to the Antarctic. The rest of you head north to the Arctic Circle. Prince Bolton, stay aboard your ship until you get there, in other words stay together as a team. We see how capable you are on a daily basis, but there's no reason to push our luck."

Sol turned to Mar-Cus who stood silently next to his young charge, "Marcus, please man the command center in case God forbid something else happens."

"I will keep in contact with both teams and relay any information I come across to you all."

"Good Marcus, thank you. Wheels up in five people." The team split up quickly, heading back to their quarters and the armory for anything else they might need.

Solaron looked at Captain Power, "How's your power levels? Are you charged up?"

"Yes I am. Whenever you're ready we can be out of here."

"I'm going to change my costume, I'll be right back."

Solaron exited the room. Cap turned to Mar-Cus, "How are you doing Marcus? Are you both holding up okay?"

"We are fine, Captain. Solaron's hospitality and the camaraderie of the rest of you has been something unexpected. We came here seeking aid against our deadly enemy, and you have all given us so much more."

Without you all we would have been killed immediately upon our arrival by the madman Zaring' forces. Now you have aided me in training my young charge in the ways of war. No, not war, survival as well as what must be done when ones back is against the wall."

Cap chuckled, "Some days it seems our backs are always against the wall. If it's not one thing it's another."

"Are you ready?" Solaron re-entered the room and asked. He was wearing a metallic gold suit. Unlike his regular costume, his head was fully covered and there was no cape. His familiar star emblem was emblazoned on the chest of this costume as well.

"What is this? Armor of some kind?" Mar-Cus asked.

Solaron nodded, "It's a lightweight armored suit I came up with for hazardous missions. It affords me a little more protection and is also more space worthy than my regular costume. A clear face shield can be lowered and locked into place from the upper part of the cowl, sealing the suit up completely."

Cap asked, "Why would you even need that? You don't breathe."

Solaron looked at his teammate in mild surprise, "You really do notice most everything don't you?"

"I try to make a habit of it. You should try to remember to do your best to keep an air of normalcy about yourself out of costume."

"Point taken Cap, and thanks. Let's go."

Solaron turned toward Mar-Cus, "Marcus, the base is all yours."

"Very good my friends, good hunting. I know I do not have to tell you both to be careful."

Solaron and Captain Power exited into the hanger area where the rest of the team was awaiting them, "Dragonfly, you're in charge. Be careful. Keep your eyes open, all of you. We have no idea what's going on here, so take it slow."

"You got it Solaron." Dragonfly replied.

Handshakes were exchanged all around, then Solaron and Captain Power flew out of the hanger deck and into the sky, accelerating to three times the speed of sound.

The rest of the team watched them disappear before entering the Stargrazer.

A moment later the small ship exited the hanger deck and disappeared into the sky heading north and accelerating quickly.

***

Far above the Earth, at the edge of the atmosphere, Solaron and Captain Power raced toward their goal. Within minutes they began to descend back through the atmosphere, arcing toward Antarctica.

"Coming up on the target area." Sol called out.

"Understood Solaro- What the hell is that?"

Both men slowed to an immediate halt. Before them a massive machine, easily a mile long and oval shaped, hovered above the Earth's surface by several hundred feet. A beam of energy blasted down from it into the ice, boring a hole through ice and rock alike. Its surface was covered in lights and moving devices.

254

Solaron shook his head, "I have no idea what that is, or what it's doing, besides boring a hole in the Earth."

"Is that thing extraterrestrial?" Cap asked.

"I would have to assume so." Solaron nodded.

"Yeah I don't think that came from Earth. Do you think this is one of Zaring's toys?"

"It's a distinct possibility."

"Okay then, time to shut it down."

Captain Power rocketed toward the mysterious device, with his balled fists extended and slammed into a force field that instantly repelled him, sending him careening through the sky.

Solaron raced after him and caught him in a glowing golden ball of solar energy.

"Are you okay Cap?"

Captain Power rubbed his head in annoyance, "I've been better. What I am now is annoyed. Be right back."

Cap streaked upward, disappearing almost instantly. Beyond the edge of space he turned around and accelerated wildly. Akin to a fiery comet he blazed back into the atmosphere, streaking unerringly toward his target.

Solaron instinctively covered his eyes, even though the plastic face shield automatically tinted on his light armored suit instantly when Captain Power slammed into the force field. The explosion was made up of pure white light so bright it was stunning and blinding.

"Cap!" Solaron shouted. He scoured the area where the power house had collided with the force field. But then Solaron realized that there was now a gaping hole in the hull of the machine.

"Did he go inside of it? Cap! Cap do you copy me?"

In answer, Caps limp form was hurled from the huge device, to land at Solaron's feet.

Out of the hull of the device leapt a creature out of nightmares to land a dozen feet away from Solaron. It was dark burgundy in color, with a huge over bite. Its bottom jaw jutted out and ended in upward tusks. Stringy long black hair covered its skull. It was massively muscled and bare chested with a large crackling mace in its hand. It wore nothing save a loin cloth. The beast-like creature snarled at Solaron, "Your strong man was as of nothing compared to Malkatrar's might."

"Well he did just drop down from orbit and crush your force field and then the hull of this device. What are you doing here, 'Malkatrar' was it? Who are you and who sent you?" Sol demanded.

"Bah you must be the puny Solaron I have heard so much about. My employer warned me about you as well as this one." He kicked ice and snow at the unconscious Captain Power.

Solaron's eyes became slits, "You didn't answer my question. Who sent you here?"

The horrible creature laughed, a decidedly unfunny sound that came out as more of a snort, "Who do you think earthman? General Zaring of course."

Solaron didn't hesitate, he immediately fired twin high density beams at Malkatrar and knocked him flying through the air, and into a cliff of ice.

Immediately he began to check Captain Power's unmoving form over, "Wake up Cap, I need you." he implored.

Without warning the mace carried by Malkatrar shot through the air and exploded into Solaron's side, sending him tumbling away.

Sol was on his hands and knees, shaking his head, trying to clear it when Malkatrar leaped from the icy cliff and grasped him by the neck, then heaved him skyward until he was face to face with the grotesque creature.

"Is that the best you can do little earthman?" Malkatrar bellowed.

"Not by a longshot, mister."

Sol instantly glowed with solar energy that exploded away from him, shoving his enemy fifty feet in stunned shock.

Solaron quickly set himself, aimed both hands and fired. This time with searing medium density bolts. Instantly Malkatrar backed up, shielding his face from the vicious onslaught.

Solaron dropped his aim down to the ice beneath his enemies' feet, turning it to vapor in an eye blink. Caught off guard, Malkatrar fell through the now liquid former ice and disappeared.

Solaron raced to his friends side, landing softly he shook the big man again and again, "Get up Cap, I have a feeling I'm going to need you."

The ice beneath his feet exploded upward from below as Malkatrar separated the two men by placing himself between them.

Sol was on his back on the ice, but he was far from down for the count.

"I've about had it with you, monster." Without hesitation Solaron again hit Malkatrar with his high density blasts, sending him rolling through the sky, to land several hundred feet away.

Cap was beginning to stir, but Solaron was not hesitating any longer.

Sol was immediately airborne and like a missile, he flew into Malkatrar with his fists glowing, sheathed in high density solar energy.

"What does that device do, Malkatrar? No more games." Solaron shouted, while hitting the big alien under the chin with a powerful uppercut. Solaron was rocket assisting his punches now, adding thrust out the back of his gauntlet for added impact. His right cross lifted the brute from his feet and again sent him haphazardly tumbling through the air.

"Why'd Zaring send you here, Malkatrar? Why do you even know about me and Hyperforce? What is your mission?"

"My mission, you little scrawny fool, is to either maim or kill whoever showed up here at the furthest kill site. Those who showed up at the closer of the two kill site's got to deal with General Zaring himself. Ha! That Zaring, he's a tactical genius. He knew you two big lugs with all your speed an' power would come here first leaving the rest of your team to take on the second site. When they landed there they must have had the shock of their lives. Zaring took an entire strike team down with him, and without your power to back up the weaker members of your team, well, it's probably a blood bath there now."

"You sunova-" golden solar blasts exploded from Solaron's gauntlets, knocking Malkatrar across the barren, frozen landscape.

Almost instantly the brutish alien hurled his energy mace back at Solaron, knocking him sliding across the ice.

Solaron slid to a stop and shook his head groggily, '*If not for my energy field as well as this lightweight armor I'd probably be unconscious at the least.*'

Solaron turned toward his teammate. Captain Power was just getting to his feet and anger was written all over his face. Cap turned toward Malkatrar.

"Cap no!" Solaron's voice shouted across his radio built into his costumes collar, "Take out that machine, its drilling into the Earth's crust. I don't know if it's a real hazard or just a way to draw us to each pole. But we can't take the chance that it's not doing irrevocable damage to the world. You have to take that thing out. Leave the monster with the overbite to me."

"Are you sure?" Cap replied.

"Absolutely, I've got this."

Cap nodded and flew off toward the hovering device.

Sol turned just in time; Malkatrar was on top of him, swinging his crackling energy mace again. Sol avoided most of the impact, receiving only a glancing blow.

'*That still hurt.*' Solaron grunted to himself.

With a blast of solar thrust he was airborne again.

"It's time to turn up the heat Malkatrar, are you ready to get burned?"

Solaron fired twin medium density blasts, at his full heat, holding nothing back; he unleashed his full fury upon Malkatrar.

Captain Power turned back toward his friend and teammate and watched in awe as the area surrounding him began to glow like a star.

259

'He's not holding back at all. This must be more serious than I thought, and I thought it was all pretty damned bad.'

Cap rocketed toward the mile long oval shaped machine. It hummed violently as energy cascaded from it down into the earth. Cap slammed into its side at twenty times the speed of sound, tearing another hole in it. This time he exploded out the other side of it as well. The great machine moved almost a half mile from where it had been hovering from Captain Powers' impact.

Cap circled around it and began attacking it with his force blasts, hammering at it repeatedly.

'This thing is so massive, so dense it may take me hours to demolish it, and once I do I have no idea what might happen to the surrounding area or the Earth for that matter.' Cap paused a moment and thought, a bulb seemingly going on above his head. *'Not here, in space.'*

Now he looped around, flying beneath it and up from below, into the very midst of the energy beam. Searing energies tore at Captain Powers flesh, as he exerted all his prodigious strength and began to force the device upward, absorbing its own mass to power himself as he got set to drive it away from the planet.

"Grrrrrrroaarrr!" he bellowed in both pain and exertion, as he flew upward lifting a million tons of alien hardware and began pushing it toward space.

***

Solaron stared in stunned disbelief as he saw Captain Power lifting the strange machine upward, slowly gaining momentum.

260

"No! What is that fool doing?" Malkatrar roared.

The alien barbarian began to leap toward the machine, when twin high density solar beams blasted him from the sky.

"Where do you think you're going? You and I aren't done yet, monster." Solaron growled.

"You foolish earthman; I will tear you limb from limb." Malkatrar roared.

The big alien hurled his mace at Solaron; but this time Solaron blasted it out of the air and knocked it into an icy glacier.

Solaron flew directly at Malkatrar now; both his fists glowed with energy. He collided with the burgundy skinned alien like a missile, his high density solar energy enclosed fists hammered at the huge brute repeatedly.

"Grrrarr! Begone you fool." Malkatrar back fisted Sol away with a savage swipe of his hand.

But the solar powered superhero righted himself immediately and renewed his barrage upon his foe from mid-air.

"Arrrgggh, do you think to stop me so easily little man? I am undefeatable." Malkatrar roared, as solar beams that could turn steel to liquid splashed against his obviously invulnerable chest.

'He's in pain. There's no way he's taking this much power hurled against him so easily. I have to keep up the assault.'

Solaron drew his arms back behind his head and grimaced with concentration; his hands glowed brighter and brighter. Malkatrar was on all fours struggling to stand after Solaron's last assault. The alien villain shook his head from side to side, working feverishly to clear

261

his thoughts and focus. Slowly he raised his head up, growling like a mad animal. His gaze fell on Solaron, whose hands glowed like twin stars now.

His growl became a full-fledged roar. Malkatrar hurled himself at Solaron, while reaching his hand to his right. Instantly the mace freed itself from where it had become embedded in the ice and returned to his outstretched hand.

Solaron waited an instant longer than stepped forward and brought both hands down, crackling and sparking with energy that fairly exploded outward, engulfing Malkatrar completely with enough heat to melt mountains to slag.

The roaring, deafening onslaught continued for interminably long seconds.

But then a burning, blistered hand reached out from within the attack and grasped Solaron by the throat! His eyes went wide in surprise.

***

At the edge of space, Captain Power concentrated mightily; absorbing mass from the machine he shoved into the void to fuel his own strength.

'I'm going to shove this into the sun, where it'll be destroyed for good. Then I can get back to see if Solaron needs any help.'

Free of Earth's atmosphere Captain Power accelerated a hundred fold and disappeared into the great depths of space between Earth and the sun. The device had long since stopped blasting its strange energy weapon from its underside. Now it was beginning to fall

262

apart under his grip. Absorbing as much of its mass as he could, Cap heaved the massive machine from him, and onto a trajectory that would lead it directly into the sun.

Halfway between the Earth and its glowing star Captain Power turned about and began rocketing back toward earth. His legs trailed rocket thrust as he focused his energy there to race back to his friends' side.

'I've got to get back to Sol. He could be in trouble from that alien bruiser. That 'Malkatrar' seemed to be taking everything Sol threw at him. He took me by surprise when I tumbled through the hull of that machine. If he catches Sol the same way, he might be able to defeat him or worse.'

Cap blazed through the atmosphere now, like unto a comet descending to Earth. Unerringly following his own trail right back to where he started from.

Dropping through the clouds his eyes went wide in surprise as he saw Solaron being held by the throat and choked by his alien adversary. Without hesitation Cap accelerated even more, barreling into Malkatrar with both fists extended. The impact was earth shattering. Solaron broke free and fell to the ground, working immediately to clear the stars from his eyes. He looked up and marveled at Cap connecting with a powerful left. The alien marauder was sent hurtling half a mile and into the very glacier his mace had earlier disappeared within.

"Are you okay?" Captain Power called to Solaron.

"Yes I am, now back off, I've got this. Not that I'm not appreciative of the last minute save, but this guy's mine."

Cap nodded, "I understand Sol. Go kick his ass."

"Thanks for the breather big guy."

Without another word Solaron streaked skyward after his enemy.

Cap shrugged and followed.

Malkatrar fell to the ice and rolled to a stop. He fought to stand, but Solaron sheathed his right fist in high density solar energy and then fired a burst out of the back of the wrist gauntlet. The blow was akin to getting punched in the face by a rocket.

Malkatrar flew through the air and again landed in a heap, sliding across the ice.

Solaron landed at his feet, his demeanor was completely devoid of anything compassionate or forgiving, "What's going on at the north pole? What'd you fools do?"

Cap landed next to Solaron, but silently kept his own council.

Solaron grasped the defeated alien villain by the throat and brought him face to face, "What is Zaring doing?"

Malkatrar laughed, "General Zaring has assuredly captured your people by now, at least the Prince of Exalander."

"What? The home world of Prince Bol-Ton?" Cap asked.

Malkatrar nodded and laughed, "Yes earther, and when he returns there he will be made to fight General Zaring for the right to rule. When Zaring kills him he shall become the one true ruler of Persoma and the ruling family will have changed for the first time in a millennium."

Solaron lifted Malkatrar into the air, "They better be all right, all of them, including Prince Bolton. If not, there isn't anywhere secret enough in the universe to hide you from me."

Malkatrar laughed, "You earthers and your dramatics, it is so refreshing to find a race that loves the sound of its own voices so much."

Touching a stud on the side of the right hand wrist band he wore he continued laughing and faded from view.

"Where'd he go?" Cap roared.

"He teleported. He got away. He must have had a ship hidden somewhere in orbit. He's probably leaving orbit as we speak."

"I'll go after him." Cap began to take off, but Solaron stopped him, "No, forget him; we beat him. He's unimportant now. We have to get to the North Pole quickly; the others may be in trouble."

"Okay, you got it."

"Dragonfly, do you copy? This is Solaron. Dragonfly, respond."

Silence.

"They must be out of range; we're on the other side of the planet."

"It doesn't matter; we bounce the signal off of comm satellites. We should be able to talk to them from anywhere on the planet."

"Then we have to get to them and fast."

"I know Cap let's go and let's not spare the ponies."

"You got it, golden boy."

Both men rocketed skyward, leaving the atmosphere completely and accelerating toward the North Pole so quickly they became blurs to the naked eye.

The two heroes broke the sound barrier many times over, covering the distance between both poles in under two minutes.

They both began to duck back into the atmosphere diving toward the last known coordinates of the rest of the team.

"How are we going to find them? This is a very big area."

"The tracking device in Dragonfly's uniform will lead me right to him. But we have to come within range of it first."

"They're in trouble; we can't waste any more time. We have to find them all before it's too late." Cap added worriedly.

Solaron nodded and began crisscrossing through the frozen arctic sky.

Suddenly the device built into Solaron's right wrist began to beep loudly and glow, a holographic map with several glowing red dots popped.

"I've got them."

"Lead us to them Sol." Cap prodded.

Solaron said nothing and merely turned abruptly left, heading in the direction illustrated above his right sleeve.

"Oh my God." Cap breathed.

"Dragonfly! Randy!" Solaron shouted as he touched down next to the still and smoldering figure of his nephew. One of Dragonfly's underarm wings was torn off.

Creature lie still, his body burned.

Stryker lie unmoving under the wreckage of the Stargrazer.

"The ship, it's demolished."

266

"I know Cap. Help me with Randy; I have to check him out."

Solaron touched the buttons on the surface of his golden metallic costume and an image of Dragonfly appeared with medical readouts, taking the place of the map that was there previously.

"He's alive. His blood pressure is low, and his heart rate is slow but steady."

"Is that all from that tracking device?"

"Hhmm? No. That is bio med data from his suit. I think he's okay from what I see here, merely unconscious."

"Should we wake him?"

"No Cap, help me with Stryker first."

"Okay."

Both men walked over to the wreckage that was the Stargrazer. Now it was a destroyed husk, literally torn in two. Its remains were scattered over a large area around them.

"Look at these blast points, Solaron. Something powerful shot up this ship."

"I saw that. Lift the ship up for me so I can check on Stryker."

Cap lifted the ship and tossed it clear of the battle area. It landed with a loud crash.

Solaron knelt down next to Stryker and examined him a moment then said, "Stryker, wake up."

Strykers' eyes fluttered open slowly, "Wh-where am I?"

"You *were* just under a spaceship." Cap replied.

"Dirty blighters dropped the Stargrazer on me. That was the last thing I remember."

"Who did this to you? What happened here?"

"Who do you think?" answered a voice from behind them. Cap and Sol turned to see Dragonfly walking up holding his right arm gingerly.

"It was Zaring. He had a whole regiment of his soldiers with him. Damned villains."

"They don't think of themselves as villains; probably as just soldiers." Sol answered. Solaron suddenly looked around, snapping his head back and forth as he surveyed the area.

"Where's Silver? I assumed Starbolt was taken, but I don't see Silver anywhere."

"Took...my...sister." Creature growled painfully. He limped to their side. Cap helped Stryker to his feet, who grunted and grit his teeth while rising.

"Are you okay Creature?" Sol asked, and then began giving him a perfunctory look.

Creature slowly shook his head in the negative. "They...took...her."

"We'll get her back, I promise." Sol replied, "We'll get them both back."

"How? We don't even know where they went. And without the Stargrazer we have no way of getting there."

Solaron frowned, "This is far from over. Far from it. We're not finished yet, not by a longshot."

"You have a plan I suppose?" Cap asked.

"I do, but first we have to get back to the solar observatory. I've tried a few times to reach Marcus, and I haven't been able to. Dragonfly, Creature, stand near each other." Solaron adjusted his gauntlets and encased his teammates in a low heat solar bubble.

"You able to fly yet?" he asked Stryker.

"Yeah mate, I am."
"Good, let's go. We have some work ahead of us."

Ralph L. Angelo Jr.

Chapter 12

The road to retaliation

"Umm, you're not even going to ask what happened to the machine they had floating here boring a hole in the ice and melting the ice cap?" Dragonfly inquired.

"No." Solaron replied, "I see its wreckage scattered around us for a mile in every direction. So you took care of it that's all that matters."

"Well, It's how I lost my wing."

"Don't worry about it, I've got a new set back at the base for you, made out of something new I just came up with, called 'solenium'. It's what this light armor I'm wearing is made of. Very tough, very light, basically unbreakable. You won't be losing half a wing again."

"Let's go. We don't know what happened to Marcus yet." Cap ordered.

"Agreed. Stryker take point, Cap you flank me. These guys in the bubble can't help us until I drop it if we're attacked. For now I want them protected as much as possible."

Cap silently nodded and the five men shot skyward, back toward New Jersey.

They raced through the atmosphere, making a bee line toward their base.

Twenty minutes later they touched down. The outside of the observatory was a smoking ruin. Warbots lie in pieces strewn about the lawn, and ARMOR forces were patrolling about the grounds holding exotic weaponry.

271

The team touched down softly and immediately
heard a familiar voice, "You're late to the party."
everyone turned to see Commander Butcher approaching
them, his signature sunglasses in place.

"It looks like you were too." Sol replied.

"Appearances can be deceiving you know."

"So enlighten us Butcher." Cap interjected.

"We were watching your place for trouble, after
Solaron's last message to us, when somethin' dropped
outta the sky-"

"Define 'somethin'." Solaron interrupted.

"I'm gettin' to that. It was a ship, and about twenty
of these goons got outta it. They kicked in yer door an'
went inside. We arrived about three minutes later when
they were dragging this old man out."

"Marcus." Dragonfly looked worriedly at Solaron,
who nodded slowly.

"We attacked 'em. But it was a tough fight. They had
air support from space. I called in some jets of our own
to take care o' these guys in the upper atmosphere, but it
was too late. They drove us back an' took yer guy. They
flew outta here, an' there was nothin' I could do to stop
'em."

Solaron nodded solemnly, "Thanks Garret, I know
you did your best." He extended his hand to Butcher,
who took it and shook heartily.

"That other thing you an' me an' your friend Marcus
have been workin' on? You might wanna come back to
HQ with us. I have a feelin' you're gonna need it."

Solaron brightened immediately, "Do you mean it's
completed? I thought your techno's said it would be a
few weeks before final testing was finished."

"That's the rub, golden boy; it ain't been tested. But it is complete."

"Sol, what are they talking about?" Dragonfly asked.

"Come with us an' find out kid." Butcher replied.

***

An hour later the battered remains of Hyperforce stood in a hanger hidden in Virginia, along with Commander Butcher. Technicians milled about them in the busy hanger, ignoring the super-heroes in their midst.

The entire team along with Butcher stared at the ship that glistened before them.

"Cor! Willya look at this?" Stryker exclaimed.

"Yeah, I'm looking." Dragonfly replied in a hushed voice.

A fifty foot long gleaming white ship stood above them. It was primarily wedge shaped, with the wings softly sweeping back from the forward compartment to the tail.

"Sol, how much did this thing cost you?" Cap asked.

"A lot." replied Solaron.

"An' it would have cost you a sight more if Solaron hadn't agreed for you all to work for us on occasion." Butcher interjected.

Everyone looked at Solaron, who nodded grimly, "It's a good trade off. We're only to be called into action against super-powered or extraterrestrial threats. Stuff the military or the various spy agencies, like A.R.M.O.R. can't handle. Otherwise we get total autonomy and supplies."

"It sounds good for now, but these deals always have a way of doing that until reality strikes." Cap admonished, "You should have consulted with us first, Solaron."

"This keeps us afloat, Cap. As it is I have to raise consulting prices for usage of the observatory. It's a good thing my equipment is top notch and in demand. This deal will take some of the edge off."

Cap nodded slowly, "I hate being in bed with the government."

"I understand. It's not my ideal situation either."

"Relax boys, have I been anything but on the up an' up with you since we met? I'll make sure no one's gonna be takin' advantage of any of you." Butcher replied.

Cap turned toward the ARMOR agent, and furrowed his brow before speaking. He grabbed Butcher by the collar, lifted him into the air, leaving Butchers feet dangling and said, "You better keep this clean. The last thing I ever wanted to do was work for the government as a hired gun, which is *exactly* what this is."

The technicians nearby looked to one another nervously.

"Okay big guy, I get the message." Butcher choked.

"Good. Make sure you remember it." hesitating a second longer Cap lowered Butcher slowly.

Butcher straightened his collar and rubbed his throat, "You've got some grip there, big guy."

"Just remember that as of now we're friends. Work to keep it that way." Cap finished.

"Okay enough of the theatrics." Solaron interrupted, "We have a major problem on hand in case you've forgotten."

"I haven't forgotten anything, Sol. I'm just making sure we don't have another problem forming down the road."

"All right Cap, as of now this is over, and we're all good."

"So what do we call her?" Dragonfly looked at the ship above him.

"Ship." Creature grunted.

"That's a little too plain, don't you think, hairy?"

"What's your suggestion, Dragonfly?" Solaron asked.

"Well it's kinda sharp, and it shines like a sword or something. How about the 'Star Rapier'?"

Stryker chuckled to himself, "Blimey mate, I'm surprised you even know that word."

"I'm not as stupid as you think, Stryker. Besides I fence in school. It's all part of my training."

"Ooo, good ta know mate."

"What do the rest of you think? Does 'Star Rapier' work for you?" Solaron asked.

"It's fine for me." Cap replied.

"I...like...'Ship'." Creature repeated.

"Ha! We know ya furry brute, we know. But I'm fine with 'Star Rapier' as well." Stryker grinned.

"This is all well and good, but we don't even know where we're going. None of us are exactly used to navigating through the stars. We have no idea where the planet Exalander is." Cap reminded them.

"No. But we all know someone who does. It's time to give the 'Star Rapier' a test run."

***

An hour later over a farm in Iowa, the sleek 'Star Rapier' began to settle down in a recently plowed and empty field.

A farmer approximately in his fifties drove his tractor on an adjoining field when he saw the ship settle down. The farmer looked up from the seat of his tractor, a straw hat sat back upon his head and a blade of wheat grass jutted out from between his teeth. He squinted and sighed.

He drove the tractor to the edge of the Star Rapier's landing ramp, stepped off of the tractor and walked toward the sleek ship. He showed no surprise at its arrival; in fact he showed no surprise at all when the five fantastically garbed figures emerged from its confines.

"That doesn't look like him." Captain Power stated flatly.

"It's him; I can see his energy with my spectroscopic vision." Dragonfly replied.

The farmer stood at the base of the Star Rapier's ramp, his arms crossed upon his overall wearing chest and he stared, as if awaiting some response from the costumed heroes assembled on the ramp of the glistening ship.

After several more seconds the older man finally spoke "Well? Are you going to say anything or just stare at me all day? What do you want here, Solaron?"

"We need your help, Nebula-Man."

***

A few minutes later, within the farmhouse the farmer was seated at his kitchen table, a steaming mug of coffee clasped between his hands with Hyperforce standing around the table staring at him.

"How'd you find me?"

Solaron shrugged, "It was difficult, until I came upon the idea of expanding Dragonfly's spectroscopic vision. I ran his vision through several satellites, and narrowed the search to the area that Silver Shadow believed you were originally from. Using the satellite telemetry he was able to pinpoint you by the amount of energy your body was using."

The man who was Nebula-Man chuckled softly to himself, "I'll have to remember to shut down my powers completely after this."

"You won't have to. If you don't want to be bothered again, you won't be. I promise."

Slowly Nebula-Man raised his eyes up from the steaming mug of coffee and met Solaron's gaze. "Why are you bothering me now?"

"Two members of our team were kidnapped."

"I'll wager a guess that it was by General Zaring. I don't see the comely female or the silver garbed boy, Prince Bol-Ton with you. Should I suppose that it was they who were kidnapped?"

"You are correct in that Nebula-Man."

"Jim. As you know, my name in this form was, and is Jim Carroll."

"Is this who you were before you were kidnapped yourself from this world, the world of your birth by aliens?" Solaron questioned.

Jim Carroll stoically nodded negatively, "No, I don't remember what I looked like. This was the face and form of the man who was my father."

"Was this his house?" Dragonfly asked.

Jim Carroll nodded affirmatively, "It was. It is where I grew up also."

"You remembered it?" Cap asked.

"Yes. Some memories were there, others just hidden below the surface. I discover something new about myself every day. This house was abandoned and decrepit. No one had lived in here for many years." He got up and walked over to a fireplace mantle. He picked up a picture that was displayed prominently and showed it to Solaron, "This is my family that I remember."

In the picture was the exact double of the man before them, a smiling and kindly looking older woman and a boy, perhaps twelve years old stood smiling between them.

"That's you?" Captain Power asked gently.

The older man nodded, "It was. This was perhaps the happiest time of my life that I remember. It was ten years later when I was taken away from Earth and from everyone I knew. My parents never knew what happened to me, or where I was. They assumed me dead. I can't say that I blame them. For all intents and purposes I was." He placed the picture back upon the mantle, and turned to face his visitors.

"What do you require of me?"

"You are the only one who knows where Exalander is. We need you to take us there."

"Why should I aid you?"

"Because you were kidnapped yourself from your home; you lost out on your life that might have been, and you became something other than human because someone meddled with your life. Now Silver Shadow

278

has been kidnapped by General Zaring as well as Prince Bolton and his mentor Marcus." Solaron answered.

"Bol-Ton. It is pronounced Bol-Ton." Jim Carroll corrected.

"Very well Jim; Bol-Ton. They've all been taken from this planet by Zaring. Doesn't that seem a bit similar to your own situation?"

Jim Carroll aka Nebula-Man walked slowly about the room looking at the fireplace and then the walls about him.

Solaron continued, "Look Jim, we could use your help, that's all. We've lost two members; you know where this world is in the vastness of space and can lead us to it. We're flying an experimental craft because Prince Bol-Ton's was destroyed by Zaring. We're almost grasping at straws here. I know we didn't get off to the best of starts the last time we met, but you were trying to kill the Prince."

"Not kill, capture. Then bring to justice."

"Which you found to be a lie perpetrated upon you by Zaring. Don't you want a little revenge for him using you like a weapon? He pointed you at a target and expected you to destroy it at his bidding."

"I am above such petty desires." Jim Carroll replied coldly.

"That sounded more like Nebula-Man than Jim Carroll." Captain Power observed.

"Perhaps Nebula-Man is all that remains?"

"Then why all of this?" Captain Power swept his arms around the room.

Jim Carroll shrugged, "Familiarity perhaps?"

Solaron rebuked, "Or because you are remembering on a cellular scale. This was where your life was centered before you were stolen from it. This is where you would have remained and had a life if you were allowed to. But the hand of fate intervened in the form of an unknown alien who took you from what might have been. You've come back to this now. You can remain here forever, happily tilling the soil. But right now we need your help, no; we need Nebula-Man's help. After this we'll never bother you again, I promise."

Jim Carroll sighed, "Very well."

Before the teams stunned eyes Jim Carroll's form twisted and changed, becoming the inhuman Nebula-Man's once again.

"I have a question," Dragonfly began, "What year did these aliens take you?"

"It was 1955." Nebula-Man replied softly.

Hyperforce along with Nebula-Man exited the house. Nebula-Man locked the door with a simple key. The key glowed then and seemed to melt into his open hand afterward. He turned and joined them aboard the Star Rapier. A moment later the ship vertically rose upward then turned and disappeared into the sky.

***

Silver Shadow slowly came to. She held her forehead and moaned quietly, waiting patiently for her vision to regain focus.

"Are you all right?" a familiar voice asked.

She turned toward the voice and recognized Mar-Cus. Behind him chained to a wall was the unconscious Starbolt.

280

"Marcus! How did you get here? What happened?"

"That devil General Zaring took you and Prince Bol-Ton into captivity."

"But how did you get here?"

"Another contingent of his forces raided the observatory. I was no match for his men. They had me before I could react. He planned this exceedingly well. No matter how much I may hate the man, his military mind is brilliant. He separated us all."

"What about the others? My brother and Stryker? Dragonfly?"

"I know not. My communications array was jammed the moment his plans went into effect. He knew to draw off the team into separate challenges. He reasoned perfectly that Captain Power and Solaron would travel to the farthest threat being the fastest among you, well fastest not counting Prince Bol-Ton that is."

"You think he knew Bolton would remain with the rest of us?"

"Of course. He was counting on the two most powerful members of the team leaving the third most powerful with the rest of the team."

"Wait, Marcus, you believe that Starbolt is the third most powerful member of this team? That's saying a lot."

"No Silver, I am saying that everyone else considers him thusly. I am convinced he is the most powerful member."

Marcus' silent gaze fell upon the chained form hanging limply from the wall.

"What'd they do to him?" Silver whispered.

"Drugged him somehow. They are keeping him sedated."

"Wonderful. We're surrounded by a force field barrier of some kind I can't do anything about this. But maybe he can."

Mar-Cus nodded thoughtfully, "He *is* an energy manipulator."

"I'm going to try to contact him telepathically. Maybe I can wake him from this stupor they have him trapped him."

"Be careful Silver Shadow. You do not want to become trapped within his mind. We do not know what they have done to him."

She nodded almost nervously, but then turned and stared at her teammate, her eyes narrowed to slits.

Silver Shadow reached out telepathically, trying to touch Starbolts' mind. After a few seconds her eyes widened, "Contact." she barely breathed.

Almost instantly the world about her disappeared and she felt herself falling into a swirling, psychedelic abyss, "What the hey?" she thought she said aloud, but almost instantly realized she was within the confines of Starbolts' mind.

She saw staggering panorama's of great cities. Skylines with multiple moons and twin suns far off in space. Great green fields that stretched seemingly on forever as well as industrial complexes with factories as far as the eyes could see.

"These are all memories of places he's been to."

Silver floated as the torrent of memories passed by her, staggering her with their depth and breadth.

"So much to process all at once." she covered her face as more rushed by her. *'This is not real. It's nothing but Starbolts' memories. I'm not even really shading my own face. This is all in his mind, and I'm along for the ride. I'm going to try something different. I just hope it doesn't kill me, or leave me catatonic.'*

Steeling herself, Silver changed tactics and flew into the flood of memories. They passed over her, inundating her with Starbolt's life experiences thus far. But now she ignored them and flew deeper toward their center. Like ghosts they passed about her, immaterial things that could neither touch nor harm her.

Flying on for what seemed to be an interminably long time she burst through the last of the memories, those memories included her, her teammates and their battle with General Zaring, who appeared gigantic and terrible in Starbolt's mind like some crazed green boogeyman with claws and teeth dripping blood.

'That's what he sees Zaring as; a monster. It makes sense though, from everything Starbolt told us, that's exactly what he is.'

She flew straight through the grasping, cackling form of Zaring and landed softly on a grassy field behind the solar observatory. Many times in the past few months she lied down in that field and watched the sky overhead in quiet moments. Now Silver Shadow saw Starbolt sitting in a cross legged position, staring down at the grass at his feet. She approached him cautiously, standing in front of him silently for a moment. He ignored her, never looking up or acknowledging her presence.

Finally she spoke, "Prince Bol-Ton, it's me, Silver Shadow. I've come to take you out of here. You're trapped in your own mind. I don't know what Zaring did to you, but you have to snap out of it and return with me to the real world."

He continued to sit there facing down with his eyes closed, "You're not really here." he grumbled, "You're just a memory intruding upon my refuge."

"No Starbolt, I am here. I can help you break free of whatever Zaring did to you to put you here. No matter if it was drugs or some psychic attack. I can free you." she held out her hand to him. He slapped it away.

"You do not understand." he replied sharply, "Zaring did nothing but prove to me the folly of my own ways. I thought I could beat him. I thought I could gain allies and save my family. He outsmarted us at every turn. He knew how to separate my newfound friends and weaken us. I was lying to myself. I never had a chance against him."

Without hesitation Silver Shadow slapped him across the face. He looked up abruptly, stunned by her reaction.

"Stand up and stop feeling sorry for yourself. If what you just said was the truth, that you did this to yourself, and Zaring did nothing to trap you like this within your own mind, you're an embarrassment to not only yourself but to the man who trained you as well. You failed him if this is your reaction to having your back up against the wall. Now snap out of it, dammit."

Starbolt looked at her incredulously, "Silver? Are you really here? In my mind?"

"Damn straight I am, mister. Now wake up and get your act together. This is not over yet, not by a long shot.

No matter what happened back there, do you really think Solaron is going to let this be the end of it? Do you think my brother is just going to stand idly by and watch me be kidnapped away to another planet?"

"But the Stargrazer was destroyed by Zaring's marauders. How are they going to follow after us?"

"Solaron will find a way. Besides, he was building something with Commander Butcher, another ship based on the Stargrazer designs. Bigger and made of a new material he had recently developed that is almost indestructible. Marcus was helping him with the engine designs."

"How do you know all of this?"

She touched the side of her forehead and smiled, "I'm a telepath, remember?"

"You really are here?"

"I am." she nodded.

"And you have not given up hope?"

"No, not at all. We'll get out of this, I promise you."

"They took Mar-Cus as well."

"I know Starbolt, he's here with me. He's fine. But we can't get out of here without your help. We need you to return to the real world and to stop hiding in your memories."

She held out her hand to him once again. This time he took it and closed his own upon hers with a strong grip.

"Now close your eyes."

Starbolt did as he was bade.

A moment later Silver spoke again, "Now open them."

Starbolt was startled. He was standing in a room, chained to a wall. Mar-Cus stood staring at him smiling. Silver Shadow stood next to Mar-Cus.

"Are you all right my liege?" Mar-Cus asked.

"I-I am Mar-Cus. I must break free of these fetters though."

"Solar beams." Starbolt spoke, almost matter of factly.

Solar rays shot out of his fingers and he aimed each hand at the opposing wrist, melting the shackle to slag instantly.

He dropped down from the wall where he was hanging weakly, and fell to one knee. Mar-Cus and Silver rushed to his side to help him up.

"Prince Bol-Ton?" Mar-Cus asked worriedly.

"I am fine Mar-Cus; I require a moment that is all."

"Very well my Prince." But Mar-Cus stood by the prince's side and slowly helped him to his feet anyway.

"Thank you Mar-Cus." Starbolt turned toward Silver Shadow, "What has happened here? Can you tell me what's transpired since I last saw consciousness?"

"The battle in the arctic was fierce. General Zaring had troops aiding him. You were attempting your Starbolt energy wave and they attacked you, knocking you unconscious. Stryker was doing his best to take out as many as possible but he was overwhelmed by their sheer numbers. Dragonfly threw his wings into the spinning turbine-like wheel at the center of that device that was drilling into the earth and it exploded. Creature was tearing through troops, both armored and super-powered. Finally he met up with an armored foe unlike the rest. This one had his own powered suit. It was really

different from the others. It wasn't a cookie cutter suit
like the rest. He beat Creature easily, throwing him
aside. Then Stryker attacked him; this fight was a little
closer. Stryker's speed and strength seemed like more
than a match for this guy. But he shot something out of
his hands that paralyzed Stryker, at least that's what it
seemed like. The next thing I knew he picked up the
Stargrazer and smashed it down on Stryker. The ship
was in pieces and Stryker was out cold, or dead. I don't
know which."

"He is tough, Silver Shadow, I am certain he is fine."
Mar-Cus replied.

"I wish I had your faith in his powers, Mar-Cus, but
sadly I don't. I just hope he and my brother are okay."

"What do we do now?" Starbolt asked, quickly
changing the subject.

"We have to get out of here." Mar-Cus answered.

"I think I can help with that." Starbolt announced,
"Both of you stand back I'm going to destroy these force
field barriers holding us captive."

Beyond the force field walls were just empty
hallways.no one stood guard over the captives.

Starbolt raised his hands and shouted, "Energy
disruptors!" Multi-hued beams blasted from his hands
colliding with the barrier that encircled them.

Almost just as quickly energy rained down from the
ceiling above them, rendering them all insensate.

The three people lie upon the floor twitching, but
barely moving otherwise.

After a moment General Zaring slowly walked up to
the cell outside of the barrier, his hands clasped behind
his back, a bemused look upon his visage, "Did you truly

think I would allow you to escape? You must be more of an idiot then I gave you credit for."

Starbolt's eyes stared daggers through the man.

"Ah there is something different about you now. I see. You do not fear me as you once, even recently, did. Good I am glad to see this. When the time comes perhaps you'll die like a man instead of a mewling weakling."

Starbolt's lips trembled as he fought to say something in return, but he could not speak.

"Perhaps you wonder why you cannot move or speak for that matter? Very well I will indulge all of your curiosities. Those rays that descended upon you all are a variation of the energy that fuels my neural axe. That is the reason you are all so helpless at the moment and were in such pain. Even your vaunted Captain Power could not stand up to my neural axe's energies. I will leave you all to your rather painful writhing's upon the floor. They should wear off in the next hour or so. At which point you will all fall unconscious from exhaustion, if you haven't already by then."

Zaring turned and walked away, his hands still clasped behind his back.

***

The 'Star Rapier' exited Earth's atmosphere blanket and began to accelerate greatly. Within its confines were Solaron, Dragonfly, Captain Power, Stryker, Creature, Nebula-Man and one other person, Commander Butcher.

Solaron and Butcher sat in the first two seats behind the controls. Behind them sat Dragonfly and Stryker. In the next row sat Captain Power and Nebula Man. Finally, behind them sat Creature.

Nebula-Man turned toward Captain Power, "You do not trust me."

"Are you reading my mind?"

"No Captain, I am merely stating what is already obvious to everyone here."

"If you're truthful with us, you don't have anything to fear from me."

"Captain, I do not fear you anyway. Remember, you came to me for aid. I was very happy upon my ancestral farm. I had no interest in leaving, ever."

Dragonfly turned around in his seat and stared at Nebula-Man, "Really?" he asked, "You can fly through space, and you'd be happy staying on Earth, on a farm?"

"Young Dragonfly, space is empty and more times than not, a very lonely place. My vast abilities allowed me the freedom to explore space from as far across as could possibly be imagined. Yet I saw the same things everywhere I went. The faces were different, but the story was always the same. There was injustice and cruelty wherever I went. It was not simply relegated to Earth. Mankind is not alone in its base behavior. There are many other worlds whose cruelties far surpass humanities."

"I thought you didn't remember much o' yer time on good ol' Earth, mate?"

Nebula-Man turned toward Stryker, "I do not. I have been back upon my natural-born world a few weeks now, and by ingesting everything I can about our world my understanding of it has grown immensely."

"So you think of us as fellow natives of the same world." Solaron called back from the pilot's seat.

"We are Solaron. I may have been gone for over half a century, but the Earth is my home too. I will continue to endeavor to learn all I can about the planet, as well as how best I can serve and protect it."

"So yer like a cop, eh mate?"

"You mean an interstellar peace officer, Stryker? I suppose that is a clear enough description of what I consider myself."

"So you go around righting wrongs on different worlds?" Solaron asked.

"Yer a regular 'Robin Hood' antcha?"

"I do not understand that term, Stryker."

"Robin Hood was a historical figure and thief who supposedly lived in Sherwood Forest in England, after losing all his own lands to an unscrupulous sheriff. He began to 'steal from the rich and give to the poor' in order to set things right in the land where he lived. Driven from his home, he and many other refugee's built homes hidden in Sherwood Forest; a dense forest that would keep him hidden for many years to the Sheriff of Nottingham's ire. He and his 'merry men' would harangue the sheriff and his own forces until they freed Sherwood Forest from the ruthless and corrupt sheriff's grasp."

"You feel I am like this 'Robin Hood' in some way because I seek to use my power to aid those who cannot help themselves?"

"That's as good a way to describe what you do as any I suppose." Solaron added.

Slowly the pale white skinned being nodded its head in the affirmative, "I suppose you are correct. Though I have not made it my mission to simply 'rob from the rich and give to the poor', no, my mission is to defeat threats deemed too dangerous for anyone else to deal with."

"I suppose," Captain Power replied, "but you're going to have to be a bit more discerning if you don't want to continually repeat the mistakes you've made already."

"What mistakes have I made?"

"Attacking us is one of them. God only knows how many others have fallen before you over the years."

Nebula-Man shrank back into his seat, deflated.

"You give me much to consider, Captain Power."

"That you even are considering it is a start, and a good one, Nebula-Man."

The strange looking being nodded his head in thanks.

"All right back there," Solaron began, "we're ready to try the jump to ultra-warp speed. Everyone buckle in."

The heroes assembled did as they were asked. Commander Butcher looked back over his shoulder at Nebula-Man before turning back to Solaron, "This guy sounds like he's got more than a few screw's loose."

Sol nodded in agreement and then replied, "He may sound and look off the wall, but believe me, he has the power to back up whatever he says."

Butcher grimly nodded once himself and then answered, "I know; I read the reports Sol. The guys a walking time bomb. Maybe we should take more precautions with him."

"No, he'll become suspicious. I believe he's telling the truth this time, and is seeking to make amends for attacking us, but no matter what we have to bear in mind that he isn't really an earthman, even though his lineage is definitely from our world, physically and mentally, he's been changed by what he faced."

"Well, I'm just glad he's on our side is all." Butcher slumped back into his high back chair and sat there quietly in deep thought.

"You and I both, Commander Butcher." Sol replied.

He turned around to face the rest of the crew, "Are you all prepared? We'll be jumping in five, four, three, two, one, ignition!"

The Star Rapier leapt forward, throwing everyone else back in their seats. Within a nimbus of lights the ship disappeared.

Dragonfly inquired, "Umm, I have to ask Sol; how'd you make this work?"

Solaron smiled, "It wasn't easy, Dragonfly. We copied the Stargrazer's technology and power plant configuration. I expanded on it slightly. It's a larger more powerful version of that engine."

"What's the power source?" Cap asked.

"Commander Butcher, I'll leave that to you." Sol replied.

"Gee thanks Goldenboy. The thing that's powerin' this is some kinda quantum whatsis that our techs were able to duplicate on the weightless portion of the space station, with Solaron's help o'course."

Cap nodded, "But of course."

Stryker interrupted, "One other thing mate, you mentioned a space station?"

"Yeah, we got a hidden and fully functional space station in earth's orbit. An' by fully functional I mean

292

it's armed to the teeth, an' is s'posed ta be our first line o' defense against anything from out there. Any other questions?" Butcher turned in his seat to stare at Stryker.

"No mate, you answered the most important one. But I have to say, so far you guys are battin' a thousand." Stryker replied, grinning.

"Glad to have been o' service." Butcher turned back around and faced forward. "Mook." he muttered.

Creature grunted, "How…long?"

"Until we arrive on Exalander?" Solaron asked.

Their hirsute member nodded slowly.

Solaron turned toward Nebula-Man, "Nebula-Man?"

"Two days at our current speed."

"Speaking of speed, I mean to ask, just how fast are we going?" Dragonfly inquired.

"In essence a hundred thousand times faster than light speed." Nebula Man replied before anyone else could.

"You knew that by the seat of your pants alone?" Solaron asked curiously, "You're not seated near any controls or monitors."

"Yes Solaron, I can tell how fast we are going just by your ships disturbance of the ether."

"That doesn't make any sense to me." Dragonfly announced.

"It was not meant to. Suffice to say, my cosmic senses allow me several added benefits your earth born perceptions cannot hope to match."

"Rriiiggghht." Dragonfly replied.

"You all might as well relax and sit back. In fact if you want to get situated in the cabins in the back now might not be a bad time to go get comfortable. We have a long journey ahead of us all."

"If you don't mind I'm going to stay right here for a while and watch the stars go by. This is something I never thought I'd see." Cap answered.

"Yeah, same here Sol." Dragonfly added.

"Why did you not believe you would see such a sight as star passage?" Nebula-Man asked Captain Power, "You are aware you can break the light speed barrier on your own, correct?"

"What? What are you talking about?"

"Your abilities. They give you the means to shatter the light speed wall to faster than light space flight. Surely you must have known this?"

"If I knew it would I have been this surprised by you telling me this right now?" Cap replied testily.

Nebula-Man shrugged, "I do not know, would you? You are not the only one of your friends to be able to do so as well. Solaron can fly faster than light also, though his approach to it is simpler and cleaner than yours would be."

"What does that even mean?"

"You will have to shatter the barrier with your great strength as you approach it. You will feel it in your path barring you. When you reach ninety nine point nine percent of light speed you will feel a barrier in your way. You will essentially be bouncing off of the light speed barrier. Once you feel that barrier resisting you, you must pull back and shatter it with your prodigious might. It should look quiet spectacular actually."

"What about Sol? How does he get through it?"

"Solaron's access to the realm of space that exists in the dimension beyond light speed will be easier for him. Like myself, he can use energy for many purposes. Since much of his makeup is akin to a star, he can use that energy to simply fly into the beyond light speed dimension."

"So where I have to brute force my way in, he can finesse his way to faster than light travel?"

Nebula-Man nodded, "Indeed Captain Power, that is a rather succinct explanation of the matter, but nonetheless it is accurate."

Butcher snorted, "Well ain't that just interestin' on all kinds o' levels?"

Dragonfly turned toward Creature and said, "This is gonna be a long two days."

Creature slowly nodded in agreement, "Doesn't matter...Whatever...it...takes. I must...save...my sister."

"We will Creature, I promise." Solaron answered.

"Well, I for one am lookin' forward to this. A whole 'nother world. This is gonna be special on so many levels." Butcher commented, while checking one of his guns.

"It is a huge and complex universe out there Commander Butcher." Nebula-Man began, "It is far more intricate a place than you can imagine. There are...dangers hidden in obvious places as well as wonders that would boggle the human mind."

"But you were human, weren't ya?"

Nebula-Man nodded affirmatively, "I still consider myself as such, at least since my past history was revealed to me by Silver Shadow, which by the way is another reason I am accompanying you to rescue her. She revealed my long forgotten past to me, and helped to clear my hindered mind. That is truly why I am going along with you all to rescue her; to repay her gift to me."

"We appreciate that, Nebula-Man." Solaron replied, "Without your input we'd have no idea where to even begin."

The strange, pale white faced being nodded once again, "I will aid you, Solaron. Of that you can have no doubt. You have my word. For this mission at least we are allies."

Now it was Solaron's turn to nod stoically and turn back toward the front of the ship.

Captain Power looked at Nebula-Man who continued to sit calmly next to him for a moment, and then he finally spoke, "Let me ask you something; did you enjoy farming?"

"Yes Captain, I did. I found it…therapeutic."

Creature turned toward Dragonfly and muttered, "Yes Dragonfly… you were…correct. A…*very* long…two days."

Chapter 13

Ten against a world

Seven figures walked amongst the milling throngs upon the streets of Exalander's capital city of Prespigus. Most wore hoods up over their heads and faces, swathed in raggedy cloaks and nondescript garments they blended in with the masses who all walked toward an outdoor arena that it seemed everyone was going toward.

Two suns hung in the sky. One cool and blue, the other a bright, fierce yellow. Tall, stunningly modern buildings stretched as far as the eye could see, and the streets were paved with an unfamiliar, yet soft black material that flexed comfortably underfoot.

Under a cloak Solaron turned toward the man walking next to him, Nebula-Man, who had altered his appearance, as he had on Earth when he appeared as a farmer, so he simply appeared as an aristocratic old man with a grey van dyke and a full head of shaggy hair. His garments were finery compared to the rest of the team, but no one gave any of them a second glance.

"Are you sensing anything?" Solaron asked him.

"I have touched Silver Shadow's mind. She is here somewhere. I did not want to startle her by probing too deeply."

"Can you link us psychically as Silver has done in the past?"

Nebula-Man nodded once.

Instantly their minds were connected together.

'Whoa, I'm not sure I'm likin' this invasion o' me privacy, mate.'

297

'Relax Stryker, whatever secrets you may have are safe.' Solaron replied.

'Besides, what would you want to hide from us anyway?' Captain Power asked testily.

'Enough, both of you.' Sol's mental voice interceded, *'Job at hand gentlemen.'*

'Agreed mate.'

'Good, let's find Silver, Marcus and Starbolt and get the hell out of here.' Cap replied.

Dragonfly looked about himself cautiously, *'I don't think I can get used to being on an alien world like this. I'm completely out of place.'*

'Relax Dragonfly it could be worse. So far no one has been hostile toward us at all' Cap added.

'That ain't gonna stay that way for long you know.' Butcher offered.

'I know Commander. We have to all be ready for it when it all hits the fan.' Sol replied.

'Gentlemen, I have found them both. They are below the ground in this arena. From what I have been able to ascertain, General Zaring is looking to make a spectacle of defeating Starbolt and cementing his role as supreme leader.'

'What about Starbolt's parents?' Cap asked.

'I have not touched their minds previously to this, so I cannot find them as easily. But I will continue to endeavor to find them.'

Solaron pulled his hood up tighter around his head. The group was approaching the entrance to the great outdoor arena.

'This is gonna be bad.' Dragonfly psychically grunted.

Nebula-Man warned, _'Keep your heads down and stay toward the center of the throng moving toward the wide arena gates. Make sure all your mechanical units are powered down. I will mask us as best I can.'_

Creature walked with his head down low and a large cloak thrown over his shoulders that dragged on the ground to hide his shaggy form.

But there were many others dressed similarly and of equal or even greater bulk than the hirsute Hyperforcer.

The group of seven made their way into the arena and up some rows of seats that were very similar to seats in a baseball stadium. They sat in two rows, four directly behind three.

'So far this has been easier than I thought, an' believe me, that's got me nervous.' Commander Butcher offered.

'I can understand why Commander. I'm feeling the same trepidation.' Solaron replied.

Nebula-Man answered, _'There is no need for nervousness, my comrades. Stay strong, for I sense this affair is headed toward its final resolution.'_

'I just hope it's in our favor.' Cap huskily replied.

'If we retain our heads and act calmly in what is to come we should be fine.'

'I'm not sure if I feel so confident with that kind of comment.' Dragonfly mused.

'Look!' Creature's gruff psychic voice exploded in all their minds, _'It is Silver!'_ He continued to shout psychically.

They all followed the aim of his mental finger and saw her sitting at the front row next to the man they all immediately recognized as

'Zaring.' grunted Captain Power.

'Remain calm, Captain. We should not give away our identities at this early juncture.'

'I agree, Nebula-Man. You don't have to worry about me.'

'I am not. I was merely stating the obvious to calm my own nervousness.'

'You nervous? You look as solid as a rock.'

'Nonetheless I am cautious of all of this. While I believe very little of the armament present here could harm any of us-myself especially, as well as you, Captain- we should still err on the side of caution until we can tell for certain where Starbolt is.'

'I can answer that,' Dragonfly interrupted, *'Look!'*

Everyone turned toward where he mentally urged them. Their hearts all stuck in their throats as Starbolt was dragged in chains out to the arena.

His once splendid costume was tattered and filthy. His cape was shredded. He bore dried scabs on his exposed flesh as if he had been beaten. In short he looked like hell.

Dragonfly looked at his uncle quizzically, *'Why didn't he just break free with his powers?'*

'Zaring probably either drugged him or threatened to kill Marcus and Silver if he didn't cooperate, or both.' Sol replied.

'That makes sense; Marcus and Silver wouldn't be covered by that clause concerning his parents.' Cap replied.

'That's right. That explains why he went back to the observatory for Marcus also. More leverage against Starbolt.' Solaron added.

300

'Look mates; the big ugly is standin' up an' pointin' at our boy.'

Hyperforce, along with the thousands more packed into the modern arena turned toward Zaring, who was now standing and pointing at Starbolt. In an amplified voice that carried throughout the arena as well as being broadcast throughout the realm by hovering camera drones, General Zaring proclaimed loudly and with much pomp and circumstance, "I challenge you, Prince Bol-Ton to trial by combat for your seat as the head of state and future leader of Exalander."

"I don't get it," Dragonfly whispered in Solaron's ear, "Can't everyone see that Starbolt's been beaten an' maybe tortured by his clothes being in tatters?"

'It does not matter Dragonfly; the challenge has been issued, and now must be met or full forfeiture by way of lineage is imminent.' Nebula-Man's voice rang through Dragonfly's mind.

'What can we do?' Stryker asked.

'For now we have to wait. We'll know when to make our move. We're not going to let Starbolt get killed here.' Solaron replied.

Suddenly a new voice interceded in their thoughts. New but very familiar, *'Solaron? Dragonfly? Is that you?'*

'Silver?' Creature replied first, anxiously.

'It is you! How'd you get here? How are you talking telepathically?'

'We'll explain everything once you're all safe. Are you okay?' Solaron replied.

'I've been better, but they beat up poor Bol-Ton.'

'Zaring did?'

301

'No, the coward had his loyal thugs do it while Bol-Ton was drugged so he couldn't use his powers against them.'

'That doesn't surprise me.' Solaron concluded.

'We should tear this place apart right now.' Cap said, *'I've had enough of watching this freak show. They're going to make a spectacle of Zaring taking on Starbolt, and the kid's in no kind of shape to take this guy down.'*

'That's not the only problem. We don't know where Marcus is.' Silver Shadow added.

'How do we go about finding him?' Dragonfly questioned.

'I believe I can do that.' replied Nebula-Man.

Solaron turned toward him, *'But you never met him. How can you find him?'*

'Through your perceptions of him. I already know what he looks like and who he is through your memories. I can find him and free him. I will apprise you of the situation when I have him in my care.'

Solaron nodded slowly, *'Be careful Nebula-Man. If you need our help call.'*

'Rest assured Solaron, if I need your aid you will know it in quite a spectacular display.'

Captain Power grimaced, *'Just be careful and don't be shy about asking for help if you have to.'*

'I will not, Captain. On that you have my word.'

With that Nebula-Man stood up and walked down and off of the bleachers disappearing into the milling crowd. His own disguise was his ability to change shape and take on the form of whoever he chose to look like,

302

now he used it to look like one of the security personnel who moved freely through the arena.

***

Up above in the stands Captain Power sat uncomfortably, almost twitching for action.

'What's the matter?' Dragonfly asked.

'We're out of our depth here kid. We're more miles from home, from Earth than I can count, and we're about to take on an entire world. Our team is separated all around this arena. If not for Nebula-Man hiding our approach I have no idea how'd we even land here to get this close to Silver and Starbolt.'

Solaron interjected, *'No doubt Nebula-Man helped us greatly. Without him all of this would have been much more difficult. But we are here. We've come this far, not because of anyone or any other reason than who we are. We are Hyperforce. That alone is going to make all the difference on this world or any. Believe in that, because I surely do.'*

Captain Power stared at Solaron for only an instant before nodding in agreement, *'Oh I do Sol, don't doubt that. I have total faith in our own powers and abilities, no matter where we are. When we decide to break all hell loose here, we have to stay together. Don't get separated at all and use our powers to keep these guards off their game, but try not to kill any if we can. That's going to go a long way toward us proving that we're the good guys.'*

'Ey mate! Eyes front, we got some action 'bout to start.'

'Where is my sister?' Creature asked.

'No hesitation in your thoughts now eh?' Solaron inquired.

'No, I've become comfortable thinking this way. No more hesitation. It is…uncomfortable for me to talk usually. At times even painful. But we can talk about all that later. Right now I just want to find my sister.'

'I'm here, right next to this madman General Zaring.' Silver Shadow replied, *'He has soldiers hidden in the crowd with weapons aimed at me so I can't hit him with a stun bolt without being shot by one of his men. I'll need a distraction to escape.'*

'Okay Silver, we'll give you all of the distraction you'll need in a few minutes, I'm sure.'

'I'll be waiting.' She replied tersely.

Zaring leaped over the fifteen foot wall and landed in the arena floor. His armored suit's boot jets slowed his landing in a cloud of airborne dirt and dust. He began to walk toward the kneeling Starbolt who was looking down at the ground beneath his feet.

"Face me, Prince Bol-Ton. For the sake of honor I will defeat you in combat. Then I will rule this world and steer our people on a corrected course toward a brave destiny worth fulfilling."

Slowly Bol-Ton raised his beaten, bruised countenance up to stare disgustedly at Zaring, "You are a mad dog, General Zaring. You seek to turn our peaceful world into a machine of war that would cross the cosmos spreading fear and intimidation, and yes, death. I will not allow that."

Starbolt stood, shakily but defiantly. He glared his hatred at Zaring, "Do your worst monster. You'll never

304

defeat me in a fair fight. We both know that. You've already had me beaten repeatedly by your loyal thugs. My body may be damaged, but not my spirit. I will lay waste to you General Zaring, no matter the cost."

"Then prepare to die, Prince Bol-Ton, for I will have your head and your throne!" Zaring hurled his neural axe at Starbolt, and the battle began in earnest.

Starbolt ducked and rolled shakily to his left barely avoiding the glowing axe, which turned around in flight and returned to Zaring's hand, all the while crackling and spitting energy.

"Why doesn't he fight back?" Dragonfly hissed.

"He must be drugged in some way yet. Either that or he's too worried about Marcus." Solaron whispered.

'What about his parents?' Creature asked.

'What about them, Silver?' Solaron asked, *'Has he had any contact with them since you arrived here?'*

'They came to see him, under a neutral guard. The king's men as well as Zaring's, so everyone was safe and accorded from brutality.'

'Was he beaten after that?' Captain Power asked.

'That had to have just happened. He was fine when I last saw him.' Silver answered.

"Look!" shouted Stryker. He pointed at the arena, where Starbolt was backpedaling across the dirt floor. Zaring was burying his neural axe to its handle in the dirt with every swing, looking to cleave Starbolt in two.

Captain Power began to stand but Solaron grabbed his arm. Cap looked down at his friend incredulously, "I can't stand by and watch the kid get killed, I've had enough of this." he yanked his arm free of Solaron.

"Cap just wait; Nebula-Man can free Marcus, he has too. If we attack before then the old man is dead. Bolton at least has a chance against Zaring." Sol breathed, "We won't let Starbolt die, I promise you. I'll put a hole in Zaring's chest from here if I have to."

Both men turned back toward the arena, where Zaring was now playing with Starbolt, swinging the axe to either side of him cleaving the ground and making him scurry like a rat.

Starbolt gritted his teeth and grimaced for a second while evading another slice of the sparking blade, then shouted "Force blast!"

Energy leapt from both his hands slamming into Zaring like a runaway freight train. He flew backward across the arena to collide with the wall, cracking it and actually going through it. He disappeared from sight under the bleachers.

Starbolt immediately collapsed from the exertion.

Instantly the crowd was on its feet cheering and clapping with a deafening volume.

Slowly, painfully, Starbolt regained his feet, audibly groaning in pain. He stood unsteadily in the center of the arena as the crowds roar reached an ear splitting crescendo.

But then the neural axe exploded outward from where Starbolt had hurled the axe and its owner. It slammed into Starbolt with the heavy blunt side of its head, paralyzing him with its horrific energies!

Zaring followed it, his boot jets roaring loudly in the confines of the open air arena. Rage colored his face a bright red. He careened into Starbolt and carried him across to the other side of the circular arena crushing him painfully against the wall.

Zaring held Starbolt close by the throat and growled in a voice only the two of them could hear. "You dare to fight back against me, whelp? Have you forgotten what I said would happen to your teacher?"

Starbolt said nothing, but instead spit contemptuously in Zaring's face.

"You dare?" Zaring hurled the boy from him. Starbolt rolled across the dirt arena coming to a stop in a huddled heap.

Slowly Starbolt turned to face his enemy, "Yes Zaring, you dog, I dare. If Mar-Cus must die to stop your madness then so be it. I know he would do so gladly to end your insane plans and machinations."

Starbolt stood now and faced his foe on shaky legs.

'He's dead on his feet. Zaring's gonna slaughter him.' Dragonfly warned.

'I don't think we can wait any longer, Sol.' Cap cautioned.

'I think you're both right. We haven't heard from Nebula-Man and we can't let this go on much more. Zaring is going to kill Prince Bol-Ton if we continue to hesitate.'

Solaron stood up, throwing the concealing robes from his shoulders. Captain Power, Dragonfly, Commander Butcher and Stryker did the same. Creature merely stood up and howled menacingly. A howl that reverberated throughout the arena. All heads turned toward the heroes from Earth, while General Zaring continued to close on the unsteady Starbolt.

Then, the ground between the two opponents exploded upward in a shower of dirt, steel and concrete, along with a hurtling burgundy skinned brute at the end of Nebula-Man's fist.

"What?" shouted a surprised General Zaring.

"Now!" roared Solaron, "It's showtime."

"Finally!" bellowed Captain Power, "Sol, look, it's that Malkatrar monster we faced in the Antarctic. I'm going for Zaring."

Cap rocketed away from the bleachers and directly at the armored General, "Zaring! Leave the boy alone!" Cap slammed into the surprised Zaring with earth shattering force. His right cross sent the stunned General through yet another concrete-like reinforced section of the stadium.

Solaron landed next to Starbolt carrying Butcher down from the bleachers with him.

"Are you all right?"

"Yes. I'm a little beaten around the edges but I'm not dead yet."

"Prince Bol-Ton!" a familiar voice shouted from behind; all three men turned as Mar-Cus climbed up out of the hole that Nebula-Man had created.

The boy ran to his teacher and hugged him, "I thought you were hurt or worse, Mar-Cus."

"I am not my prince. I am here. Now quickly, you must heal yourself and then your hand must be the one that defeats Zaring once and for all."

"Heal myself ? But how?"

"Use the enervator rays. They will heal your flesh."

"Enervator rays? You've never even mentioned them before. How am I supposed to just call them up?"

308

"You can because you are the Starbolt. You are the heir to the throne, and also because you must. Concentrate on healing. This is your final lesson, and everything depends on you learning it well!"

Zaring appeared again at the edge of the arena, whirling his glowing axe over his head. Captain Power stood his ground, his hands glowing with pent up explosive energy.

Across the Arena, Nebula-Man traded blows with the savage and monstrous Malkatrar.

"You are the legendary Nebula-Man? You don't seem so tough." the bestial warrior growled.

"Dim witted brute, I've been holding back." Nebula-Man threw both his arms forward, unleashing cascading energy that hurled Malkatrar skyward across the horizon.

"Go after him," Solaron shouted, don't let him escape, he's too dangerous.

"Agreed." answered Nebula-Man a heartbeat before streaking after his foe.

Across the arena, Creature landed with flapping leathern wings amidst those soldiers surrounding Silver Shadow. Then with armor quickly spreading across his body, and razor sharp talons growing from his fingertips, he slashed and fought his way to her side.

"I was wondering when you'd get here." she chided.

"Bah...women...all...the same." He grinned as he hurled soldiers from them.

A shot rang out from above and Creature hurled himself in front of his sister, the ray blast sizzled across his now armored skin painfully.

"Creature!" Silver Shadow screamed. Instantly she sighted where the blast had come from and unleashed a powerful psychic stun bolt. A heartbeat later the aggressor tumbled from the higher bleachers to the ground far below.

"I...am...okay." Creature stood, "We...must...rejoin the...others."

"Let's go." Silver agreed. The two siblings flew off toward the arena's center.

***

General Zaring hurled his neural axe at Captain Power, "Not this time Zaring." Cap roared. He unleashed his powerful force blasts at the axe, sending it crashing to the far side of the arena.

"My soldiers to my side," Zaring shouted, "The intruders must be dealt with, permanently."

Zaring's personal troops began to flood the arena floor. Dragonfly, Stryker, Solaron, Butcher, Silver Shadow and Creature stood surrounding Starbolt and Mar-Cus, encircling them and protecting them from the encroaching troops. Amongst them was a strange looking man, Grey and blue armor covered his body and seemed to move like flesh.

"That guy," Stryker pointed, "he's the one from the arctic circle what dropped a space ship on me noggin. When the time comes, he's mine mates."

***

"Your enervator rays, my Prince, hurry."

"Mar-Cus, I-I have never tried this before. We never covered this lesson."

310

"It does not matter Prince Bol-Ton. You can do this, you must! Only you can defeat Zaring and permanently end his threat."

"I will try Mar-Cus."

The older man grabbed Starbolt's arms and stared into his students eyes, "No! You will not try, you will succeed!"

Starbolt nodded quickly and began to concentrate.

"Here they come!" shouted Dragonfly.

"Let 'em have it!" bellowed Butcher.

Butcher hefted a rifle and began spraying the troops as they closed in. The bullets bounced off their armor, but began to drive them back.

Dragonfly and Creature flew into the alien soldiers, scattering them with powerful blows.

"Stay with me, kid." Stryker shouted to Dragonfly.

Dragonfly's rising punch sent a soldier hurtling across the arena. He turned toward Stryker and said, "Don't call me 'kid', old man."

Stryker smiled and blasted another group of soldiers from him, "Sure kid whatever you say." he grinned.

Solaron sprayed the arena with burning solar rays, melting armor and scattering troops.

Suddenly the suns were blotted out by a massive shadow. Everyone both on the arena floor and those who remained in the stands turned toward the sky to see a huge flying warship hovering there.

"Oh no…" Solaron mouthed.

"That's the same ship we took on above the Earth." Dragonfly advised.

Immediately those left in the stands scattered in panic and fear for the exits.

Without hesitation, Solaron shot skyward, high density solar blasts blazing from his hands, hammering the hovering warship.

Below General Zaring laughed, "Your friends are doomed, Captain Power. My attack ship will burn you all to ashes, and then I will kill Prince Bol-Ton, becoming this world's next ruler."

"Like hell, you madman."

Cap streaked through the air and connected with a mighty left, hurling Zaring again into the arena's wall behind him. Zaring sunk to his knees, his armor dented, cracked and ruined. Cap turned toward the ship hovering overhead. He girded himself to fly right through it, when Stryker shouted, "I got this mate, take care o' that rotter."

Stryker disappeared; his instant acceleration power hurled him from zero to fifteen hundred miles per hour in less than an eye-blink.

Cap turned his head skyward and saw two puffs of smoke, one where Stryker entered the ship and one exiting exactly opposite where he exited.

"Impressive." Cap nodded.

***

High above, Solaron grimaced. Solar blasts exploded from his hands, hammering relentlessly at the ship and its quickly failing shields. Solaron was leaving nothing to chance now, *'I'm using my full power on my attacks. I'm not going to hold back at all. This is for all the marbles. If we don't win here, it's over for all of us.'*

***

Aboard the ship the captain shouted, "Get him! Blast him out of the sky."

The gunner replied, "I-I can't sir, he's too small and too fast. The few hits I've scored against him are blunted by an energy field surrounding him. To break through that field I'd have to hit him with enough power to fry or kill anything that it might hit on the ground. I could wipe out everyone in that entire arena."

"I don't care, just do it, you fool. This is the second time those earthmen have attacked this ship. It will be the last." He turned toward his tactical officer, "What about the one who punched a hole in us?"

"I can't get a lock on him, he disappeared after ramming us."

"Find him!" shouted the maddened ship's captain.

***

Solaron fired his high density blasts again and again, each time the ships shields lit up from their impact.

Again and again he released enough solar energy to light a city and each time the shields lit up with more and more visible cracks throughout them.

'Have to keep darting back and forth. I can't give them a bead on me for too long or they'll take me out.'

Solaron's blasts shook the great ship repeatedly.

***

Aboard the ship the gunner shouted gleefully "I've got him!" and stabbed the fire control.

***

Immediately Solaron was engulfed in an energy blast and knocked from the sky. He landed in a heap in the dirt of the arena floor. Silver Shadow instantly sprayed the soldiers surrounding him with her stun bolt, dropping them like flies.

"Sol!" she shouted fearfully, "Sol!" Silver ran to his side and helped to prop him up. He shook his head groggily.

"W-what hit me?"

"That space ships entire weapons array I think. I don't think you should move."

"No. No, I'm okay." he brushed her hand aside and forced himself painfully to his feet. My energy field blunted the attack. It still hurt like hell though. I think if there was any more to that blast I wouldn't be here talking to you."

"Look! It's Stryker again." Silver shouted.

Solaron followed where she was pointing and saw the black and gold garbed Hyperforcer cleaving through the sky like a missile. He impacted the ships shields and then went through them, causing a blindingly bright explosion as the shields shattered in another spot. He careened into the hull and through it. An instant later he exited the other side.

"Wow. I'm impressed. I didn't know he had that in him." Dragonfly offered. He had run up to Solaron's side

314

to make sure his uncle was okay during the continuing melee.

"He must be invulnerable when he's flying like that. Probably an energy based power that plays off of those explosive beams he fires." Solaron postulated.

The ships forward guns fired again, this time tagging Stryker hard. With a cry that echoed to their ears below the big Aussie fell like a bird with its wings cut.

"I've got him. I have to amend that though, he's not *that* invulnerable." Solaron announced, catching Stryker in a solar energy bubble and lowering him to the ground.

"Look!" Dragonfly shouted. He pointed to the ship above which had begun disgorging familiar shapes that flew down toward the heroes in the now mostly abandoned arena.

"Warbots!" roared Captain Power. He held Zaring by his armored suit's collar against the wall of the arena. After watching Stryker fly through the ship above he had returned to Zaring and held him in a vice-like grip. "It looks like hundreds of them."

"This just went from bad to worse." Solaron commented.

Mar-Cus looked at Starbolt, "Only you can end this my Prince. Heal yourself. You can do this and then defeat Zaring in combat."

"I-I'm trying…"

"Do not try, do!"

"I-I will, I am!" Starbolt shouted, as he began to glow.

"Nooo!" shouted Zaring, pulling free from a startled Captain Power and running toward Starbolt, just as the healing energies finally engulfed the struggling young prince.

Both men were now bathed in the healing glow emanating from Starbolt's body.

An instant later the glowing energy subsided, leaving both men on their feet and staring balefully at each other.

"I am fully healed. My injuries from that brutes attack are gone." Zaring announced gleefully. "Now it is but you and I, finally, Prince Bol-Ton. For all the world to see."

Slowly Starbolt looked up, raising his head from staring at the ground until his eyes met Zaring's, "Good, you insane animal, I wouldn't have it any other way."

"Explosive blast!" Starbolt shouted.

Energy ripped from his fingers and blew Zaring off of his feet, hurling him into the bleachers. Without hesitation Starbolt flew after him.

Solaron turned toward Cap and the others, "Let him be. Starbolt can take care of himself. We have to deal with that ship."

Solaron threw his hands up and put a solar force field dome over them all. The golden energy field was tested immediately. Blasts from the ship rebounded off of it again and again.

But each one drove Solaron to his knees. Grimacing he looked at Dragonfly, "We need to take the offensive."

Dragonfly streaked skyward and began sweeping the ship's shields and hull with his dragonblasts. Each time the beams stabbed outward they destabilized the ships hull's molecular structure.

316

On the ground Captain Power looked up, and then he rocketed toward the ship, fists clenched and accelerating quickly.

He punched a hole through the weakened shields and then through the ship itself, quickly passing through the other side.

"Dragonfly," Cap called, Get back down there and help Butcher, Silver and Creature with the Exalanderian soldiers. Sol is going to have to come up here and give me a hand taking this thing apart. When Stryker comes to, you and he take on what's left of the Warbots. Sol and I will be right behind you both."

Dragonfly smiled and nodded, "You got it Cap." He flew away in a burst of boot rockets, arcing down toward the rest of the team.

"Sol! Do you read me?" Cap called.

"Not so loud, Captain. I almost heard you without the comm headset."

"I need you up here buddy. We're going to have to tear this thing apart."

"On my way Captain."

Solaron blazed through the sky, joining Captain Power almost instantly.

"Are you okay for this Sol?"

"It depends on what 'this' is."

"We have to cripple this ship once and for all and drive it out past the city where it can crash harmlessly."

Solaron nodded stoically, "Yes, I'm ready. Let's do this."

"Hit it Sol!" Cap ordered.

Solaron began blasting at the ship again, this time with his medium density blasts. They splattered against

317

the ships weakened shields which became more and more visibly cracked.

"That's how Stryker got through them before. My high density beams had weakened the shields enough for him to pass through them as if they weren't there."

"Not important now, just keep hammering away at the shields where they're weakest." Cap howled.

"You got it Cap."

Solaron fired powerful beams of solar energy again and again at the ships forward shields. Visible cracks appeared on them. Finally they failed all together and the blasts now scorched the hull repeatedly.

But the ship was not finished yet. It continued to fire at Solaron.

"Okay, enough of this." Sol roared. He raced across the front of the ship, the ships guns blazed repeatedly, sometimes only missing him by inches. In mid-flight he'd turn and fire his own solar blasts strafing the hull repeatedly and tearing holes in it large enough to fly through.

"Finally! We're getting somewhere now." Sol shouted.

Captain Power rocketed down from up above and slammed through the ship's hull and once again, out the other side.

"It's working, Cap." Solaron shouted.

"I know Sol, I know. Let's get this thing out of here." Cap hauled back and punched the ship directly on its front or nose. Sparks flew everywhere. Great blasts of smoke were escaping from the many holes in its hull now.

Down below, Dragonfly and a just revived Stryker faced off against the encroaching Warbot's. The tall and powerful robots attacked with unstopping precision and cold, calculating efficiency.

"On your left kid." the big Aussie shouted.

"Got it." Dragonfly replied, turning and firing his dragonblasters again and again at the mechanical monsters, "Explosive fletchettes are having no affect, I have to stick with the dragonblasts."

"Kid I don't care if you spit on 'em at this point, just take 'em out."

Dragonfly rocketed through the air toward a Warbot and slammed both his fists into what passed for its skull; then he reached in and pulled its head apart. The decapitated Warbot took two steps, spun on its heels and bowled over. Dragonfly turned back toward Stryker and said, "I thought I told you not to call me kid?"

Stryker grinned that big, silly grin of his and replied, "You got it mate; you proved yer point."

Stryker took off and flew into the robotic troops, shattering them and heaving them aside with each quickly thrown punch. Then he saw him, the grey and blue armored warrior, whose own eyes locked with Strykers'.

"Time for a rematch tin can; let's see how you do without yer boss backin' ya up."

The mysterious blue and grey armored foe replied, "Our new battle will end the same way the previous one did, you backward earth-born dog. With Kalatrar the Marauder the victor!"

"So ya do know how ta talk , eh Kaly? All the better. Ya can scream while I tear yer liver out!"

Stryker rocketed into his foe, and both men careened to the opposite side of the arena, throwing punches all the way.

***

Silver Shadow, Butcher and Creature were battling the more human-like soldiers, which meant Creature was tearing through their ranks in his own inimitable style. Half his hide was covered by a thick, natural armor, the rest by his normally thick, black hair. Several soldiers began backing away from him. In response he growled menacingly, drew his arm back, its surface changing instantly. He slashed forward and quills flew from it as if from a mutated porcupine.

'Silver!' Solaron called along the telepathic link, *'It's been too long since we heard from Nebula-Man. Try to reach out and find him if you can.'*

'You're worried about him? He fought all of us to a standstill.'

'I also know the monster he's fighting. He could be in trouble.'

'O-okay I'll try.'

'Hey thanks for bein' concerned about me an' all.' Commander Butcher's characteristic telepathic voice intruded, *'I'm just the soldier from Earth in the middle of a firefight usin' an alien rifle 'cause my own ran outta bullets long ago. An' I'm doin' fine, thank you.'*

'Butcher, Solaron began, *'Just stay with Silver and Creature against the more human appearing enemies. Let the rest of us handle the heavier threats.'*

"Sol!" Captain Power shouted.

Solaron turned toward his friend who was hovering a hundred feet away from him.

"Sol, it's starting to go down." Cap pointed at the severely damaged ship that was now listing to its right side and losing altitude quickly. "Get out of the way; I have to get this thing away from this city or a lot more people are going to be hurt or killed."

Captain Power flew upward, but instead of punching his way through the hull of the big war ship, he slowed and dug his fingers into its steely hull, bending the armor into handholds, "Okay girl up you go." Cap gritted his teeth and began to push. Energy thrust out of his legs in a larger, more powerful volume. His legs looked like twin rockets blasting upward.

'This thing is incredibly heavy, I'll have to re-power myself by absorbing its mass as I fly it away from this city.'

Far below the stunned and frightened populace of the sprawling city held their breath in awe as he slowly but surely moved the ship away from crashing in the city's heart and killing so many. He began flying it toward a desert on the outskirts of the city. Solaron watched him disappear in the distance carrying the great ship.

***

'Nebula-Man, where are you? Answer me.' Silver Shadow called.

"I am right here, Silver Shadow." A voice called from above her.

Silver looked up to see Nebula-Man landing, and carrying Malkatrar like so much dead weight. He

321

dumped the unmoving brute to the arena floor, and then touched down softly.

"My God, what happened?"

Nebula-Man shrugged, "He was a very tough opponent; strong, resilient and savage. Ultimately he fell to my power. It just took a bit longer than I originally expected it to."

Marcus and Butcher ran up and joined them, "Things are goin' our way now Silver. The tides definitely turned. We've got the guards on th' run and Dragonfly an' Stryker are tearin' up those robot things pretty damned good."

"But where is Starbolt and that damned General Zaring?" Silver asked.

In answer a portion of the stadium exploded. General Zaring hurtled out of it, followed closely by a flying Starbolt, his hands glowing.

Zaring rolled across the arena's dirt floor and righted himself. He thrust his hand out, awaiting the return of his neural axe. The blade began to fly to him from beneath rubble when Starbolt aimed at it and shouted "Disintegration beam." Twin blasts flew from his fingertips, engulfed the Neural Axe and destroyed it, turning it to atoms instantly.

Then with a sneer of rage he turned toward Zaring once more. "Explosive blast!" He hurled energy that smashed Zaring from his feet.

Again the older man struggled to rise; cursing and shouting epitaphs at Starbolt. Starbolt looked at Dragonfly and smiled then shouted "Electron power bursts" The same energy Dragonfly called his 'Dragonblasts' shot from Starbolt's hands and engulfed

General Zaring's armored suit. An instant later it fell off of him in pieces.

"No more toys, Zaring. No more powers. Just you and I, man to man, fist to fist to end this. I have had enough of you hounding me, threatening my family, sending madmen and bounty hunters after me. This is now between you and I, and you and I alone!"

He hurled himself at Zaring, grasping his foe in a crushing grip about the waist and heaving him to the ground. Atop him now, Starbolt pummeled Zaring with blow after blow.

"Mad dog! Did you think this was going to end differently? Did you think the weakened and wounded boy would just lie down and die? Never Zaring! Never! I will fight you to the death if need be! Yours or my own!"

"I'm glad you said that." Zaring grunted through bloody teeth. He reached behind himself and in one lightning quick movement, stabbed Starbolt with a knife he had hidden under his armor, even as Starbolt continued to punch him repeatedly.

With a brutal kick he knocked Starbolt off of him.

The young hero lay there gasping for breath.

"*This* is how it all ends, whelp; with my victory, with your death. The only way it was *ever* meant to end. Your friends cannot help you here. All the world will see my victory, my ascendency to leadership of this realm.

Starbolt grimaced and pulled the knife from his side. Instantly Silver Shadow and Creature were at either side of him, Creature growling at Zaring. In a cloud of dust both Solaron and Dragonfly landed between Zaring and Starbolt. Solaron raised his right fist and pointed his finger at Zaring.

"You're done here Zaring. You lost. Starbolt won. You're right about one thing, your entire world saw what happened. They saw you pull a hidden knife and in an act of desperation and they saw you stab your opponent after he had utterly defeated and humiliated you. This is finished, you lost."

"This is not over!" Zaring screamed madly, "This will never be over until I sit upon the throne!" he continued to shout, spittle spraying from his mad lips.

"Wrong you coward, this *has* ended." A new male voice interceded. Everyone turned toward the source and saw a man in blue and white robes and a cape, with greying brown hair and a full beard crossing the arena toward them. Behind him were a woman equally as regally attired, two younger children, a boy and a girl and a half dozen armed guards.

"The King!" Mar-Cus breathed heavily.

Zaring began to stammer, "K-king Mal-Car, you-you cannot interfere. The laws state-"

"I make the laws, you mad dog! You can be certain this is one that will be unmade before this day is through."

King Mal-Car knelt beside his son. Touched Starbolt's head and face and nodded, smiling gently at his boy.

Then he stood and purposefully made his way to Zaring, his own face twisted in rage, "You were wrong Zaring, *this* is how it all ends!" The king jammed the knife that had been used against Starbolt into Zaring's own chest, then he pulled down and across.

Zaring's eyes went wide in shock and pain. He grasped the kings' robes, staining the white to blood red,

324

and then wordlessly his corpse slipped to the ground and lie still.

Stryker walked up bloodied and haggard looking, but he dragged the unconscious armored foe 'Kalatrar the Marauder' with him, then released him so he hit the ground with a thud.

Captain Power landed next to his teammates, having just returned from setting the damaged ship down safely, while everyone saw to Starbolt's wellbeing.

Ralph L. Angelo Jr.

Chapter 14

The Cleanup

Two days had passed. Hyperforce had been put into the most opulent guest rooms the palace had to offer. Starbolt was too weakened to use the healing rays upon himself again, at least at first. The palace physicians saved his life and when he stabilized and regained enough strength he used the enervator rays once more and healed himself completely.

King Mal-Car treated the heroes like the finest royalty from a visiting world.

"I thank you once again my friends, for saving my sons life and for following him back to Exalander. Without your aid my boy would have been dead by now and my kingdom in the hands of that madman Zaring." He turned toward Captain Power, "My entire planet saw you save the throne city from total destruction when you flew that war ship away from here to set it down safely in the desert. You are a hero to my people, you all are. Once again, I cannot thank you all enough."

They were all gathered at a sumptuous repast made in their honor. The royal family-Prince Bol-Ton included-sat opposite Hyperforce. Mar-Cus sat next to Bol-Ton.

"We were more than happy to aid him, King Mal-Car. He is a good son and a wonderful teammate. We'll miss him." Solaron nodded, smiling.

"I understand my friends, but for now I would like to spend time with my son. It has been too long since his mother and I have seen him. Perhaps one day he will return to your world, if you would welcome him that is."

Solaron continued to grin, "Both he and Mar-Cus are always welcomed to rejoin us any time they want."

Butcher raised his hand, "If I may interrupt your highness, I'm empowered by my government to extend an invitation to welcome you to Earth at any time as well. My people would welcome the opportunity to greeting peaceful new friends from across the galaxy."

Mal-Car nodded, "I believe that will be something that could benefit us all. I look forward to meeting your world's leaders, Commander Butcher and extending our hands in friendship, as I do to you now."

The King stood and offered his hand to Butcher, who took it and shook it strongly.

"King Mal-Car," Solaron began, "That law that caused all of this, may I ask, did you do away with it?"

"Yes Solaron, immediately upon our return to the palace. It was an ancient thing from a thousand years agone that no one had ever called into use since that day. General Zaring found it while looking for a way to legally overthrow my rule and return this world to a military leadership. If not for your intervention he would have done so. I thank you again. Now please, no more talk of politics and the corruption of the throne. Let us simply enjoy the rest of the day as friends would. I have much of my worlds' wonders to show you all yet."

Epilogue

A week later the 'Star Rapier' landed in the hanger bay underneath the Solar Observatory. Hyperforce exited the ship grunting and groaning from the long journey home.

"I can't wait to get into a hot shower." Captain Power grunted.

"Aye mate, I haveta agree with ya there."

"I'm just glad to be home again." Silver Shadow added.

"My parents are going to kill me." Dragonfly muttered to himself.

"No they're not, Randy." Solaron replied.

"No? Why not? I've been missing for over a week now."

Solaron placed his right hand on Dragonfly's shoulder, "Randy, they know."

"W-what? You told them? When?"

Solaron laughed, "Months ago." I even contacted them again when we were leaving. I know you told them we were going on a camping trip for a week or so to record star light data in the wilderness, but I had to let them know the truth. Relax Randy, they trust you. Or I just have to keep you safe, because they'll kill me if I don't. Besides, I also contacted them from Starbolt's world, once we were ready to leave for home."

Dragonfly looked at Solaron and grimaced, "Thanks for telling me. You could have let me know sooner. It woulda saved me a lot of worrying." then changing the subject Dragonfly continued, "It's a shame Nebula-Man left after the feast in our honor. I thought we were making another friend there." Dragonfly commented.

"We did Randy, at least I hope so. But he's a loner, and I think seeing Starbolt's family at the dinner reminded him of what he had lost."

Butcher grabbed his gear and began walking toward the hangers exit, stopping to shake hands with Cap and Sol, "I'm outta here gents. It's been a pleasure, an' I'll seeya next time."

A black SUV pulled up outside the facility and Butcher hopped in the front seat. The vehicle immediately drove away.

"We were wrong about that guy. He's okay." Cap said to Sol.

"What about him?" Solaron nodded toward Stryker, who was chatting up Silver Shadow as they entered the door to the interior of their headquarters.

"The jury's still out on that one." Captain Power replied grimly.

"You're being too wary with Stryker. Are you sure it's not simply that he's hitting it off with Silver and maybe you're a little jealous?"

Cap shrugged, "It could be but I don't know. There's something about the guy that just rubs me wrong."

***

Minutes earlier, and many miles away in upstate New York a figure sat behind a desk and watched the 'Star Rapier' land at the observatory. A metal gauntleted hand reached out and shut the monitor.

"They have returned. Good. Now the game will begin in earnest." He stood from his plush chair and with a dramatic swirl of his cape, 'Mind Master' left the room.

***

Thousands of miles away in an island headquarters we have seen before, hidden in the Caribbean, a hulking grey skinned brute wearing all black save for red chains around his wrists and the tops of his boots as well as a black belt of skulls watched Mind Master leave his command center, and in a voice like gravel being crushed added "Yes indeed, Mind Master; let the games begin, Hahahahaha…"

The End…
For Now.

Ralph L. Angelo Jr.

Hyperforce Appendix

A.R.M.O.R- *Advanced Reserve Military Operations Response*- a special high tech military unit.

Brotherhood of the blade- Ninja clan Silver Shadow trained with.

Captain Power-The strongest member of Hyperforce, and possibly the strongest man on Earth. Absorbs matter to power himself and can use that power for strength and flight as well as force blasts from his hands. Must recharge himself occasionally by absorbing more matter. The more difficult the task, the more energy he uses. Unstoppable and invulnerable. The team's powerhouse, as well as its moral center.

Creature-Hyperforce member who has shape shifting powers that are instinctive. He draws his abilities from the animal kingdom in super-charged versions of natural animal abilities. His First name is Billy.

Dragonfly-Randy Anderson, nephew of Solaron. Has natural super strength, agility and reaction time. Also has a power called 'spectroscopic vision' which allows him to see on all levels of the visual spectrum. His battle suit allows him to fly, fires energy blasts called 'dragon blasts', which stop the electron flow in atomic structures, as well as firing explosive fletchettes. The underarm wings can be thrown as a slicing blade that can sheer through just about anything. They are remote controlled by circuitry in Dragonfly's cowl.

Epherezus-Underground city Gravity King rules over.

Exalander- Homeworld to Starbolt and Mar-Cus.

General Zaring-Exalendarian warlord who wants to kill Starbolt and take leadership of his world. Wears a superstrong armored suit and carries a 'neural axe' whose energies scramble the brain of whoever it hits. Can also fire the neural scrambling energy as a blast of energy.

Gravity King- Mysterious subterranean 'king' who rules a civilization many miles beneath the Earth's surface. Has vast and powerful gravity manipulating abilities.

Groundpounder-Villain who grows to giant heights, possessed of extraordinary strength.

Kalatrar the Marauder-Alien mercenary with grey and blue organic armor. A powerful foe.

King Mal-Car Starbolts father and ruler of Exalander.

Malkatrar-Alien powerhouse. Burgundy skinned, huge underbite with upward thrusting tusks and stringy black hair. He carries an energy mace that returns to his hand at his mental command. Extremely strong and powerful. A barbarian of sorts who is also a mercenary arm for hire.

Mar-Cus- Starbolts' teacher and mentor.

Mikuro- Leader of the Brotherhood of the Blade

Nebula-Man-Impossibly powerful being who flies amongst the stars as a cosmic force of nature, settling wrongs no one else has a hope of righting. Possesses Cosmic strength off of the scale.

Presipigus- Capital city on Exalander

Silver Shadow- Sister to Creature, able to fly and fire a psychic stun bolt from her forehead. She is also a highly trained fighter, a female ninja.

Hyperforce

Skyrocket-Villainess, Super strong, durable and flies very fast.

Solaron-Able to fire solar blasts and fly at incredible speeds. Able to encase his body in a solar energy field or project solar force fields. He can change the density of his blasts from a low density, to a medium, laser-like beam to a high density force blast. Also able to lower the temperature of his blasts. Ronald Anderson is a solar energy researcher by profession. Team leader and financier.

Starbolt- Prince Bol-Ton of Exalander. A mighty energy manipulator.

Stormsurge-Villain who controls water and can call down lightning from storm clouds.

Stryker-Super-Strong, instant acceleration to 1500 MPH, limited invulnerability, fires explosive energy blasts.

Ralph L. Angelo Jr.

Other books by Ralph L. Angelo Jr

- Redemption of the Sorcerer, The Crystalon Saga, Book One: A mighty sorcerer and ruler of his world is deposed and exiled to a world identical to his own, save for one difference, magic doesn't exist there. Now he must fight against seemingly insurmountable odds to regain his powers in time to save both parallel universes from utter destruction. ISBN# 0615763030
- Torahg the Warrior, Sword of Vengeance: In a land before recorded time, a world of warriors, monsters and wizards, a young prince is framed for the death of his father by his own evil brother and riven to exile. For twenty long years he wanders the world, until finally he is coaxed into returning to his homeland seeking justice for his father and bloody revenge for himself. ISBN# 1490516263
- The Cagliostro Chronicles: In the depths of space awaits danger for all mankind. When man's first faster than light space flight begins, it opens up a whole new universe for mankind. But it is a universe filled hostile enemies as well as a century-long conspiracy against humanity. Will mankind survive? ISBN# 0615854427
- Help! They're All Out to Get Me! The Motorcyclists Guide to Surviving the Everyday World: A Non-fiction motorcycle

safety and instructional manual for the new
and returning riders. A 'Must Read' for those
seeking to better their motorcycling
experience. ISBN# 0615756786

- My Enemy, Myself, The Crystalon Saga,
Book Two: It has been two years since
Crystalon defeated the mad warlord Maceyis.
Much has changed in that time. Crystalon has
become his adopted world's hidden mystic
guardian, protecting the Earth from those
who would threaten it with evil, sorcerous
intent.
Until a visitor from his past, one he never
expected to see again would appear within his
very home. Now he and his companions must
travel between worlds to his home dimension,
a universe where he is hated and feared, to
face a threat that dwarfs any challenge he has
ever faced before. The challenge of an enemy
who wears his very face. The challenge of
'My Enemy, Myself'. ISBN# 149950523X

- 'The Cagliostro Chronicles II: Conflagration'
After an almost disastrous battle in space, the
star cruiser Cagliostro must land on an
unknown alien world to make repairs only to
discover a new threat to Earth and humanity.
But alone and unable to return to Earth until
they can complete repairs will they be enough
to stop this new threat by the Agalum
empire? And what of the strange new foes
they encounter upon this world of prehistoric

monsters and aliens? It's more fast paced, interstellar action in the sequel to the best-selling 'The Cagliostro Chronicles' ISBN# 978-0692255506.